To Olivia Rock on

PLASTIC
CONFIDENCE

BOOK ONE

THE GOOD BYE SERIES

A Rock Star Suspense New Adult Romance

A novel

By Alisa Mullen

This book is a work of fiction and all persons appearing in this work are fictitious. Any resemblance to real people, living or dead, is entirely coincidental.

Plastic Confidence is meant for mature audiences (ages 17+) only. Due to explicit sexual scenes and murder details, please do not read this book if you are sensitive to that subject matter in any way.

ISBN-13: 978-1500494889

ISBN-10: 1500494887

Edited by Melissa Borucki and Krysta Anderson

Cover Design by Margreet Asselbergs

Rebel Design and Edit

DEDS AND CREDS

~ To my editors Melissa Borucki and Krysta Anderson. There are no words and I am a writer.

~ For my fabulous assistants, Marina Acosta(US) and Kelly Byrne (INTL). You keep me from drowning daily.

~ LOVE and GRATITUDE to Rachael Berkebile, Sarah Ratliff, Alexandra Lied, and Vanessa Lofton.

~ This book required a plethora of research so thank you to Nikki Deatherage, Matthew Kohl, I. McFarland, and Jeff McDonald.

~ To the Official Street Team Boston Babes– Find the words.

~ Thanks to the beautiful Margreet Asselbergs at Rebel Edits and Design for my awesome cover design. You are a miracle worker.

~ Thank you to Dana Hook and Nina Ceves just because.

~ Love and hugs to William, Shea, and Tyler.

"The past does not have to be your prison. You have a voice in your destiny. You have a say in your life. You have a choice in the path you take."

–Max Lucado

~For the twelve year old girls out there who live by their labels.

You are you in SO MANY words and beautiful is one of them. ~

PLASTIC CONFIDENCE

BOOK ONE

THE GOOD BYE TRILOGY

A ROCK STAR SUSPENSE NEW ADULT ROMANCE

PROLOGUE

2009

I woke up singing Don McLean's *American Pie*... again. It wasn't the first or the last time the up tempo opening notes would startle me wide awake. No–I most certainly did not write the book of love–and God? We still weren't on speaking terms. It went hand in hand with the nightmare or dream or whatever it was. Memories. It was the memories from one summer when I was twelve years old and lost a great chunk of my innocence. This morning, however, was different for one reason. I woke up naked and sweating, smelling like body odor and sex. I felt like I was going to throw up. The dream was so real this time. I was living it all over again and I didn't fucking want to. I wish there was a button I could press or a pill I could take that would erase that one stupid summer from my brain. I would pay millions of dollars, travel to any psychic healer, invest in any drug company, and maybe even cut off a finger. I would do anything. I just wanted it gone from my head.

Grace Miller. Jason #2. Emmy. Angie.

Kids from my past were making their casual and unwanted appearance in my present. It wasn't that the dreams necessarily haunted me but this one was so extremely vivid that it left me feeling like I was missing something. Over the years, I had purchased every dream book out there. From the murder to the OUIJA Board to the night I lost my virginity, the books all said that I am facing a big change. A brand new path. It was time to let go of what is comfortable. Whatever it was, it had been years and my path was steady and solid. No changing paths now. My life was pretty fucking great.

I rolled over to try and locate the blankets but found a blond haired, tatted up hunk of sex laying next me.

In my hotel bed.

In the morning.

Oh hell no! Sure, he was cute but I was most definitely too far gone last night to kick his ass out after we screwed.

I racked my brain, as I tapped my fingers to my head. Oh! He kissed like a lizard but that was okay when he went down south. No! Shit! That was the guy from the night before.

Oh! He was the one that had a small dick but still knew how to use it... pretty well actually. Multiple times. Yes, that is why he was still here. I was too exhausted after three hours of him pleasuring me.

Still, it had to be done. I smacked his shoulder.

"Wake up, Casanova. Time to hit the road," I shouted at him. He groaned and as he rolled over to face me, he slowly opened his eyes.

"Jules Delaney," he smiled as he, too, remembered who he was in bed with.

"Up and at 'em! Now you have to get out." I was a little more forceful with my tone.

"What? Why? We could... you know," he said suggestively as he started for my neck. I pushed his face back with my entire palm. Hard.

"Hell no! You were lucky that I didn't toss you at four this morning. Time to go," I repeated and I swear to fucking God if he didn't listen this time, I would start screaming rape. *Grace Miller was raped. Shut up, shut up, shut up.*

I started off the bed and purposely shoved the memory back into my brain. I didn't have the energy to think about what I was supposed to do. Obviously it was something huge since my subconscious was bringing it to my conscious once again.

He grunted out something foul in reference to me. Cold bitch, fucking tease, slutty whore, or you label it. I had heard them all. *Just go, douchebag. Yes, I am all of those filthy names but much, much more. Now leave...Please.*

Plastic Confidence - Prologue

"Hey," I called out. I hadn't bothered to learn this one's name. "I am going to take a shower. If you aren't gone by the time I am out, consider spending the next four hours in a police station, answering the age old question about what the word 'no' means. Okay?" I smiled brightly at him. "By the way, you were amazing last night."

I walked into the bathroom and grabbed my toothbrush as I looked in to the mirror. Not too bad for a late night gig, hours of sex, and hardly any sleep.

"The name is Jason by the way," he shouted to me. I heard the door of my hotel room close.

"Jason," I repeated. "Of course it is." The memory of that summer pops up everywhere. Call it serendipity. Call it fate. I call it suck ass.

The Good Bye Trilogy

Plastic Confidence - Prologue

ONE

1993

Merrimack, New Hampshire

JULES ~AGE TWELVE

I leaned into Frank for a final kiss good bye. He was twelve like me and had been my first kiss ever. *Sigh.* I was now a person who kisses. A kisser. I kiss boys. Well, I kissed a boy. I knew how to make out. All thanks to you, summer camp! Rock on.

Camp Wimberley sat in the White Mountains and had been a constant summer staple for me and my two best friends. Angie, Emmy, and I booked early for two weeks at the end of June every year since we were eight. We would skip out of the last day of class and know in less than two weeks we would be in one of our favorite places. We loved the crystal blue pond with the mountains surrounding it. Mom always commented on how great I was at taking pictures of them but all anyone had to do was point and click. Every view was a post card waiting to happen.

The log cabins were hot but so comfortable. Emmy, Angie, and I took up three of the cabin's four bunks and every year we made a fourth best friend forever in the last bunk. Throughout the school year, we would keep in touch with that girl until the next summer when we would get a new bunkmate. We told her how lucky she was because we knew the ins and outs of Camp Wimberley. We knew the ropes. We were sleek and total mission impossible at night to retrieve food from the cafeteria or enjoy a late night walk around the lake. We got away with a whole heap of stuff over the years.

Swimming, boating, and field games took up most of our daylight camp hours. The mess hall was a huge building and it allowed us three or sometimes four a place to play tricks on the camp counselors. One little frog dropped in the pudding made for a lot of ruckus but no one could pinpoint us as we were already walking through the sea of campers back to our reserved table. I think they eventually caught on after two years but they loved the three of us nonetheless. We were entertaining.

Now that we were in the older group, we enjoyed more freedom–nightly dances, later curfews, and interactions with boys from the camp down the road. Frank and I kissed the first night we showed up for registration and the opening dance. I liked him right away. He was funny and made me feel special. We swapped love notes and slow danced to *American Pie* at every dance, where he would sing all the words to me. It became *our* song. Angie and Emmy also met boys but Frank and our love connection cemented my growing up. Being twelve was so rad. Boys and Junior High were the future life of Jules Delaney.

I heard someone clear their throat behind me and I turned my head to see my mother with her hands on her hips.

"Jules Delaney!" She admonished me. I immediately stepped back from Frank and flushed.

"Mom! You are early! Pick up isn't for another two hours," I stated firmly.

"Yes, well, all of us wanted to get you girls home now. Something extremely tragic happened yesterday and we got permission to pick you girls up early." She was her normal, cold self. No hug, no smile. *Pick up the kid from camp, check.*

I looked around to see Angie with a miserable face and speaking to her parents, who were comforting her with hugs and hushed tone. Emmy was listening to her parents–stoic and emotionless–with no reaction at all. She nodded every once in a while but seemed resolute. Obviously she didn't mind our early departure. I turned back to Frank and smiled at him. I pulled out an envelope with pre-stamped postcards, addressed to me. He grinned down at them.

"I will send one today. I will put my phone number on it for you to call me, okay?" Frank seized my hand and kissed it. I blushed again.

"Jules!" My mother snapped. I rolled my eyes as I twisted back to face Frank. Catching his wondrous gaze, I mouthed 'I love you'. He brightened up and mouthed it back to me. *Yes!* We finally admitted it. Summer camp was magnificent through and through. I could go home knowing that I was a new girl, almost a woman. A boy had kissed me and he told me he loved me. There was no better feeling.

With one final look at Frank, I trailed my mother with my trunk in tow. I waved over to Angie and then to Emmy. They made the phone signal with their hands and I nodded quickly with wide eyes. Something was most definitely happening. Were we all in trouble for something we had done before we left for camp? I tried to remember but all I could think of was Frank. I sighed as I looked back to him, but he had already moved from our spot. I looked at my best friends again. Both girls had stunned and freaked out expressions on their faces as they handed their own trunks over to their fathers.

I had what my mother referred to as an absent father. He was alive and well, but to me, it wouldn't affect my daily life if he wasn't. He left Mom when I was five. He got himself a brand new family, who I liked enough to visit on occasion. Okay, that wasn't true, I didn't like his wife. I called her my step-monster.

The day my dad left my mother for that woman, two things changed. I knew what it actually felt like to hate someone and the joyful light in my mother's eyes completely flickered out the day my dad left for good.

My brother, Kent, and I are our father's afterthoughts. To be fair, he is *my* afterthought, too. Rarely do I have memories of our family all together and they fade just as quickly as I try to grasp more detail from my brain. I don't remember very much of my life back then. Everything I know is from what mom tells me. I believe what she says because, well, he isn't around to give me his side of the story. It is times like these that I wish a fatherly figure could make an appearance and show everyone that I am loved by two parents.

As I hoisted the trunk into the back seat, I dismissed the thought. I was a twelve year old who was in love for the first time. *Nothing* else matters. I just wish I didn't appear different in any respect from my friends. Explaining a divorce to my friends is just as uncomfortable for me as it is for them. Daddy just didn't love us anymore.

I threw my seat belt on and played with my silver bangles on my wrists. Mom started up the old Buick and I watched the luscious green grass and trees as we made our way out of the most magical place. My summer camp experience was unforgettable and I sighed heavily as I started to long for it already. I had to switch gears and get back into home mode which was heavily clouded by my mother's mood. Mom was upset and more than a *usual* upset. It wasn't like she was a cold person but hugs and kisses just weren't her way of showing affection. Talking was her thing.

"Communication is key," she announced at the beginning of every argument. I decided to take her stance and use it against her. I would not let her mood ruin mine.

"So what is wrong with you Mom? I like Frank. He is very sweet. We kissed. So what?" I asked incredulously.

"Frank? Was that the boy you were with? Yes, well, I suppose it is time for a trip to Planned Parenthood. I suppose you are growing up, huh? I was around your age for my first kiss, but my mother would have cut off my lips with an exacto knife if she saw me. *See*, I can be hip." Her humorous laugh faded off into silence." She shook her head. I balked at that image. Geesh, it was only a kiss.

She continued.

"As much as I would like to be solely concerned about you kissing a boy, that is not what is upsetting me and the community back home," she croaked out, as she started to straighten her body in a protective stance. She meant business. I, myself, sat up a little taller in the seat.

"What is going on, Mom?" I asked, alarmed. "Are you mad at me? Did I do something wrong at home before I left for camp?"

She shook her head again. She was silent, probably trying to figure out how to fix the problem inside her own mind. She could do it, too. *My mother, the world class Ms. Fix-it.* The pipes are leaking? Call the plumber. Failing math? Hire a tutor. Kissed a boy? Go on the pill.

My mom was good to us despite the circumstances. With a full time job and a single mom, she was stretched thin. Kent and I got away with a lot. Her expression morphed back into a nervous consideration as she handed me the *Merrimack Daily* newspaper and asked me to read it. A photo of Grace Miller was on the front page. She was a year ahead of us in school. She was already in Junior High, so we would be at her school next year. Pretty blond. Popular socially. Trendy clothing. Sometimes snobby to people outside her circle of friends. On the rare occasion, she said "hi" to Angie because they knew each other from gymnastics camp. Emmy and I would give Angie crap for that. We teased mostly, saying she would ditch us for the popular crowd when we started school.

As I read the story below her photo, I saw the words rape, strangled, and murder. How was Grace's picture associated with murder? I tried to tamp down the car sick feeling when I read words in the car but it was too late. I was focusing too hard on each word and my head started to throb. My stomach became a pit of snakes that were eating their way underneath each rib.

"Mom, reading is making me car sick and I don't understand what I am reading here. Just tell me what you want me to know. Gracie Miller is dead?" I asked as the sluggish, nauseated words stumbling their way out of my mouth.

"She was strangled to death," she emphasized, and then paused so she knew that I understood the enormity of what she was telling me. "She was riding her bike home from the camp at Merrimack Elementary."

She looked at me pointedly like I should have already been aware of whatever she was telling me. My friends and I, and especially Grace, were too old for that camp at the school. It only went up to fifth grade so it didn't make any sense that Grace would have attended. The words from the newspaper replayed over and over in my head as I felt the headache start to subside.

"Whoa, that is... " I didn't know what to say. I suppose I had more questions than knowing what to say. *A murder.* That didn't happen in our daily life. Murder was made for television and newspapers that highlighted those high crime areas in the bigger states. New Hampshire was safe. I felt safe but maybe now, I wasn't? Was I?

"Mom, what is rape?" I felt my eyebrows were pinched together with curiosity and it seemed to make my head feel better.

My mom's lips went into a thin line and she paled. I could tell she was trying to reign in her feelings. Maybe she didn't mean to show me that portion of the newspaper story? It appeared that before she was strangled, she was raped. Whatever that meant. Mom took a deep breath like she always did when she about to say something that she didn't want to, like the day she told us our father was never coming home.

"Rape is something that is very cruel. It is an illegal crime when someone makes someone else do things they don't want to do," she explained. "Sexually," she added.

"Oh," I peeped. I couldn't manage to say anything else. Rape wasn't something I knew about but the word itself sounded awful. I had seen someone being strangled on television and it was a cruel way of killing someone. I couldn't imagine trying to suck in air. The victims always fought against the hands. They always shook their heads and bodies to get out of their grasp. The fear hit me then.

"Mom, did they get him? You know, the man who strangled Grace?" I asked, as I felt my stomach inch its way into my esophagus.

Mom shook her head. I watched her shake out her hands and firmly put them back on the steering wheel. I stared at absolutely nothing for a long beat before I sat back in my seat. I stayed silent while she sniffled and looked devastated. She was driving but her vision was all over the place, like she was looking for something. I wanted to ask her more but this woman was someone I hadn't seen before.

Her face proclaimed that she was furious. Her jaw set implied that she didn't want to start crying. Her absent minded hand to rub her breastbone admitted that she was scared. I watched her and wondered what else she knew about Grace Miller's murder that I didn't. What was she not telling me? Did Emmy and Angie know more than I did? I would call them as soon as I could.

She held the front door open for me at our white ranch style house in Merrimack. The familiar country smells were welcoming. I was home. Our home was set up in a small but family focused town. Everyone knew everyone. I had great memories of camp but the summer still had a great deal of time left. I couldn't wait to get on my bike and spend every day scrounging up coins for the penny candy down at the MM Country Store. Emmy, Angie and I would ride the long country roads for miles and enjoy the butterflies and small lakes. We were always on a mission for an adventure.

My brother, Kent, was in the front room reading a magazine. He was seventeen and I was surprised to see him home. He was never ever home. Either he was playing baseball and hanging out with the *Jasons*. Yes, all three of his good friends were named Jason. If he wasn't with them, he was trying to stick his tongue down his girlfriend's throat.

Krysta, a petite blond that went a little heavy on the makeup, was nice to me. They had been dating for a couple years and my mom really liked her. She showed me how to apply my own make up one day and I sort of looked up to her, since I didn't have a sister. I told Kent that if he breaks up with her I would never talk to him again.

"Hey, twerp." He stood up and whoa, he was taller. He threw the magazine on the table and enveloped me into a hug, while mom observed us with a faint smile.

"Hey big brother. Whatcha doing home?" I asked, as I wrapped my arms around his lanky frame. My brother was super nice, but he was kind of a geek. He wore thick lens square glasses, but listened to heavy metal. He head banged, for God's sakes, to The Cult,

Guns and Roses, and Metallica. He was a walking contradiction.

"I just wanted to see my Julia Child before I headed out," he smiled at me. That nickname was ridiculous. I tried to speak like her once. I sounded more like a drunk cat, not that I had ever heard one. But that is what Kent and the *Jasons* said, and I went with it, laughing right along.

"Where are you going? Can I come?" Excitement streamed through my veins at the idea of chilling with my *big bro*. Sometimes, he would let me tag along and I would be the special little sister for the day. It made me feel somewhat superior to my friends.

"No way! Jules you are staying home until I tell you that you can leave!" Mom bellowed with the sternest voice in history. Kent and I were taken aback.

"Oh... kay," I drew out. This stern attitude was a little over the top, even for Mom. I mean I would just be going to hang out with Kent. He would watch over me the whole time. What was the big deal?

Kent gave my mother a look that my Dad would have given her, if he was still around. Kent must have felt uneasy with her temper, as well. For the second time that day, I thought about my Dad. *Weird.* He left when I was five and we hardly saw him. He lived about two hours away in Massachusetts, but since he had a new family, the drive was too long for frequent visits, he had argued once. Birthday cards and Christmas gifts were Kent and my only expectations out of him.

I don't know why he didn't want to see us but I think it had something to do with seeing my mother at drop off. She tried so hard to say something nice to him. He would nod at her, without even looking at her, and get us in the car as quickly as possible. Kent and I slowly accepted that we would never be fans of our father. Our loyalty remained with our Mother.

"It is so great to be home," I sassed at them, with a slight pucker, and made my way back to my room. My room was big and it was set in the far back corner of one side of the ranch home. I thought about the car ride and my mother's outburst. What did she mean I couldn't leave the house? I was considering sneaking away for the day. I mentally thought of everything I needed to pack in my backpack. Water, change for candy, a swimsuit, towel, and... as I started for my empty backpack, the lawn mower's loud reverberation started up outside my window and I drew back the blinds to find my brother. Kent was head banging to his Walkman, pushing the old lawnmower over freshly mowed grass. I rolled my eyes at my mother's deceptiveness. Obviously, Mom sent him out because she knew I would crawl out my window to go to Emmy's house. She was so annoying. And right.

TWO

Returning home from camp was a big, fat mistake. The days dragged on and on without anything to do. It was like going from a roller coaster to the merry go round in two minutes. I was bored out of my skull, brain, body, house, and everything else in between. I wanted out of myself and fast.

I watched the local news every night with my mother and brother, while we ate dinner at the table. Mom had dragged a TV in to the kitchen, so we could get updates on the murder and what parents were doing to make sure their kids remained safe. When they said safe, I always muttered prisoner, drawing looks from both Mom and Kent. I was dying. I even hated eating because that was all there was to do. So I sat and watched the updates on my jail sentence as I forked the veggies around on my plate.

When Grace's story came on, Mom made a loud clanking noise with her fork as she set it down and I hung onto every word. It didn't feel real. They had buried her the day before and I thought maybe I would go to the cemetery just to... I don't know. Say hi, maybe? People talked to gravestones. I saw it on television. It was so sad on those shows, so I tried to think of other ways I could tell her that I was sorry she had to die.

The days went by in true prison fashion. Breakfast, shower, dress, television, lunch, play games, snack, look out the window, dinner, television, and bed.

Hit repeat.

During the play games portion of the day, I acted as teacher with my stuffed toys. Mom had put a huge chalkboard on one wall of my bedroom so I lined all of my dolls and animals just as I gave them their math pop quiz. The groaning answer I got from my students was so annoying to me, the teacher.

I hung out in our basement a lot. It was cool and damp and far away from the woman who was set out to ruin my life for the unforeseeable future. Mom wouldn't let me do anything outdoors. I couldn't even go to the supermarket unless she was within eyesight of me.

I exhausted all of our old Atari games over and over. Pac Man, Asteroids, and Centipede weren't as visually stimulating but they were hard to beat nonetheless. While everyone else had the newest PlayStation, Mom insisted Kent scarcely used the game console to begin with; therefore, constituting that it needed more wear. I rolled my eyes at her but covertly had a serious obsession with Kaboom. I treasured that game until I had beaten it so many times that I disconnected the whole system and put it in a box for our next garage sale.

Mom owed us that upgrade since the system was thoroughly played. As I added the last of the wires to the box in the garage, I made a note to mention that at dinner that night so she knew that I couldn't handle solitary confinement much longer. Not one to back down on what I thought was right for world peace, every day I begged Mom incessantly for Emmy or Angie to play. What was her repetitive response?

"We'll see," she proposed with a frown. Why not just yell no to my face? That would be some excitement for the day. I watched Kent mosey in and out of the house with Krysta or one of the Jason's. I begged them to go for ice cream. I begged them to take me for a five minute drive. I begged them until my sobbing, reddened face, and their pathetic apologies made me hate them forever.

Mom caved in on the fourth day. I could play with chalk on the walkway leading up to the front door. I had to report anything suspicious because according to the evening news every night, Grace's murderer still hadn't been caught. They had a few people that they were looking into but no arrests had been made. My defense to my mother went something like this:

"Mom, I didn't even know the girl. She lives a town away. Grace was alone when she was taken. If I go to Emmy or Angie's house, I won't be alone. I will be safe there. I will watch out for any strangers who stalk the house. I will do whatever you want me to, but if I don't get out of this house, I am going to hate you forever." I confidently blasted into her face.

Her reply was not to have a reply. *Typical Mom.* Stone cold until she probably got behind the closed door to sigh and roll her eyes. Ignoring me and walking away to prove that my argument wasn't up for discussion was more annoying than a fly that wouldn't stop circling my head. I would smack at it only to miss. My mother was officially that annoying fly. I was too keyed up to take pleasure in soaking in the sun. I took the stupid plastic tub of chalk out to the driveway, not the walkway (thank you very much), and colored all of them down to the nub so that she could never suggest such a juvenile activity.

That night, I snuck phone calls to both girls after I knew their parents would be in bed for work. Sometimes I hated that my mother was a secretary librarian at school, allowing her the late nights and sleeping in. Their parents weren't allowing them to do much either but Emmy did get to go to Wild World for a day with a cousin who was visiting. I secretly disliked her very much for that. It had been four days with minimal communication with my best friends. It was the longest, most agonizing time I had ever suffered. I felt like I was being starved. It was child abuse. I threatened "red rum" regularly, hoping my drama would force my mother to give me my life back. She told me I was watching too many horror movies and to knock it off.

One morning, Mom called out to me while I was beginning the boxes of Hopscotch with the leftover nubs of chalk.

"Both Emily and Angela are on their way over. I will sit outside with you girls with lemonade and a book. All the parents have discussed it and every day you girls can have two hours at each other's houses. Tomorrow, you can go to Angela's," she declared.

I sprinted to her and hugged her so tight that I knew she was flinching. She hooted at me and I pulled away. I kissed her cheek, ran inside for a couple of board games, and headed out to the warm green grass to wait for their cars. I started to notice dandelions and butterflies. Nature had color once again and I couldn't be more enthralled with life that day.

Angie was first to arrive and we squeezed one another like we hadn't seen each other in years. Emmy showed up in the middle of the hug and we had a five minute group hug as we jumped up and down. I noticed we had all dressed in the requisite best friend attire. Solid colored tank top from Old Navy, khaki short shorts, and the Tevas we had all grown to love. They were all the same design, of course. We were the triplets. We made sure that everyone knew it just by the way we coordinated our outfits. We no longer needed the phone call the night before. We just managed to do it somehow. I laughed at the familiarity of our friendship and was instantly content. I pointed to the blanket Mom had put out and where the board games lay.

"Payday? Or do you guys wanna play Hopscotch" I asked with excitement in my voice. My friends were actually here. It was glorious.

"Hopscotch," they answered in unison and it made me giggle. My friends. I was so happy. We searched the front yard for stones as we talked about camp and how we all wished we were still there hanging out in our cabin.

"Frank sent me a postcard the day before yesterday. It has his number on it but I don't think I will call," I twisted my lip into a frown.

"Why not?" Emmy asked. She threw her rock and started to hop.

"I don't know. When am I really going to see him? I only get two hour supervised visits with you." I made a groaning angry sound that I had been using quite a bit. I was learning the art of being angry.

"True," Angie said with a shrug. "I don't care much about seeing or talking to Kevin either."

We all let out an exhale and moved on to the topic of starting Junior High in the fall. That conversation took up the rest of the two hours and as I waved goodbye to both of my friends, I thought about how much I wished Grace's murderer would get arrested already. He was ruining the lives of all children in the area.

That same night there was a small knock on my door. I muted a rerun of "The Wonder Years" and called for whomever to come in. Krysta hesitantly stepped through the room with a board game in her hands. I looked at her puzzled.

"What's up? Are you here to pity the little sister?" I was finished with niceties. She smirked at me and shook her head.

"This was mine," she addressed a game box as she handed it over to me. The box read OUIJA in big bold letters. "I thought maybe you and the girls could play it when... you know, things are over. I played it with my friends when I was twelve and we had a pretty entertaining time with it."

"OW-EH-JA?" I asked looking up to her with a perplexed expression. I had never heard of it before.

"WEE-GEE," she laughingly answered.

"That is not proper English. Who comes up with these words?" I asked as I slid my hand over the worn box top.

"No idea. But try it out. It's fun. It's a board and you basically call in ghosts," she smiled with a tinge of sarcasm as she air quoted ghosts.

I was instantly interested. I sat up and forward with my eyes wide.

"Really, like what do you do?" I asked. I opened the box and saw a sun and a moon, yes and no, the alphabet, and the words GOOD BYE in big font.

"You and someone else or whoever can fit their fingers on this thing," she said pulling out a triangular pointed plastic piece. "You ask it questions and you try not to move your fingers but somehow, probably like how trees sway or something, it moves to different places on the board."

I looked at it with rapt fascination. "Can we try?" I asked looking up to her, begging with my eyes. She shrugged her shoulders and we got on the floor and positioned the board and the pointer. Krysta asked it what year Kent and she would get married. I rolled my eyes but kept my fingers very still. It didn't do anything. It just sat there. And so did we, for like twenty minutes. She asked the same question over and over, increasingly irritated each time. Finally I popped my fingers off and got up. With my butt now asleep and my interest totally lost, I frowned.

"I guess it doesn't work with me," I lied, kind of thinking that they would never get married. Krysta let out a breath and popped the game and pointer back into the box.

"Well, it's yours now, Jules. Have fun with it, if it even works for you," she said, flinging her blond hair behind her back. I watched her walk out of the room, quietly closing the door. I felt bad for her in that moment and yelled out a thank you.

I pressed the mute button and laid back to watch Kevin and Winnie walking down the street, hand in hand.

THREE

It was a week after Krysta had given me the OUIJA board and I had forgotten all about it. Emmy, Angie, and I were outside on my lawn, within eye sight of my mother, playing Scrabble. I hated Scrabble. Our daily play dates were becoming so dull and we grasped on to whatever we could to keep our friendship alive. We couldn't go biking. We couldn't play in our fort in the forest behind Emmy's house. We couldn't do anything fun.

Angie placed the tiles down to make the word Donkey on the board after Emmy played the word Rocket. I threw my pieces up in the air and growled out in frustration. *Stupid Scrabble.* At the least, I could have been winning but no. I was so done with being a bored twelve year old. Mom looked up from the newspaper ten feet from us and gave me a disapproving look. It was actually the look she saved for when I was being a total brat. I was getting that look a lot lately.

"Jules Delaney! Why are you acting like you are two years old?" Mom snapped at me. The two other girls looked wide eyed as their eyes jumped from me to my mother and back. I started to cry and ran into the house, yelling that I hated my life. This was the worst summer ever. Not even the glorious time I had had at camp could make this summer a memorable one. I felt like a hostage. No, I *was* a hostage.

I threw my head into my pillow on my waterbed and sobbed. Minutes later, Emmy and Angie were standing against my bedroom wall, waiting for me to stop my crying fit. I was embarrassed that I had ruined our game.

"I'm sorry that I ruined the game," I whispered, as I hiccupped in my post crying fit. My friends were prisoners, too, but I seemed to be the only one taking it so hard.

Both girls climbed on top of me and we all hugged. I heard them muttering that they hated this summer and they just wish that we could go play on our own for just one day. I nodded, as I sniffled, and tried to muster up a smile for them.

They could barely smile back and we all knew why. This was the worst summer in the history of all summers. Emmy got up and started eyeing everything in my room with fascination. I did have a cool room. I watched her go through my CDs and books. When she saw the OUIJA Board, she picked it up. As she turned the box over and over again, she smiled broadly.

"I played this once with my cousin in her back yard! It was so much fun! I begged my parents for one but Mom and Dad said it wasn't a nice board game for the house," she said. She was clearly excited. She could have the stupid thing if she really wanted it.

"Oh yeah? Krysta gave it to me. We played it about a week ago and it didn't do anything," I replied, noticing Angie peering over at the box with interest.

"Let's play it now," Emmy clapped her hands with glee. She giggled to herself as she started to open the box. I inwardly sighed. I didn't want to play another board game. I officially despised them all. They were mind-numbing. Nevertheless, Emmy hardly came up with ideas when we played anything so Angie and I got on the floor and waited for Emmy to set it up.

When all of our hands were in place, we peered at one another expectantly.

"What do we do?" Angie inquired.

"We say hello and ask them who they are," Emmy announced, nodding in determination down to the board. "So I will ask. Hello. This is Jules, Emmy, and Angie. We want to talk to you. Are you here?"

Emmy asked as she looked at the board with rapt attention.

I sighed and just watched Emmy and Angie. I loved my friends and I didn't know what I would do without them. They were keeping me together this summer. I had not even noticed that the pointer was moving. Emmy smiled and Angie looked confused. I looked down to see that the pointer was right over "Yes".

"Hey! Did you guys move your fingers?" I chided, startling them both. The board hadn't moved a lick when Krysta and I had done it. *Nothing.* Now it was clearly on the word "Yes" and I yelped, a little freaked out. I started to pull my fingers back.

"No, don't," Emmy admonished loudly. "Leave them on or they will leave." Who would leave? What the hell was going on? My upper body started to shake which made my fingers a little shaky, too. I took a few calming breaths to make them stop moving.

I firmly laid my four fingers back on the pointer, never losing the connection. Thank God I didn't break the connection or whoever would have left. Wait, did I believe this? I looked around to see if the other girls were as quizzical as I was. Was this thing actually real? Emmy looked amused and Angie was intrigued. I was scared and hoped I wouldn't pee my pants.

"Who... are... you?" Angie asked very slowly, but her voice shook noticeably. A huge bubble of unease rose in my chest and I swallowed really hard. I watched our fingers–looking to see if any of them were moving, even if unintentionally. But we were all still. We were hardly touching the plastic triangle as it flew across the board with disjointed speed. G–R–A–C–E

We all gasped. Angie's eyes got so wide, she looked like a bug. A beetle. Emmy didn't look so amused anymore.

"You are Grace? You were just murdered!" I screamed at the board like it was going to yell back at me. I started to sweat and I watched the two other girls' mouths drop open. Either they couldn't believe that we were supposedly talking to Grace or that I had screamed murder at the board. Either way, no one was saying anything as we waited for a response. The pointer moved to "Yes", moved away, and went back to "Yes". Yes, it was Gracie. Yes, she was murdered.

Emmy cleared her throat and it looked like she couldn't get her mouth to work. "Who... who killed you?" Emmy asked. We all watched the board with rapture. The pointer didn't move. Several seconds went by. Just as I was going to ask again, the pointer slowly moved. We watched it as it slowly went through the three letter word. It was going so slow, we were all holding our breaths for it to stop on one letter. When it did, we looked up to each other with horrified expressions.

D–A–D

The pointer quickly zipped out of our hands and landed on "GOOD BYE". I couldn't breathe. Tears were in Emmy's eyes and Angie was shaking her head in disbelief.

"Her dad killed her?" Emmy asked softly.

I couldn't believe it. It was a dumb game and one of my friends had just punked me. Someone punked me and that pissed me off and made me feel a bit of relief. I threw my head back against the wall and exhaled in relief. I would make them play again. I will watch them very carefully.

"It's not real," I stated firmly. I picked the board and the pointer up and threw them in the box. I stuck it in my closet on the highest shelf. I turned around to see both girls looking at me like I should know what to do next.

"What?" I asked.

"Shouldn't we tell someone?" Angie asked. Moments passed in silence.

That's when I knew. If Angie moved the pointer, she wouldn't be asking me this. If it was Emmy who moved it, she would be objecting to telling anyone. She was too nice to lie.

"Tell them what? We played the OUIJA board and it said that Gracie's dad killed her?" I asked incredulously.

They both shrugged. I shook my head at them. Sometimes, my friends were clueless.

"Tell you what," I started. "Tomorrow, I will bring it to Angie's house. We can do it again. We can ask her if there is proof." I said, as I started flipping through a Seventeen magazine. Pretending that I wasn't scared was hard, but both girls looked convinced as they made their way out of my room to meet their parents outside.

Minutes later, Mom and I waved to the cars. I apologized for my outburst as she put her arm around my shoulder.

"Mom, does anyone think that Grace's father is the one who killed her?" I tried to act cool about it but she eyed me with little bit of suspicion.

"I don't think so," she said slowly and wearily.

I nodded my head and went back to my bedroom. I didn't sleep at all that night. I knew who had murdered Grace and there was nothing I could do about it.

The next day, I fumbled with the OUIJA board box before I gave up, by stuffing just the board and the pointer into my backpack. Mom had called for me to go for the third time and I rolled my eyes at her impatience. She didn't know that important things were being prepared and I, too, couldn't wait to get with my friends and try to talk to Grace again.

The three of us begged our parents off and headed into Angie's room. The Offspring and Goo Goo Doll posters adorned her walls. Angie was also an amazing artist and had several of her canvases leaning up on every wall, with open and dried up oil tubes littering her floor. The smell of her room sometimes made Emmy sick but for me, it was relaxing to be among creativity. I hadn't found my real hobby yet. I liked to sing along with male lead bands because my voice was low enough. That, however, was the extent of my musical talent.

I took the board and pointer out of the backpack and tossed it on the bed.

"We are not doing that where I sleep at night," Angie scolded me. I nodded in understanding while Emmy gracefully took the board and with great care, as if she was going to break it, placed it on the floor like she had done the previous day.

35

We quickly sat down, placed our fingers at the same spots, and look at each other. Without asking a word, the pointer moved to yes, move away and then went back to yes.

"She is here," Angie whispered. "What do we ask?"

The pointer moved and we watched as it moved from D to A to D. It did this twice before I realized that she would probably leave again.

"What am I going to be when I get older?" I asked in a hurry. "Oh, this is Jules."

The pointer didn't move for a while as I thought about an early death. Would I get older? Was it like Krysta? Because last I had heard, Kent was fighting with her over the phone. A lifetime they would not last. Finally it moved. Slowly it moved to S. It sat there for several seconds. What was I going to be when I grew up? A singer? A songwriter? A salesman? A sales clerk? Oh god, I was going to be pathetic.

The pointer moved quickly to L. I couldn't come up with anything before it moved to U. Then rapidly, it shot over to T. The pointer gained momentum and repeated the word.

S–L–U–T.

S–L–U–T.

I looked at my friends in confusion.

"What's a slut?" Emmy whispered. We both shrugged our shoulders and then Emmy asked the same question. I didn't see what the pointer answered but she looked just as dumbfounded as I did. I blanked out, trying to figure out what a slut was. When Angie asked, I was about to jump up and run to a dictionary but I couldn't let go before we were done. Emmy and I both stared off at something in the room as Angie got her answer. I looked down to see the last two letters were Z-Y. Angie gasped and withdrew her hands from the pointer. Without her fingers, however, the pointer made its way to GOOD BYE.

We all started talking at once about how the board was a fake and one of us was moving it. When I asked them why it moved on its own without our hands the previous morning, I was met with silence.

Angie got up and with shaking hands, put the board and the pointer back into the backpack. Emmy cleared her throat.

"Let's go play hopscotch," she said numbly. We all nodded. As we made it out of the house, Angie's mom came up and clearly she had been crying. She hugged Angie so hard and then continued to hug both Emmy and I, as well.

"Mom, what is it? Why are you crying?" Angie asked.

"Oh honey. They got him. Grace's killer. They found evidence and he was arrested this morning. You are all safe now. It is so sad for her family but such a relief to us parents," she said grimly. Her head fell back as she wiped the mascara from under her eyes.

"Who? Who killed her?" Emmy shakily asked.

"It was her father, dear. He is a very, very sick man. But that isn't your problem so you don't need to worry about it one bit. Here, let me get you some candy money and you can walk down to the corner store," she said as she scurried out of the room and gave us each a five dollar bill. We all looked at it perplexed.

"Is it too little? I can get more," she said, sounding panicked. "You girls have been holed up for three weeks now. Maybe I should get more."

"No." We all said it in unison and Angie's mom nodded slowly. We filed out the front door and started walking on the sidewalk in a line. We didn't say anything all the way to the store. We all knew who had killed Grace. But the shock that the board was right was what made us realize that we probably couldn't escape who we would be as we grew up.

FOUR

I was anxious to get home that night. I immediately went to Kent's room and banged on his door. He was playing his electric guitar and the amp was so loud, I could hardly hear my knock. Krysta opened the door, sucking on a lollipop, and smiled. "Did you hear? That asshole dad killed his own daughter. What a freak," she said.

Kent looked up and gave her a weird look and then smiled at me. "I guess this means you are off house arrest now, huh Jules?"

"Yeah. I guess. Hey Kent? Can I talk to you a minute?" I asked and looked at Krysta. "Privately?"

Krysta bounced out of the room, claiming she needed to touch up her makeup and Kent rolled his eyes. I shut the door and sat on his bed, closest to the chair that he sat in when he played. "You sound good," I said.

"Thanks, Jules. I doubt that is what you want to talk to me about though. If it is a boy, I will... " he started, cracking his knuckled.

I shook my head. "No. No. No boy. Kent... What does the word... slut mean?" I asked him cautiously and watched for his expression. It grew dark and he stood up quickly.

"Did someone call you that?" he yelled.

"No. I mean, yes. But no. It was just a game," I said, trying to calm him down. It wasn't working. He was pacing back and forth.

"Just *tell* me what it means," I pleaded.

"You don't want to know, Jules. It's a mean, mean word." He snapped.

"I need to know," I said quietly.

He let out a loud exhale and sat down on the bed next to me. He looked at me and then back down at the ground. "A slut is someone who has sex with a lot of people."

"Sex?" I asked. "Like intercourse? What they talked about in maturation classes?"

He nodded, looking completely uncomfortable. I closed my mouth on the subject, blinking over and over. I had both embarrassed him and me. Why would I grow up to be a slut? That doesn't make money or provide for my family. Did it mean something else? Kent started to talk again but I couldn't hear him. All I could see was the pointer moving to the words over and over again. I was lost in the visual, lost to the word, lost to all the questions I had that probably would never get answered.

"Cool. Well... thanks Kent," I said awkwardly.

"Jules," he said.

"Yeah?" I answered, turning around from my door.

"Make sure you love the guys that you have... umm" he coughed and I nodded.

"Like you love Krysta?" I countered. I didn't wait for his response. I ran out of his room so fast that I almost slammed into Krysta who was obviously eavesdropping. She gave me a sad look like she was going to say something. I shook my head, bee lined it for my bedroom and slammed the door.

I knew in that moment that nothing would ever be the same between Kent and me again. We had officially stepped over the brother/sister boundary line. Of course, I would never ever discuss the word slut with my mom. She didn't know that I was going to be one. Or was I?

That night in bed, I fell asleep repeating the word "slut" over and over in my head. I tried to sing a song. I tried to think of *any* other word. God help me, it just kept popping back into my head, like a bug was implanted into my ear. I squeezed my head. I screamed into my pillow. I shoved my head into my stuffed animals at the wall side of my bed. I did everything I could do to detach my brain from my head.

The next morning I canceled on Emmy and Angie and stayed locked up in my room. I didn't feel like seeing anyone. Would they know? Would they be able to see that I was losing my mind? The canceling continued the following day when Emmy called. The next day? Angie.

It was my thirteenth birthday that hot August day. I had asked Emmy and Angie over for cake and ice cream but both of them said they couldn't. No excuses. They just couldn't. I was confused and lonely. Mom had made the obligatory call to my favorite bakery two towns over and reserved a Boston Crème Pie Cake for that night. Other than that, it was just me and the house. All day. All alone. Happy 13th birthday to me.

It was the middle of the afternoon when I heard a knocking at the door. I lifted up on my tippy toes to peek through the view hole and there was Jason #2 with a wrapped gift in his hand. I immediately opened the door with a wide smile.

"Hey Jay," I welcomed him excitedly.

He smiled at me and handed over the small present.

"Do you want to come in? Kent isn't home yet but you can wait for him," I offered the idea, as I looked down at the gift. It poorly wrapped, but it was such an unexpected surprise. It felt like it was probably a tee shirt that was bunched together to not waste too much birthday wrapping paper. Either way, someone was thinking about me that day.

"I know he is at work. I just swung by and he wanted me to tell you that it is going to be later than usual. He feels really bad about it, Jules, so he said maybe he would take you to Dairy Queen after he gets home," he said solemnly.

Jason was sixteen and going into the eleventh grade. Grade cut offs put us at a four year scholastic difference, but out of all three Jasons, he was the one I got along with the best. I was old for my grade and he was young for his. Kent and he were super good at sports, and since he lived right around the corner, their age difference didn't matter to either of them.

"Oh, well. I guess that is as good as it is going to get today," I shrugged, still holding the package, and looking off into space.

Jason stepped way too close in my personal space and my heart kicked up in speed, as I realized he was coming in to kiss me. Shocked, I didn't move my lips like I had with Frank. I didn't let him feel my tongue with his. I just stood there, like a statue, not understanding why he was kissing me.

He pulled back and smiled at me innocently.

"Jules. Julia," he started. "I have noticed that you are growing into a woman now. When Kent told me it was your birthday, well... I found a little something that you might like. You know, since you are older now."

He nodded his head at the package, but I was still reeling from the kiss that my big brother's friend, who was both seriously hot and seriously older than me, had given to me. Maybe it was just a fluke. Yes, my birthday! You know, it was like 'Hey, let's give Julia a fifteen second kiss to make her feel like a teenager!' Okay, it was seventeen seconds because I was counting. And I was counting because it was the only way I could maintain some semblance of sanity. Jason had just kissed me and he had given me a gift. Did he? Did he like-like me? I mentally shrugged that preposterous idea off and looked at the package. I ripped it open to find an adorable outfit. I pulled out a cute pink tank top with small boy shorts that had less material than the tank top. Jason had purchased underwear for me? No, it wasn't underwear, but certainly I would only wear this to bed. Bed. He had gotten me sleep wear. But, why?

I looked up to him puzzled and that is when I saw it. He had the look that Frank had at camp when he was just about to kiss me. Jason wanted to kiss me? He wanted... me? I don't know how it happened, or why he felt that way, but wow. His eyes were blazing hot and only for me.

"Will you try it on for me, Julia?" he whispered with an eagerness I had never heard from him.

"Um. I don't know. I mean I think it is very cute but I guess I didn't think you thought of me like that." I tried to stay cool. Inside I was freaking out. Where were my two best friends? I needed them. I didn't know what to do.

"You are still a virgin, right? You didn't lose it to some jackass at camp?" he teased in a really awkward, almost jealous way.

"That is none of your business, Jason." No way was I telling my brother's best friend if I am a virgin or not.

I nodded at the gift in my hands and headed back to my bedroom, slightly mortified and somewhat wanting him to follow me. When he did follow me into my room, I looked up to him with apprehension.

"Are you ticklish, Jules?" he asked. I shook my head because I knew better than to confess that I was.

"I don't believe you." He waved all his fingers in a taunting threat. I moved closer to the wall on my bed, but the water below didn't help me move far enough.

"Please don't tickle me," I whispered.

On cue, Jason was on top of me, tickling under my arms, on my sides, and soon in between my legs. He slowed as his fingers and started to lightly tickle up my legs towards my core area. I stared at his hands as I tried to calm my breathing from the excruciating pain of just being tickled. His two fingers clamped over my cotton panties.

"Okay, okay. Stop. I am a virgin, yes. Are you happy now?" I breathed out heavily as his lips came crashing down on mine. I opened my mouth, my arms, and my legs for him. He was super good at kissing and I tried to learn what I could from this moment. He shuddered and pulled away.

"Will you try on the outfit, Jules?" Jason asked as he kissed the back of my hand. That simple gesture was so gentle and in that moment, I wanted to be a couple with Jason. Mom and Kent could never know but we would be secretive. He really was so sweet for bringing me a present, although a little weird for me, and spending time with me on my birthday.

I nodded slowly. I started to get up to go to the bathroom when he demanded that I change in front of him. He lay on his back with his hands behind his neck. I made to double check the lock on my door and quickly undressed.

When my shy face looked up to see what kind of reaction he would have, I was taken aback. He was looking at my every private area with rapt attention and I saw the spot near his zipper on his jeans where his penis was growing. Frank's penis had changed like that a few times and I did touch it once. It was soft, and I liked touching it, but Frank quickly put himself away when we heard people coming down the trails at camp.

I never did make it into my outfit that day. Jason took my virginity away and gave me the first orgasm I ever had. I did wear it the next day he showed up for another round of "tickling", as he continued to call it. Jason was hot and so sweet to me. To some degree, I knew he was taking advantage of me, but I grew to enjoy our time together. I was addicted to sex, to him, and I was always ready for Jason when he called. I got jealous when he dated other girls and I sometimes kept him waiting to make a point that I wasn't just anybody. The only thing he ever promised me was that there would be a next time.

Nevertheless, we had a secretive affair for two years. We either met at my house after school and before we expected anyone home or we used a guest bedroom that was on top of his garage when his parents weren't home. From seventh grade until the night before Jason left for college on the west coast, we learned everything and anything we could about each other's bodies. He said he would miss me. I told him life wouldn't be the same. I cried the day he left for college, but not for very long, since I had a date that very night with the sexiest guy in the tenth grade.

By the end of our senior year, my childhood friends and I never acknowledged one another, Jason was long gone from Kent's and my life, and the OUIJA board was but a faint memory. It wasn't until I was twenty nine years old that it came back to haunt me.

FIVE

SIXTEEN YEARS LATER

2009

New York City

My dream about the OUIJA board from last night was just another repeat memory to me now as I set up the stage for our show. I sensed something looming over my head all day, like a dusty cloud that never dissipates. It had been a while since I had the dream. Weeks? Maybe months? I wondered why I had one today. Normally, it had something to do with my mood, but I was fine. Everything was right as rain. Putting all that aside, I had to focus. Too much bullshit from the past would mess up my game tonight.

Tiny droplets of sweat appeared in my cleavage just as I took the stage. Dex, a beefy dark haired muscle man, started the beginning drum beats for our first song. It was a chaotic beat that got the whole crowd rip roaring and jumping. I smiled and threw my hands up to the crowd in an all-encompassing welcome. They flailed their arms right back in response. Johnny, the bassist and my former surfer looking blond boyfriend, gave me my signature silver and black Fender guitar and made sure that I saw him wink at me. Every single show, he had to give me that stupid wink. *Ass hat.* He joined Dex in the beat with his perfect bass banging. I bobbed my head side to side, in an attempt to loosen up my neck for the next forty minute set. One of the worst things about singing and playing guitar was my neck always throbbed in pain post show.

When I strapped on the guitar, my foot immediately found the pedal to fine-tune the distortion. I adjusted the microphone to my five foot three inches and waited for my cue. I closed my eyes and counted down four, three, two, and one... *I Sang for You* was met with another hurricane of praise. It was, after all, one of our most widespread and popular songs these days.

We are Love Sick Ponies. No, it wasn't *my* favorite name at first but it grew on me after about ten minutes. Johnny's pep talk which outlined how famous we would be with such a rocking name made sense. We had the perfect story to go with our rocking band name. Love Sick Ponies or LSP, voted unanimously by all three of us, was founded on a hilarious, albeit a drug induced memory. Dex, Johnny and I have been friends since college, our band started in our sophomore year. Johnny and I were living together in a small two bedroom apartment in Baltimore after we graduated from the University of Maryland. For years, we took odd jobs and looked for gigs everywhere we could get in, just to pay for rent for that dump.

One night, maybe two years after we moved in together, we decided to eat tripped out mushrooms. After several hours of laughing and chatting a mile a minute, we fixed ourselves on the couch to watch television. While we flipped through the channels on cable we stopped and became instantly fascinated by the cartoon, My Little Pony. I commanded that Johnny record the first episode half way through. We then proceeded to record the following two episodes and scrutinized them over and over until the sun came up. As we started to come down off the high near dawn, we both abruptly noticed that were tangled in a conversation about the sparkles and colors. We were intimately close. He was right there. *Delicious enough to kiss.*

We found ourselves making out on the couch, while My Little Pony's theme song rang throughout the apartment. The kissing directed us to my bedroom. There he threw me down on the mattress and started licking my ankles for what felt like hours. His beautiful blonde hair and tanned, muscled chest, Johnny held himself over me in a frozen push-up for three solid hours while he devoured every part of my body. When I finally saw Johnny completely nude for the first time, I had to ask myself why I went against the grain with him. I loved sex, he was hot, and yes, I got the stink eye for at least a full day when I brought any guy home for the night.

Johnny and I fit. We were wild about each other for twenty four hours straight only stopping for food and a quick nap. It was extreme. We didn't leave our apartment for days, ignoring the phone, ordering delivery, and enforcing a no clothing rule in effect for the duration. I loved Johnny. I loved him solid. Sex with him was not ever what I would call 'making love'. I was mesmerized by the incredible pleasure he gave me and he was clearly taken with me, as well.

To the outside world, we were the levy that everyone was waiting for to break. I mean break *up*.

Effortlessly, we announced that we were a couple to three older hunters and a metrosexual bartender, who was on the phone the whole time. We still got the applause we sought after... from Dex. Then he begged us to get the show over with so that he could get back to his own girl. We were together for a few years and it was a fun, laid back relationship.

I guess somewhere along the way, Johnny and I started to focus more on the band than our relationship, because when we landed our first real headlining tour, Johnny celebrated by blatantly getting so plastered that he fucked another girl in the back stage bathroom. It was a night to remember because not only did the band get noticed and our relationship went into the gutter, but it was the first time I had ever had the dream about the summer of 1993.

Of course, Johnny claimed the busty blonde threw herself at him, so it wasn't really his fault. I still account the incident as nature's way of telling us that we were better as friends and bandmates. I mean, shit. He didn't even bother to look ashamed when I watched him exit the bathroom, pulling up his pants, and Blondie hanging on to his every word for the rest of the evening. I didn't feel hurt about his infidelity, but embarrassment was the killer for me. The pitying looks I received from the tour crew were infuriating.

Due to my mortification, I felt the urge to act upon my own sexual desires from that very night on. I kicked Johnny out of our place in Baltimore for good measure. He moved in with Dex until we all left permanently to go wherever our label told us to. I was somewhat disappointed in the expectations I had put on a man, especially Johnny. I had never trusted men before him and I guess I fell into the trap that nothing bad would ever happen. I assumed we were something special and our relationship would never get so boring that one of us would stray. I was sorely wrong since he still had a penis and it evidently needed the endorsement of numerous women.

I closed my eyes against the pink, green, and yellow strobe lights. Why on earth our tour manager, Danielle, required our band to look like a kaleidoscope on stage, I would never fathom. I twisted to sing to Johnny to dodge being blinded or seeing spots for the rest of the night. I examined his fingers smacking down on the strings and gave my plaid school skirt a little jiggle. He and I did a back and forth guitar dance and as the song neared the ending, I turned to face the masses again.

Once again, the flashes and strobe lights caused me momentary blindness. Most nights I really didn't care that much. It was part of the gig. Tonight, however, I was uptight about it. If I went blind from being a rock star, I wouldn't know who to sue.

"Hello, New York City!" I roared into the microphone. The crowd went mad and then hushed down to wait for my obligatory speech I made at each show.

"I'm Jules Delaney. That crazy drummer is Dex Parker and the sexy bassist over there is Johnny Lennox. We are Love Sick Ponies and we are so thrilled to be here tonight with Desired Pitch! Lizzie was incredible, yeah?" The crowd screamed and I giggled at their fervor.

"So we are going to bring it down a notch. How about a slow one? Can you guess what it is?" I probed.

The crowd chanted "Leg up, Leg Up, Leg Up." It was out of control.

I nodded my head enthusiastically and put my mouth back on to the microphone. The beginning solo vocals were sweet on *Leg Up*. The reverberations, the lyrics, and the energy were more elegant than who I really was beneath all of my eye makeup and piercings. Total contradiction. I don't know why Dex wrote this song exactly. I considered that his girlfriend had broken up with him for something like the fifth time and he was tired of spending their few days apart drinking himself into oblivion.

Dex would write songs for days and nights around-the-clock. I am a firm believer that these two new songs were the reason for why we were ready to record with Nick Sawyer Productions for our next album. Based out of Boston, NSP was huge because Nick and Lizzie Sawyer had serious abilities and contacts. They had built an incredible company over the past few years and Love Sick Ponies was there every step of the way.

Nick and Lizzie always set us up in a bad ass apartment downtown Boston and it was a blast while we hung out with Desired Pitch. They were like family. The production company became just as widespread as both bands in the past few years. I busted out a wide smile at the thought of spending the ensuing two months in their studio as I initiated the first verse.

You haven't been home

I called around

No one knows where you can be found.

If I found you, I'd hide you well

I'd make you scream with one leg up. One Leg Up,

I got you baby with one leg up.

I started to play the lead guitar solo in the song when my eyes landed on *him*. He wasn't jumping or screaming. He was a stone statue and wholly contented to watch my individual act. He was stunning. He was a man I could look at for days. His black blue hair, his stormed dark eyes were disguised with brown square rimmed glasses and a brown beanie hat. *Hot.* One full tattooed sleeve peeked out from his Henley and I peered at the arm to make out some of the design. I shook my head in exasperation when I couldn't see anything that far away. The fucking white spotlight that found my face made me want to throw my guitar across the stage.

After my solo, my eyes danced up to his face and his expression looked intensely thoughtful for a man. I grinned to myself as I looked down at my fingers flying across the strings. He would obviously never know that I was checking him out. People in the crowd never did notice that we, too, looked at the crowd one by one. That was one of the best parts of being on stage. Sure, they were all watching us but we were inspecting them just as much. I was the actual stalker in a room. A big belly laugh erupted out of my throat as I automatically chimed into the chorus.

One Leg Up, Up, Up

One Leg up, up

One leg is all I have when I am with you.

That's it how it will always be.

I looked to my right and saw him again. He was marginally moving his head back and forth. So the guy liked slow songs, too? *Very mysterious man.* He looked like a death metal fan and yet he was digging on this love ballad. *Oxymoron.* The song finished on one long note as I pursed my full lips in his direction as if I was giving him a kiss. His answering smile made me stumble backwards.

My boobs were officially drenched.

Danielle, stealthy as she was when we were on stage, handed me a clean towel and my first bottle of water. It was going to be a long soaking wet night. Johnny and Dex started the next song and fortunately Johnny was on vocals for this one. I hung back and let him take the show over. It gave me time to admire my admirer. His piercing dark eyes took me in. No, he was visually molesting me. They perused me, drinking me in, from my black cowboy boots to my dark hair pulled back into a spiky ponytail. I considered my guitar and was thankful for the first time ever that I had something to focus on. I grinned. If I had it my way, that chunk of sex would be licking my body sweat off in the shower back at the hotel.

Six songs later, I was convinced that I was in love. The fiery looks and burning bursts of energy we exchanged were intense. We were undoubtedly having visual intercourse. No matter how distracted I was, I was spot on with every queue and every lyric. Even the four shots of vodka I had taken before I jumped on the stage didn't make me lose any brain cells. I was singing to my beanie wearing tatted up hunk and he knew it.

Johnny hurled inquisitive looks my way throughout the last songs. I hit every beat and every breath. He probably had never seen me play so well and maybe I hadn't. Damn jealous ass face. He recognized that something was going on with me and looked over the crowd to see who I was playing for because it was obviously *not* for him.

Even though I broke it off with Johnny that night he fucked the busty blonde, he never had another serious girlfriend. He made it clear to everyone who would listen to his love woes that he was waiting for me "to come around".

He would be waiting a long time. I saw him hook up with indiscriminate chicks under the radar. He wasn't waiting around for me. His head was just trapped in the past. It was hard not to think of *us* and that night when we had to say Love Sick Ponies at least twenty times a day. But damn if I wasn't a love sick pony for erotic beanie guy.

SIX

I sauntered back stage into a flurry of activity. Fans were already waiting for us to sign shit and have a beer with us like we were old buddies. No one knew the true Jules Delaney, the face people associated with our band. Sometimes even I didn't know me. I was Jules to some, Julia to others. Johnny liked to use both names to let me know which mood he was in at that moment.

Despite the ardent fans that were actually very cool, this was the focused part of my night. After the show is when I found my male conquest for the evening. Johnny had nothing on me as far as 'under the radar' goes. I signed a few posters and tickets. I found Danielle on the side of the room. She handed me the obligatory shot and a beer. As I took them she rattled through the list of people that I needed to talk to and handed me a new shirt.

"What? I don't look fucking sexy in this?" I asked, laughing at her disgusted look. I hugged her and then handed her the empty shot glass, threw the shirt over my shoulder, and headed for the restroom. She called out somebody's name I had to find after I went to pee. Someone extra important? *Yeah, whatever.* I nodded back to her like I cared. I would do what I wanted tonight. Tonight was off limits and while we are at it, please make a fucking appointment. Don't these people know I just sang my guts out for hours?

Just as I got to the open door, I slammed right into one of Lizzie's friends. I had seen him around at the last few shows on this tour. He was attractive. Even the tattooed sleeves on both arms didn't take away that he was hot. With a wide grin, he excused himself.

"Sean, right?" I pointed at him. His expression was priceless. He must have thought I had ignored him outright when Lizzie introduced us. I knew names like my lyrics. They were part of my database vocabulary. I laughed at his bewildered look.

"Yeah, I'm Sean. You are Jules. Or is it Julia?" he questioned. I shrugged.

"We've met a few times over the years but I didn't know that you were paying attention," he grinned. Over the years? Shit, I thought I had *just* met him. Well hell. So much for attempting to get my head out of my ass for this conversation. I wondered if he detected my sudden flinch. I tried to save a shred of poise.

"Sure! I love Lizzie and her friends. That means I love you!" I laughed. It was fake as shit. It was like me sticking out two finger pistols with the accompanying smirk that jested, "You matter to me, buddy!"

"Hey, I have to run–gotta put this shirt on since I am drowning in this one," I said as I considered the sad excuse for a shirt. When I pulled my eyes back up to say bye to Sean, his hand was on someone else's shoulder. *His* shoulder.

"Hey Brennan! Lizzie got your pass all straightened out?" Sean asked, not detecting that I was transforming into a love drunk adolescent.

"Yeah, man. Liz got it set up. I am good," he affirmed, staring beautiful slivers of truth into my eyes. He was more than good. Was he a mind reader because I swear he knew exactly what I was thinking...which was... hell if I knew?

I held out my hand to introduce myself, waiting in anticipation for his touch. I waited for the sizzling electricity that I already knew was there between us. I was thirsting for it. It *had* to be there. That was one fact I knew for sure.

"I'm Jules. Or Julia. Julia Delaney." I wanted to make sure he knew that he could call me any name he wanted. Bitch would even be okay if he was going to stick around and talk to me.

His hand was immediately in mine, stroking it with his thumb like it was itching to stroke all of me. Yes, yes the electricity was there and scorching my hand. I felt it all the way to the nails on my toes.

"Brennan Curtis," he confessed.

His smooth, rich, fucking delicious voice combined with his dark brown, *'please take me now'* eyes demanded my skin to ripple ubiquitously. *Heavenly Father, please forgive me because I am about to sin…again.*

We stood there, neither one of us wanting to let go of the other. Sean caught on, suggested something dismissively, and strolled into the room of people.

"I… uh. I am going to head to the bathroom to change," I insisted as I held up my shirt. Brennan nodded at me but his eyes told me I needed to stay in this spot for a little longer. Maybe even forever. I was barely breathing. Nope, scratch that. I wasn't breathing.

"Where are you from?" I inquired after my lungs discovered air.

And what the fuck was that? I never ask guys anything. Normally by this time, we are taking shot after shot and making out like juveniles in a dark corner, far away from Johnny's peripheral vision. Why did I *care* where Brennan was from?

"New York. Brooklyn, more specifically," he answered with a blaze in his eyes. "I met Sean at a tattoo conference and he mentioned he was going to come to the show tonight. I wanted to come meet you."

Air escaped my lungs and I coughed at his blatant statement, causing me to drop my hand from his. He looked disappointed at my response. I had never thanked personal connections to gain backstage access as much as I did in this moment.

Johnny came up behind me and kissed me on the cheek while he flung his arms around my waist. He was already half tanked and laying on his nightly moves, hoping that tonight would be the night that I reformed my mind and fell to his feet with burning love. I extricated myself from his arms and gave him a scathing look. Feeling self-conscious and disgusted, I brushed past Brennan, his muscular build, and leather scent to bolt to the bathroom. *Johnny has to stop this revolting game.*

I slammed the bathroom stall door shut and sat on the toilet. My brain was fried. I didn't care about Johnny and apparently, I just shit the bed with Brennan. It was the same shit every show with Johnny. I could never find it in me to stand up to him and tell him to fuck off. I wanted to hide in this stall for the rest of the night. I wondered if James, our occasional tour driver, was easily accessible for a ride back to the hotel. I dragged out my cell phone and sent James a text.

Me: Ready to leave. Help?

James: Got it. Meet me in the back parking lot.

I flung my new shirt on and thought about going to Danielle for my personal shit. I sent a quick text to her asking to return my stuff to my room when she got back there. I dashed out of the bathroom and headed out to the back door. Luckily, nobody I knew was in the hall. I made it out the town car. The rain fell in cold splinters against my skin. James opened the door and gave me a lopsided smile. The guy was cute. He was probably my age and our best driver to date. He was always looking out for me. Although he would never bring up my issues, I knew he was well aware of my shortcomings.

I watched the beautiful buzz of downtown Manhattan. People were lost in their surroundings as they observed the bright lights of signs and billboards. The city wasn't a place to make friends. New York City *became* your friend. It was a city that compared to no other. I loved it but, as a New Hampshire native, I could only take it in small doses. Just the idea that I was on the small island and among so many people boxed in, I was more uneasy than enchanted. Nevertheless, it was exceptional to watch our crowds and their reactions to our band. I sucked it up. Coming to New York City was well worth the show.

James made it to the Hilton Midtown in record time and I flew out of the car. I ran in before I realized that I didn't have a key card or that I didn't say goodbye to

James. As I stood in the lobby, feeling misplaced, James presented a card before my eyes and I hugged him in thanks. He rubbed my back in silence until I pulled away. I was just hugging my driver. *Really?*

"You better be good to yourself tonight, Jules," James whispered. "Glad to see you taking the night off from the after party."

"Why don't you head back there and pick up that red head you were drooling all over before the show?" I laughed as I turned away but not before I saw his clever grin and heated blush.

As I headed up to my floor, I replayed the whole scene with Johnny and Brennan in the backstage room. I cringed at how inferior Johnny had made me feel once again. No doubt that Johnny would end up with some dumb bitch tonight and I would never see Brennan again.

I was no one's bitch. No one owned me. No one stakes a claim on me. The more people tried to rein me in, the more I pushed against their restraints. Tonight I was worn-out from the battle. I met a man who I was instantly fascinated by and Johnny slaughtered any further conversation by making it look like we were together. He would never let me be happy with anyone else. One way or another I needed to set the record straight with him once and for all.

I picked up my phone and shot Johnny a text.

Me: We need to talk tomorrow. Not happy.

A few minutes passed and my phone chimed.

Johnny: Does this have to do with tatted nerdy guy?

Me: Tomorrow. Sick of your shit.

I silenced my phone and went to the full length mirror. Time to rehearse the speech. I put my hand up against the wall and leaned into the mirror.

"Listen, Johnny... " I started. I shook my head and started again. I needed all my expressions accomplished, my words articulated. I needed him not only to listen but to finally *hear* that I would never desire him romantically or sexually again. It was going to be a tough conversation but it had to be done.

SEVEN

When Love Sick Ponies first started to tour, the accommodations we were given weren't exactly five star. Those dingy motels, God they were disgusting. The room consisted of beds covered in polyester floral blankets over hard smoke scented sheets and a five station cable television that was always on its last leg. We slept five people deep in a double bed room. Technically there were only three of us in the band but Johnny, Dex, and I usually had one or two people tag along after a show. We didn't call them a groupie. The victim was a far better label. The victim usually left the next morning looking like death had taken them multiple times.

From the very first night, I told the guys I would leave the tour if I didn't get my own bed. Dex and Johnny constantly fought over the second double bed but the one with the scissors or rock normally won. Paper just never made the grade. Johnny once waited until I was dead asleep to do his thing with a girl. It was evident when Dex, a buddy of his, and I all woke up to a female voice crying out Johnny's name until his final two thrust grunts. *Dumbass.*

That night, I locked myself in the bathroom and slept in the bathtub with a pillow. I remember chanting, "Anything for the music", while the girl's screams of ecstasy threatened to tear down the fucking walls. Fuck nugget thought he was being all stealthy. Habitually, he hooked up with his conquests either back stage or at their house first and then crashed at the hotel but I guess that night he was clearly out of his brain. I told Dex the next morning that if I had to listen to my ex bang out another chick, I was gone. It didn't happen again. And so... we endured each other's disgusting sweat, dirty underwear, and major gas spells city after city. Grimy hotel after grimy hotel. Some nights, I didn't think I would make it.

I reached the forty second floor and passed my card over the panel to prove that I had secure access to the floor. Nick Sawyer would only pay for secured floors for his beloved Lizzie therefore we all got to enjoy the benefits of being in an exclusive group. I found my way to Room 4210 and swiped the card to enter a beautiful suite. It was plenty of room for one. It had a brand new leather couch and a monstrous king sized bed. The Jacuzzi and spa style bathroom was calling out. "Jules, come here. I want you naked now," coaxed the bathroom in all of its marble and fluffy towel glory.

I didn't have to listen to boys farting through the night. I didn't have to smell the pot smoke lingering its way from underneath the bathroom door, the flimsy white towel stuffed under it be damned. I didn't have to look at Johnny the next morning and wonder if he enjoyed his sexscapade as much as his verbal conquest did. Now that our band was bigger and, well, we finally grew a pair and made strict demands for boarding, we got decent rooms to sleep in. Decent meaning that I got a room to my own self. *Hallelujah.* I looked forward to drinking a bottle of wine, taking a muscle relaxer, and soaking in a bath... all by myself. Tonight, however, I didn't even make it to the white fluffy robe before a loud banging started on my door.

"Juliiiiaaaa," Johnny yelled as he attempted to replicate the spirited line from Rocky when he called out to his wife. I held my breath. I didn't want him here. Why *was* he here? He knew to always leave me alone after getting back to the hotel. Perhaps, I wasn't clear that I would not spend the night in his company when I pulled out of his embrace back at the show? Or maybe I wasn't clear when I told him to basically fuck the hell off via text message? *Mother fucker.*

"Jules, open up. I know you are in there. James told me you came back early." Using his authoritative voice that I used to mock back at him during relationship squabbles reminds me of that awful time.

"I saw you looking at that dude."

"You forgot to pay the electricity bill."

That hard tone used to both turn me on and make me laugh. The make-up sex was always out of control impressive. We could never stay mad at each other for longer than an hour.

"When are we going to fuck again?"

I slapped him across the face and inquired how many times a day he anticipated sex.

"Six times doesn't seem too much to ask, Pony," he smirked and kissed me hard on the mouth. I suppose I missed having him to sleep with. We knew each other's needs and we could bang it out in minutes. I did miss that. He was familiar. Safe, maybe. Beyond that physical security, there wasn't anything left between us. So again, why the fuck is he outside my hotel room door?

I threw open the door instinctually and the instant smell of hard liquor met my nostrils. Wincing, I placed the back of my hand both underneath my nose and over my mouth.

"Jesus, Johnny, booze has taken over your body," I admonished him with disgust.

"Oh Jules. You know you love me no matter what I smell like. Let me come in. I want us to talk... you know... talk about the show and shit," he scrambled out his words.

He didn't want to talk. He wanted ass. I wasn't a friggin' idiot. Okay, maybe one time I fell for his drunken charm, but I was wasted. It didn't count. I chalked it up that we did it again for old times' sake. And, humiliated, I left before he woke up and pretended that I didn't remember us having sex at all. Faking a blackout has always been my excuse of choice. It's flawless really. How can someone truly put the blame on you if you don't have the foggiest idea what they are talking about?

"Nah. I am going to bed," I begged off, as I started to close the door on his smiling face. He was still so adorable. His tall, slightly built tattooed body was beautiful. His silky blonde hair could put him in the California beach boy category. Johnny didn't break my heart. He broke my trust. Since him, I sleep with guys and then I leave. I am not reckless or dumb about it. I am safe. I take all precautions. I didn't know if I could say the same about Johnny. I don't think he knows what the word protection even means.

He stopped the door with his hand.

"Just let me come in for one drink. I will be good. I promise. I know you aren't interested Jules. I just... I just fucking miss you. I miss us," he slurred as he crooked up one side of his lip. This was a side to Johnny that only came out to play every once in a while. Vulnerability. *Neither* of us showed it often and when it happened... well shit the last time it happened, I had to beg off a blackout.

Tonight, he had me with his rare helpless plea and he knew it. Besides, I was a sucker for waxing nostalgic with him and Dex. I loved to listen to the old stories about our college days and our first few tours. I loved talking about how we made up dinner recipes from a can of tomato paste, shredded cheese, peanut butter, and toast. Best damn sandwiches to this day. Actually, I could go for one right now.

I waved my arm with a flourish and let the door automatically shut. I immediately went to the bar, popped open the wine, and poured two glasses. Johnny sat on the couch. Actually he sat in the middle of the couch and his tall frame crowded most of it. If he wanted me to sit there, I would basically be on top of him with either side I chose. I shook my head at him as I handed him a glass and laughed.

"Not falling for that one, beach boy," I warned.

I carefully lowered myself into the business chair at the cherry wood desk. It wasn't as comfortable as the couch but I was sure it was far more comfortable in other ways.

Johnny clucked his tongue at me and winked.

"So, no hot chick to bang out tonight?" I questioned nonchalantly over the top of my wine glass.

He had the audacity to appear embarrassed. Everyone saw his obvious promiscuity. Was he really that dumb to think I hadn't noticed too? *Blind fool.*

"Well... if you *must* know." he started. I rolled my eyes.

"Must? Oh yes, Johnny, please. Please tell me. I am on the edge of this business seat. I can't wait. I *must* know now," I laughed with nastiness.

Ugh, he just brought out the worst in me. He looked at me like I had lost my mind and then wobbled his head a few times and took a deep inhalation.

"I met a smoking barbeque blond tonight. God, I would have devoured every rib on her until she was licked clean."

Oh. My. God. Did he just compare a woman to a rack of ribs? He didn't notice that my wine was stopped half way to my mouth as I gaped at him. I cleared my throat of the nausea inching itself up from my stomach.

"We were all set to go back to my room. In the elevator, she started... you know, working on me." His face flamed red hot as I listened but I was unresponsive. Why did I ask him about this again? Oh yeah, I am a masochist. I *must* know.

"So, she was taking care of business but she didn't really know what she was doing and then I thought about you. Something about how you know every inch of me. For just a tiny minute, I pretended she was you. I tried to guide her like you would do it. I just wanted it to feel like you again and then I guess I moaned out your name," he admitted as he shrugged one shoulder. I was unquestionably and outright thunderstruck. My eyebrows were aching from the force of my eyes being pushed so hard together.

"So!" He slapped his jean clad leg that was crossed over his other one. "She got pissed and took the elevator back down. It made me think. I mean, really think. For the ten seconds that it took me to walk to your room, I came to the conclusion that you, Jules Delaney, are hands down... wait for it... wait for it... the *finest woman* at giving head."

His voice was like a game show host's telling the winner that they had just won a brand new car. His expectant expression for my thrilled moment of joy slowly faded with the seconds that ticked by.

I coughed. He did not just say that. Part of me wanted to throw my wine at his face. But then I felt it. A little sense of vanity. Acknowledgment. Admiration.

"Well, hells bells, Johnny! Where the shit is my fucking gold painted plastic trophy? Put best blow jobs right up there in my accomplishments column. Maybe right above the one that says I am the most popular singer-songwriter in the new millennium?" I was fucking fuming. Despite that small feeling I had a few moments before, did he think I was going to drop to my knees and give thanks?

"But what *makes* you such a good singer, Jules? Think about it. You are making love to the microphone and the mic is a dick," he snickered as he popped one of his eyebrows up in a way that only concluded that he was right.

Touché, Johnny. Tou-fucking-che.

Did the microphone really symbolize a proverbial penis for me? Maybe. Yes, it probably did but what the fuck ever. The microphone was not an *actual* dick and why the fiddle fuck was I even having this conversation with him or myself?

I laid my head back on the chair and swigged my wine. I grew introspective as Johnny started to get more comfortable in the leather cushions. I never tried the whole girl on girl scene for sure but I was flawless at having sex with men. I had a lot of practice growing up and I paid rapt attention to what they desired from me.

Although most lovers, including Johnny until I trained him on a thing or two, didn't know the first thing about a woman's anatomy, I didn't mind. I was there to serve their desires so that in the end, they gave me the attention I craved. It gave me great satisfaction to give them the memory of being with such a skilled woman. It made them want me more and the thought of that is what got me off. It was a confidence enhancement and I wouldn't trade that feeling for anything.

I didn't consider that I was a whore. Nope, not in my eyes. I chose the guy... always. I had to be with a guy that was sexy. He *had* to be funny. He *had* to like to listen to music during our time together. It was what got me in the mood. Despite those specifications, I didn't really mind who the guy actually was as a person. For all I knew, they had zero money and still lived with their momma. However, I needed to know how they evaluated my mad skills at the end. One hundred percent of the time, I was hands down *the* best lay they ever had by their looks of satiated bliss. I always patted myself on the back as I showed them the door. I knew there was one more guy out there that worshipped me.

"Gee whiz, Johnny. Thanks so much for your praise," I regarded at him with a cheeky smile. He rolled his eyes and then drank the whole glass of wine in two gulps.

"Is sharing time over now?" I asked. "I want to get a bath in."

"I don't *want* our time to be over. Can I just sit here while you take a bath? I'll watch TV or something. I just don't want to go to my room alone." He sounded tragic. Was he just lonely or was I a constant that he had come to rely on? Maybe he just missed the idea of me being there every night.

I nodded, making a *poor you* face at him, and grabbed the bottle of wine. With both the bottle and the glass clutched in a one handhold, I slinked into the bathroom and shut the door with the back of my foot.

As I filled up the tub and mixed the lavender bath oil with the water, I thought about how I didn't miss Johnny at night. I enjoyed the peace. I had my fun devoid of him. Being alone was calming. It was my time. I could write music and sing to myself without criticism or his voice joining in. I could watch "The Cosby Show" reruns and laugh at Dr. Huxtable's idiotic jokes without Johnny stealing the remote and shouting obscenities at a Patriots game for an entire afternoon. I was my best friend. I was self-confident in my body around others and in those inaudible times that I made love to myself.

Thirty minutes later, I heard another knock at the door. I glided out of the bathroom and yelled, "Damn it, Johnny. If you were going to leave, you should have... " the rest of that sentence was cut off at the sight of Brennan Curtis leaning into the door jam. His large hands on both sides made me feel small and slightly unsteady. I faltered and tripped over my robe as I took him in. His dimpled smile was first. His leathery masculine smell was second. His animal, please come have sex with me, energy was next.

"Uh... gah... hi," I offered, trying to regain poise, and maybe relearn the English language. *What kind of douchebag hello was that?* Oh right, this guy made my hearing, speech, and brain to body synapses cease to work properly.

"Ugh, hi," he quipped, clearly mocking my lacking use of words. "How are you, Julia?"

His eyes measured my body up and back down only to settle back onto my face to await my response. He was fascinating to look at. He was the actual tall, dark, and handsome man that all those books and fairy tales dreamed and screamed about. His tattooed sleeve made him less human, more of a super-god, and definitely mysterious. But I liked him. I liked him a lot.

"How... or who let you... did you get up here?" I probed as I poked my head out the door frame to see that the hotel hallway was empty. On my retreat back inside the room, Brennan tilted his cheek just the most minuscule bit so that my damp hair could graze his cheek. I stilled, frozen in that spot. Yes. Please graze me. Graze away. The barbeque comment came back into my head and I pulled back. He was not a slice of meat. He was a sexy guy. No more animal references to the human body.

"Lizzie. Sean. Sean... shit. Well, it was Lizzie," Brennan puckered his brows. He was evidently having a disagreement with himself and I watched with fascination. I could watch Brennan argue with himself all night long. It was, to say the least, adorable.

I just nodded. "Okay. Great! What can I do for you?" I requested sunnily. Why was I being fake plastic right now? Why did this guy unsettle me? If it had been anyone else at this hour, I would have probably verbally punched them in the face and sent them on their way to hell. Not Brennan, though. No, he did something to me that made me second guess the meaning of life entirely. He had a purpose in everything he did. There was something in the handshake, grazing my wet hair, and searching for who I was with his eye. He was a scientist who was compulsive to answer the equation of Jules Delaney. That was evident since he sought me out on stage, in the back room at the show, and now here, on a totally secured hotel floor. I decided to let him experiment away. What did I really have to lose?

It was then that Brennan's face went from amusement to pure disappointment. I followed his gaze to my couch where Johnny was passed out cold.

"I'm sorry, Julia. I didn't know. I thought... " he began. I quickly shut him up. There was no way in hell that anyone would ever get the impression that I took Johnny back.

"Johnny and I aren't together. I mean, yes, he is here but he was drunk. Then I took a bath, while he... shit... that didn't sound very good either, did it?"

I laughed as I tried not to fuck up anymore words. What was it about this guy? He made me babble on, like a little school girl. *Unnerving.* He grinned back at me. It was a big goofy grin that made my damp legs a little too warm and I quickly tried to dry off the wetness with my robe, but to no avail. That was the only action that either of us made. I still had no idea why he was here and so we stood there staring at each other like fucking idiots. I didn't know what the hell to do next.

I cleared my throat and waved him in with the hope that he would make his intentions clear behind the privacy of the door.

"Just... come in," I finally said on an exhale. He was a human being. A fine human being but nonetheless, he was just a guy. I could have company. Johnny was company and we weren't doing anything inappropriate. Nevertheless, where was the first place I drew him into?

I led Brennan back to the bedroom because I might get to fuck him after all. I closed the door quietly, because obviously, I did not want to wake Johnny from his alcohol induced sleep. I was being considerate of Johnny. That was the story I was telling Brennan and myself.

EIGHT

Brennan shadowed me into the big hotel bedroom and as he perused the room he rubbed the beanie off of his head. No flat hair head. In fact when he tore that beanie off, hair sprung to life. A plethora of black curls were shiny, thick, and wrapped around his striking face. I was immediately jealous of his no frizz hair. I spent so much money on products to preserve my straight hair. Some mornings, I had knots that were so bad that I could grow dreadlocks from them. Guys had it so good. Brennan's hair was the epitome of perfect hair. I itched to run my fingers through those long locks.

I turned into his personal space and placed my hands on his chest. I noticed his heart started to pump harder at my touch and he smiled softly, as he regarded my hands. He really liked my hands on him. Thank God.

"Why are you here, Brennan Curtis?" I seductively probed. There could be only one reason why he was here. He wanted to bag the lead singer of LSP and I was ready to let him try. What he didn't know was that my abilities would make him feel all of me on my own terms. Johnny reminded me only an hour ago just how good I was at taking care of a man.

Brennan looked into my eyes with confusion taking over his pupils. He placed his hands on top of mine. He wasn't giving off the horny vibe that I was used to. He was courteous and had better manners than the other guys. I didn't understand why. I tried to get back into my sexual confident self, as he held my hands, and only my hands. He wasn't touching me anywhere else. And w*hy the hell not?*

"I think there is something special here," he said soundly, taking one hand off of mine to motion the space between us.

"Special, huh?" I smirked, as I started to brush my lips against his. They radiated sweetness and inviting warmth. They were soft, but I could feel the trillion muscles in them as they started to flex upon my lips.

Holy shit. The. Best. Kiss. Ever.

As I deepened the kiss, Brennan's lips were definitely special. The purposeful melding of them made me want more of his muscles. My hand found his abs and as I started to move lower, his hand firmly grabbed my fingers, and he took one full step back from me. I was left there with my lips still lingering into dead space and I was totally fucking confused. What the fuck just happened?

"What are you doing, Julia?" Brennan asked taken aback.

"What are you doing, Brennan?" I asked, at the same time. We both smiled in unison. I stepped up and brought my smiling lips back to graze his and hummed. He hummed back into mine and tingles dragged up and down my back. I wanted his hands there. I wanted his hands everywhere.

"Hmm... I am doing what you wanted to do when you knocked on my hotel room. Lie down on the bed and let me show you how special we are together," I smoothly cooed. I owned the seductive voice on the stage and in the bedroom. Perhaps, it was from all the voice lessons in college or the summer I took the undercover job at the phone sex company. All the callers wanted "Pony Girl", which was the first thing that came out of my mouth when the owner asked me my call name. I even had a few female callers that loved to listen to me coo to them as they took care of their business.

Johnny never asked how we managed to pay our bills with left over cash. He just expected that I would take care of it. When he did have money, he made sure to hand over half of what he had on him, even if it was just a twenty dollar bill. Johnny did contribute, but certainly not as much as the sixty year old in Idaho who said he imagined me riding him like a pony. Ugh, the thought of what I said for money was disgusting.

Brennan pushed back from me a little and shook his head slightly, looking down at the ground with a frown overwhelming his beautiful face. Dark eyes, lush lips, beautiful straight chin, and dimples that made me want to lick again and again. This man was going to make me beg. Hell no, I never begged.

"Did I say something?" I asked, incredulity bleeding from my body.

"I did not come here for sex, Julia. I mean, I am attracted to you. God, I do want you, but I came here because I have a compulsion to be near you. Maybe I want to get to know you, or understand why I feel this... this pull towards you. We don't have to do anything. I just want to be in your presence. I know you feel it too... or am I all wrong here?"

Brennan was nervous but the confidence he exuded when he spoke about me was palpable. He knew there was a magnet between us and yes, I did feel it too, but I couldn't tell him that. I smiled inwardly at his declaration–his words about just wanting to be near me–as he ran his fingers through those silky black curls, I watched the way he moved with pure fascination.

Brennan looked uncomfortable under my scrupulous and drawn out examination of him. I crossed my arms over my chest and decided to throw him a bone, the poor guy. A small smile on my face got his attention and I almost heard the moment when he exhaled the breath he was holding. I held out my hand in greeting.

"My name is Julia Delaney. Friends and family call me Jules and strangers call me the singer from *that* band. I grew up in the state of New Hampshire. I tour with my band and I love to have sex. I would like to have sex with you," I stated, looking his square in the eyes. "So, that's it. I don't have any hobbies. I don't play sports. I don't remember the last book I read, and I think my favorite movie was released five years ago, but I only saw it once."

I waited for him to say something about himself, about what I admitted to, or just anything at all. He watched me in amusement as I started to twirl my hair.

"What was your first concert?" he asked softly. He had his easy composure back. His heart wasn't thumping as badly through the pretty shirt he's wearing. His eyes, however, still burned fire into mine and my stomach clenched.

I felt like he was poking at the secret insides of me, that no one ever dared to touch. My heart? My soul? Did I have those? No, my heart is solid rock and so is my band. It has been my mantra for years. But... with Brennan? It didn't feel truthful to chant the mantra with him around. He was poking at my plastic shield just with his eyes. It was unnerving, threatening, and I was going to get out of this exchange with my shield intact.

"What the fuck are you talking about? My first concert? Really?" I spat out with incredulity. That was what magazines asked, not guys who wanted to really know me as a person. Brennan smiled easily at my attempt to be forceful and in control. His look kicked my fear down a notch and I was excited to see what happened between us next.

"Julia, what was the first concert you ever *went* to– not played at," he probed. He came closer to take my hand into his. It was like sticking my hand into a warm bowl of bread dough. His hand secured mine and the rest of my body despised my hand in that moment. Shit, now my body was arguing with itself.

"Lollapalooza," I said, in a rush because I still really didn't want to talk. I wanted to feel the soft comfort of Brennan's whole body melted around me, thrusting into me.

He nodded his head and took my other hand, intertwining our fingers as he looked down at them in wonder. "Good show, I went to that festival, too." he confirmed.

I nodded absentmindedly while I watched his face. It was lovely. I already knew his different expressions from our ten minutes together. His wondrous look. His offended look. His patient look. His look of... was that adoration? For me?

"Which band did you like the most?" he asked me. I pondered that for a moment and tried to remember the lineup. I nodded slowly as memories started to rush back to me. I was in the ninth grade and I was dating a boy, whose name has slipped my mind now. I squeezed my eyes for the name.

Nate, Nathan Williams.

It was our second date; he had bribed me with the tickets, so he was motivated to make it past the first two bases. I watched Billy Corgan and The Smashing Pumpkins with rapt attention, while Nate successfully got his hand down the front of my jeans. I didn't care. We sat off on the side of the lawn and had a great view of the stage. He made it under my panties to play with me, but I was too entranced with Billy to notice. When they had ended their set and we all starting clapping, Nate pulled his hand out of my pants and cleaned himself up. He smiled and kissed me on the cheek, like I was the best date ever.

Now that I think about Nate, I am revolted at his behavior. At my own ambivalence! What the fuck was

I thinking? Nevertheless, I do remember that night to be special for something completely different. That night might have changed my life.

That was the night I decided that I wanted to be the female version of Billy Corgan and I craved to sing like nothing I had ever wanted before. The next day, I begged Kent incessantly to teach me everything he knew about the guitar. I played day and night. My fingers bled but I didn't care.

I joined the high school choir and was basically the only class that I attended on a regular basis. I just wanted to sing. The teacher was impressed, but gave me odd looks as she praised my improvement. I imagined she heard stories in the teacher's lounge. The gossip was full of "what Jules Delaney had done that day in class" talk. But in choir sessions, I was attentive and I was granted a solo at nearly every high school performance.

"Why are you smiling, Julia?" Brennan asked softly. He cocked his head to the side in disbelief. I don't think he had ever seen me smile before, because he stared at my mouth and then my eyes, only to smile right back.

"Billy Corgan," I declared. "You know him? He is the lead singer of Smashing Pumpkins? It was *that* guy that made me the person I am today. He is the whole reason I am a musician and the lead singer of a killer rock band. We are *incendiary* because of him." I smirked.

Brennan nodded his head with an appreciative grin. I waited for him to say something about how dumb that was. What was he thinking about me? It couldn't be good. I had ditched him, jumped him, spaced out on him, and then shared where my inspiration came from— a forty-five minute concert.

"You know, one person can't turn someone into the lead singer of a popular rock band. You might have been motivated to learn but y*ou* actually did all the work when you learned to sing and play the guitar. It came from a deep place inside of you, Julia. Don't ever give credit to anyone or anything else. It is all you." He kissed the back of my left hand, and then looked up at me as he blew a black curl from his right eye. It was so sexy and I wanted him... badly.

I couldn't accept his compliment about it being all me and shit. I didn't accept any compliments about my work because I simply learned to play and sing. The rest of it was timing and who Dex and Johnny knew. Yes, there was a lot of pounding the pavement to market our band, but that didn't feel like work to me. Music–this band–was my life. I didn't know any other way to live.

"Thanks," I said flatly. He smirked at my lack of enthusiasm. Maybe one day I would look back on these years and find the pride. *Maybe* that would happen, but not likely.

Johnny's voice boomed through the hotel suite.

"Jullliiaaa" he yelled once again, with the Rocky referenced tone. *Jesus Christ.* Johnny needed to leave. The door to my bedroom flew open. Within mere seconds, Johnny's jaw dropped when he saw Brennan and my hands intertwined. Brennan's hands squeezed mine, reminding me that he wanted to be there, with me.

"So. Being a slut again, are we?" Johnny sneered. I felt Brennan's posture tighten up at Johnny's crude question, and I wearily looked at Johnny.

"Shut the fuck up, Johnny, and go sleep it off. In your *own* hotel room."

"And don't you ever called her a slut again," Brennan warned.

Johnny stumbled back a little, probably because of all the booze, and laughed. He bent over and bellowed out so hard, while Brennan and I gave each other random looks of apprehension. I felt the foreboding moment when I looked back at Johnny. He was about to destroy my chances with Brennan forever. It was the train wreck moment that people talked and wrote about. I saw the collision coming and there wasn't a damn thing I could do about it. I prepared my shield for battle. Drunk Johnny always came out firing.

"She is a slut, man. She is damn proud of it, too. Aren't ya, Jules?" he sniggered.

I didn't say anything because he was spot on. Good one, Johnny. Shield was effectively up and strong. I let my head fall in a moment of humiliation and resolve. I let my hands slip away from Brennan's. I closed my eyes, and exhaled my guilt, my shame, and my embarrassment out in one breath.

I considered the scene, tried to find the best way to get out of it, and pointedly regarded both guys. Johnny was an automatic boot. Brennan was just a bad moment.

"Please. Leave. Both of you," I answered shakily. I turned around in a flash, grabbed my phone, and proceeded to lock myself in the bathroom. *Really, Jules? No rebuttal?* That wasn't like me at all and Johnny was probably standing out there, completely dumbfounded at my lack of reaction.

I always took Johnny's shit and gave it right back with pleasure. Brennan witnessing our exchange changed everything about my reaction. I didn't want him to know I was a slut. I didn't want him to think that he would be one of hundreds. He was different. So... I ran.

NINE

When I didn't hear anyone in my bedroom anymore, I opened the bathroom door cautiously. My eyes went to a hotel note pad on the end of my bed. I walked over to it in a flash. Brennan had left a note. Well, he wrote one sentence and his phone number.

I walked out to the living area and picked up the phone.

"Lizzie?" I asked when I heard her cheery hello. "I need a different place to stay in Boston." Minutes later, she and Nick had it all worked out with no questions asked.

The next morning, we all climbed into the town car to the airport. Johnny and I wouldn't look at each other. I patted my jeans pocket to make sure Brennan's note was still there. I looked out the window and slowly began to close my eyes. I had hardly slept. Once again, Johnny had reminded me why men sucked. I was so tired of playing the game, and considered leaving the band. I knew it wasn't smart, since we already signed a contract but after the recording, I wanted to be as far from Johnny as possible.

How we went from amazing friends to worst enemies, was beyond me. Times were changing. *The dream.* I had the dream on the same day that Johnny ruined any hope of my actually liking another man. It made sense now. Well, fuck him, the OUIJA board, and everyone else in the world. Maybe I didn't want to be that girl anymore. Is anyone listening? I wanted to change to be with Brennan. I needed to see him again.

"So, what happened to the love sick babies today?" Dex asked, looking from Johnny to me. I opened my eyes, startled at his amused voice. I scowled and briefly flashed my eyes over to Johnny, where he looked embarrassed and sad. I pursed my lips and went back to window watching.

"I fucked up, man," Johnny said firmly. "Jules is never going to want me again. I ruined it all last night."

It was nothing like Johnny to accept all the blame, so when he said that, both my body and my breath froze. I listened to him explain that he was a son of a bitch and that I had every right to never like, or even trust him again.

"Dude, what the hell did you do? We all know you'll never give up on Jules. Where are the roses?" Dex asked as he looked over to me. I felt his gaze on the side of my face but I still didn't move. Johnny always thought flowers fixed things. He would buy roses and paint them black. It was so romantic.

"He told it like it was," I said blandly. "No roses left, Dex. No fucking roses."

Johnny pulled his knees up and placed his fists into his eyes. I glanced over to see him start to shake. Was he crying? *Jesus.* Dex watched him, dumbstruck, and that was the end of the 'morning after' conversation. I had no more words for Johnny.

Everyone remained quiet as we made our way to the plane. Without looking at seat assignments, Dex took the aisle seat blocking me from having to look at Johnny. When we arrived at Logan Airport, I was so relieved to see two driver signs. One for Delaney and one for LSP. My solo ride was here, thanks to Lizzie. The guys looked thoroughly confused, as I strode up to the driver, tore the sign from his hands, and kept walking towards the town car.

Luckily, we didn't start recording for a few days, so I took time to explore after I moved into a small furnished studio in Boston. I was close enough to walk to Nick's recording studio and close enough to catch the train anywhere else. First thing first, since I would be here for a while, was finding the second hand shops in and around the city.

I loved shopping at thrift stores and I was determined to find one here that would outfit my entire upcoming tour. My favorite outfits came from women who were obviously either in a nursing home or are dead. Today I wore a 1950's polyester, pleated dress. It was a white button up, sleeveless with a brown collar. I added my polka dot silk scarf, my brown clogs, and put my hair up in a half pony tail. I threw on my sun hat and sunglasses, to avoid recognition, and stepped out on the downtown streets of Boston. I smiled at the change in scenery. I loved this city.

As I walked down the street, I tried to get the iPhone app to Yelp so I could find the closest thrift stores. The music kicked on through my ear buds and

Dinosaur Jr. rang through my ears. I stopped in my tracks, remembering how they were one of the first bands to shape my music style. They were phenomenal and helped me to envision the kind of lead singer I wanted to be. I got lost into the song. As I started to play the air guitar, someone tapped my shoulders, breaking me out of my reverie. I spun around, with eyes wide open in shock, and found the smiling brown eyes of Brennan Curtis.

It took me a moment to understand that he was standing in front of me. I pulled the ear phones out of my ears and gawked at him.

"Brennan?" I asked.

That was an absolutely pathetic thing to say. Of course, it was Brennan. I was officially pathetic *and* lost. Great. But why was he here? How did he know that I was in this exact spot outside the Prudential building? Was he following me?

"Julia?" He chuckled with those damn dimples, as he poked me on the arm. All further questions escaped my mind. I looked down at his finger, his touch, the way it automatically made me feel uncomfortable, but in a good way. It was in that moment. *That simple touch.* It was the mammoth 'aha moment' that I would never forget. He came to me in Boston. He came to touch me? And I felt the magnitude. I knew it for the first time. Brennan made me feel. I had feelings and excitement for another person. He wasn't Kent or Johnny. He made me want to do life right by him. He made me want for more than just boozing, music, and sex.

"How... did you know I was here?" I asked, looking around to all the people walking in every direction around us. My eyes landed back on Brennan. I noticed his glasses were gone. He had a dark blue mechanic's jacket with a patch on the left side that read, "Brennan". It wasn't dirty with stains, but crisp and obviously well taken care of. Underneath, he had a white v-neck tee shirt on and gray jeans that were worn and ripped. His black leather belt made him look both sophisticated and fashionable. It was exactly what I would have dressed a guy in. I wanted to call him mine and I didn't know anything but his name.

Brennan held up his hands in defense. "Before I tell you, promise me that you won't freak out," he said cautiously.

I smiled brightly at him. "I don't freak out, Brennan. I get even." His eyes searched mine, like was waiting for me to tell him that I was just joking. I wasn't. I would surprise him one day, too, because this guy wasn't going anywhere. I saw a future with him. Us standing on the streets of every city–staring at each other. Okay, I wanted in.

"Is that why you aren't living with Johnny while you record your next album?" he asked. I cocked my head to the side with continued interest. Brennan had done his homework and knew a lot about me. *Julia, you need to stop smiling now.* I nodded once.

"I thought you would call me last night or this morning, Julia. I thought we had... I thought we decided to get to know one another. It's the pull. Shit, I can feel it now. I felt it the whole drive here," he shook his head with embarrassment, and looked down to the ground. I said nothing.

"You affect me. I thought you were interesting before, when I hadn't met you yet. I thought you would be a rock star bitch," he laughed. It was hollow. "You are a bitch but a good one and you are so much more than that. I don't see you as a famous rock star.

Don't get me wrong, I downloaded all of your songs and your voice is amazing," he rambled, starting to sound a bit like a fan. I waved my right hand in a circle, telling him to move along.

"So, when you didn't call, I guess I became obsessed to know why not. I contacted the studio and Lizzie told me that I was *fan boying*?" He quirked his left eyebrow up and he smiled wide. I blushed, as I barked out such a loud laugh that people stopped in their tracks to look at where the noise came from. I put my hand over my mouth and started to giggle. I giggled and it felt so damn good to giggle with Brennan.

"She had to explain what that meant. So, yeah, I guess I am fan boying," he conceded, suddenly looking uncomfortable as he put his hands in his pockets. I suppose that didn't sit well with him. I mirrored his stern face until it morphed into a smirk.

"You are not a fan boy, Bren. Fan boys ask for autographs, pictures, and as the shutters go off, fan boys feel me up," I assured him. "You wouldn't even let me kiss you."

"You just called me Bren." he said it in awe, his hand going up to touch the underside of my cheek.

I shrugged my shoulders, not understanding. "I don't want to be all serious with you. I want fun."

"That's really... perfect," he said, as he let the words linger in the air. I waited for the rest of his story to come but he just stared at me. "This feeling is so weird, Julia."

"So how did you find me *here*?" I asked, pointing down to the ground.

"Oh right," he chuckled. "So. You didn't call, Julia. I needed to see you. I closed down the shop and drove up here, only to realize that Boston is kind of a big city."

He scratched the back of his neck and looked perplexed.

"I called the studio and as luck would have it, the phone was forwarded to Lizzie's cell. She told me about your apartment and where to find you. When I pulled up, you were leaving. I found a place to park and ran after to you. So... *here* I am," he said as he mimicked my pointing down to the ground.

"Hmmm. And you want to know why I didn't call?" I asked.

He nodded as he searched my eyes, even though my sunglasses were firmly in place. I knew these glasses still showed my eyes up close so he wasn't looking at reflective mirrors.

"I think Johnny made it pretty clear the type of girl I am, Bren-nan," I answered, using his full name.

"What type of girl is that?" he asked, moving closer to me. His chest was almost touching mine and I readjusted my hat.

"Umm," I said, enunciating the *m* with a quick end to the word. "I am a slutty lead singer of a rock and roll band. That is my type."

I took off my sunglasses and stared straight into his eyes to show that I wasn't joking. It wasn't self-deprecating. It didn't feel like it anyway. It was a factual statement that had always been about me. I couldn't remember a time that I didn't just sleep with whomever and whenever and for absolutely no reason. I wanted to sleep with Brennan when I saw him in the crowd that night but at the hotel, he had turned me down–so he wasn't *my* type.

His note afterwards that read, "You are so beautiful inside and out" left me breathless and confused. Those foreign feelings were short lived as I remembered what happened. He didn't really know me and I realized I didn't *want* to fuck him. He wasn't my type of people. He didn't know the rules of the club. He didn't belong at that concert or in my hotel room that night.

"A slutty what?" he asked incredulously. "No, no forget it. I don't want to know. So, that's why you didn't call me?"

I nodded with a look that said *obviously*.

"Bad move, Julia," Brennan retorted. He closed the space between us and enveloped me in to a firm hug. I felt him shaking a bit and all the wind knocked out of me. I put my hands up and hugged him around his hips, as I closed my eyes into the sweet oblivion.

He kissed my temple and grabbed one of the earphones dangling from around my neck to put it in his ear. I pressed play on the iPhone still in my hand. Dinosaur Jr. rang through again as Brennan put the other plug in my ear from behind. J. sang about how he knew she was out there to love and Brennan smiled into my cheek.

"*Such a* perfect song about us." His voice vibrated soundly against my cheek. "J. Mascis wrote about true love, you know. I know you're in there."

He hummed over the music while he insistently hugged me for what felt like hours. I was falling hard, and fast, and I didn't know what the fuck to do about it.

TEN

Boston, Massachusetts

Brennan pulled away from me and smiled down into my eyes. His lips touched my cold nose and I closed my eyes at the warmth of them. He slid his hand down my body and intertwined our hands. I looked down, regarding them quizzically. Had anyone ever held my hand like this? It felt amateur before but so deeply intimate with Brennan. Little sparks of excitement spread all over my skin.

As I gazed at our fingers, and turned our hands around in examination, a face flashed into my mind. A little twelve year old boy. I saw him there, smiling at me, as we headed down to the canoes at camp. Fred? Frank? Frank! He was the first boy I held hands with. The first boy I kissed. It was also the beginning part of *the* dream, that I could never remember when I woke up.

I remembered that part now because holding hands with Frank was the last time I recall having this feeling of excitement for a boy. It was thrilling and new. It was fresh, like cut green grass, and yellow butterflies looking for the flowers on the edge of the large lawn. It smelled delicious. It looked brand new. Only amazing things happen in this feeling and I never wanted to let it go.

"Julia?" Brennan broke into my thoughts.

"Hmm?" I hummed, looking up into his dark eyes.

"Where did you go, Julia?" I closed my eyes, inhaled the cold air, and his sweet scent of attraction in one breath. I am right here. I am letting you in.

"I was thinking about the last time I held a guy's hand and when it made me feel this... this special," I answered quietly. I felt like a little girl, vulnerable, and naïve. Something in the back of my mind screamed that this wasn't me. I am Jules, the lead singer of a rock band. I can have anything or anyone I want. I am a bad ass, bitchy, slut.

"I like your hands," he smiled as he took both of them into his. "They are small and very beautiful." And just like that, listening to his words and holding hands, Brennan erased that rocker girl and replaced her with the little girl once again.

I looked at him and squeezed his hands. I didn't want to break our moment so I cuddled back into his chest, over our adjoined hands.

"Tell me, Brennan. Why are you here? Don't you have to work tomorrow?" I probed. I knew what I wanted his answers to be and I sent up a silent prayer that he would tell me he quit his job to be with me. He was in love and wanted me all the time. Damn. Did I just think that? I must be going crazy.

"Well, like I said, I came here for *you*. I want to spend time with *you*. Let me spend time with *you*. As for work, I own a graphic design company and work from home. As long as the hotel has internet, I can work from here," he stated. He moved his lips to my ear and kissed them softly, making them warm. "The answer to your questions will always be because of you, Julia." This was so deep. It caught me off guard and I remembered that we were standing here, practically feeling each other up in public.

"Graphics?" I asked, pulling back and trying to regain composure for public. I adjusted his shirt sleeve to see his tattoos. "Did you design these?"

Brennan hesitated, took a piece of my black hair, and tucked it behind my ear. I knew he wanted to tell me more but he simply nodded.

"And you met Lizzie's Sean at a tattoo show? Are tattoos all that you do?" I asked.

"Yeah. I met Sean at a design convention. Tattoos are small jobs. I design logos, album covers, book covers... you know, lots of different stuff. I have a partner and we split the work," Brennan informed me like he was rattling off something he had said a million times. It felt bland. He didn't seem passionate about his work. I didn't want to pry too much. I suppose when you do something so long it becomes so familiar that there isn't any more excitement. I know playing music is exciting and I felt it. But what so many people didn't know is that I am most passionate when they lock me in the vocals booth and I sing my heart out just for myself.

"Album covers? Have you approached Nick yet?" I asked, poking him in the stomach. He winced but then smiled.

"If I made your album cover, Julia, Johnny and Dex wouldn't even be on it," he said in a low, husky voice.

He closed into my face and placed his lips on mine. We leaned into each other's lips like they were supposed to be attached in a sensuous play of skin and muscle and passion. We didn't open our mouths to explore for more. My heart and lungs felt like they were going to abruptly stop.

It was so overwhelming and it felt right. I didn't even know Brennan and I broke the kiss for fear that I was going to start crying. I had the sudden urge to bawl and I *never* cried. I don't even remember the last time I did. Something about Brennan made me want to throw up everything in my soul and make him want every bit of it, despite its ugliness.

"May I buy you a cup of coffee, Julia?" he whispered into my ear. He leaned down and placed a light kiss under my ear. I nodded as I caught my breath.

"I suppose since you drove all this way the least I can do is have a cup of coffee with you," I smirked. I grabbed onto his hand harder and we swung our hands as we walked down towards Newbury Street.

That night, I asked Brennan to forego the hotel and stay with me. He was cautious. It finally took me telling him that I wouldn't jump his bones in his sleep for him to concede.

"I am not worried about *you*, Julia. Shit... I am really not good with words." He looked terrified.

"I think you are magic with words," I countered. I put my hand on his tatted arm and noticed a tattoo of three building blocks. A, B, and C. Childlike. Cute. *What the hell did it mean?* I shook my head and brought myself back to the moment. "Tell me the facts," I said.

"Ok. The *facts*. Yeah, I can do that," he said on a large exhale. "I wanted to meet you in NYC because I watched an interview you did one night and there was just something about you. I couldn't escape thinking about you as a real person. You weren't on some music high horse but when you sang, it was so passionate. You are so talented but so guarded. You don't want people to know you, do you?"

I shook my head and twisted my lips into a thin line. "Nope. Very few people know me. And even they don't know it all."

"So I wanted to see if you were like that in real life. Call it a science experiment. I had to get this idea of you out of my head. When we met, it was so much more for me. I need to be next to you. If I sleep over, I might lose all hopes of being a gentleman," he admitted, with a blush. I kissed him on the cheek and smiled brightly at him.

"I want to be near you, too, Brennan. Maybe we could just go with the flow and see what happens? It isn't like we live in the same city," I said, feeling like my gut was twisting into a ball of cement and surging up into my throat. Shit, I was going to cry again. What the hell is going on with me? I wanted to hug him again and I did. Through coffee, shopping, and walking around my side of Boston, we hugged. It was awesome.

That night, we played cards. He read to me from a newspaper article about how all art was going digital and what would we leave for archaeologists after our extinction. Brennan made me think. He made me want to tell him everything I thought. I held on to every word he said to me because each word was a gift. He was careful and thoughtful when he spoke. Sometimes it took minutes for him just to think about a question before he answered. I was normally like that with everyone, but with Brennan, I spit out everything I thought before I even thought it. He laughed at me while sneaking kisses and touching different parts of my body.

He would take his thumb and brush it over my ankle bone for long minutes. He took the back of his hand and felt my shoulder and biceps with it. He used two fingers and rubbed along the middle of each of my fingers over and over again. Each touch was endearing and a turn on. Heaven help my vagina. He was amazing.

Despite the small foreplay, we fell asleep fully clothed on top of my covers. He snuggled up into my neck and whispered about his childhood in Brooklyn as I felt myself fall asleep. I felt like a virgin that night. I had never spooned with a man before. I never wanted to. I laughed at people who thought it was the best part of sex. Brennan's tight grip around my waist made me self-conscious, but as he continued to talk, I felt myself mold into him. I understood in that moment what it felt like to feel the intimacy. It was comfort and security. It was safe.

The next morning, I had to go into the studio for some initial solo voice layouts. Brennan and I hit the coffee shop on the short walk to the studio. Hand in hand, we walked through the doors, laughing at how we both wanted to open the door for each other. I didn't notice Sean and Johnny standing in the reception area until Brennan dropped his hand from mine. I frowned down at the break in contact and looked up to see Sean and Johnny both scowling at our arrival.

"Boys," I addressed them instead of a hello, walking by to the inner studio's hallway. Brennan didn't follow me and I turned around to question why. He looked uncomfortable. Was he still thinking about the night in the hotel with Johnny?

"I think I am just going to hang back here with Sean for a while," he said. I looked at Sean who was only staring at Brennan with a coldness that made me shiver. Johnny was the first to lighten the mood in the lobby.

"Jules, Nick wants me here to do some of the duet harmonizing. Let's go," he said as he pushed by me and opened the door to the studio for me. Brennan's searing gaze on Johnny was impenetrable. He *was* upset about that night.

Nick and Lizzie greeted us in the sound room and pointed me to the voice mic that hung from the middle of the sound proof room inside the window. Johnny followed me but sat on a chair as far away as possible while I placed the earphones on and warmed up my vocals.

The buzzed intercom rang through the room. "Jules, let's start with *I Don't Give a Damn*," Nick said.

I nodded and I heard the techno beats of the song come through. This wasn't my band playing but Nick's attempt to replicate it for me to see how well my vocals were in sync with the song. He had some scientific method that he was working on and every time he tried to explain, Lizzie's eye rolls would make me laugh.

You don't want to know

You don't want to care

And for the record, I don't

I don't give a damn.

Nick's voice cut through the intercom.

"Uh, Jules. This is supposed to be an angst song. You are singing it like a love song," Nick stated as his eyes looked sincere. Lizzie was biting her nails in the background.

I nodded and we motioned it from the top. I tried to reign in my Alanis Morrisette and Tori Amos and I started again.

No more than two lines in, he cut in again. "What the hell, Jules? Normally, we can't get you to tone down the anger. Where are you? Do we want a boy band pop song on this album?" He sounded a little more peeved now. Shit.

"Nick!" Lizzie gasped. Nick shook his head at her and muted the intercom to say something. She left the room, looking thoroughly pissed off.

Johnny jumped up off his seat and motioned to Nick to give him a minute. Nick crossed his arms and leaned back in his chair. He only wanted the best for our band. He was mad at me and it wasn't the first or last time he would call me on my shit.

"You want to find your anger, Jules?" Johnny taunted.

"What? Should I think about the other night?" I asked, noticing that Brennan had just walked into the sound room and shook Nick's hand.

"No. Don't think about that," Johnny laughed. He cut his chin over to Brennan.

"Your guy there? Married, Jules. *Fucking married,*" he said in a low growl. His *holy shit and you are fucked* expression drove the words home.

His eyes stayed on mine as he backtracked to his seat and crossed one leg over the other. My mouth was dry from the long exposure to air without saliva. I guess that is what happens when you can't close your mouth. *Married*? To another woman? I slowly lifted my eyes to Brennan who smiled and winked at me. He might as well have kicked me *Kill Bill* style in the chest.

"Nick?" I asked shakily. "I got this." Four, three, two, one...

I nailed it on the first take. Johnny slowly and deliberately clapped his hands at the end.

"*There* she is," he said with a wicked smile. I wanted to projectile vomit in his face. My tyrannical mood was a full blown animal and I knew I wouldn't be able to keep it on a leash. I needed the mic again. I needed another angry song.

ELEVEN

For the rest of the session, I was a zombie. Life was stupid. If people tried to talk to me, I wouldn't answer or I scowled. I felt betrayed, duped. *Why did I keep getting fucked?* Why would beautiful Brennan come into my life, bring out feelings I didn't know I had, and then remind me that I was stupid slut? I heard the high school girls in my head, circling me down the halls, calling me an easy lay, a slut, and their laughing expressions making it all worse. Endless loop of bitch slaps. Fuck them and fuck Brennan, too. I was a gutted fool to mock.

Johnny peered at me with suspicion, as I pulled on my grey pea coat.

"Are you crying?" he asked, in bewilderment. I touched my face and felt wetness on my cheek. "You never cry. I have never seen you cry," he balked at me. "Is it… because of that douchebag? Jules, for real?"

"I am not crying," I snapped sternly, teeth clenched. "It's allergies. My eyes have been watering since I got here." I turned to walk out the door, but Johnny stopped me with his hands on my shoulders.

"Despite what I said that night, and every night before that, I will always be here for you. You know, to talk, or whatever. I am *here*." He released me as I nodded once. I suddenly felt bad for being a bitch to him that morning on the way to Boston. Johnny wasn't a saint, by any means, but he spoke the truth. I could rely on that, at least.

"Thanks Johns," I whispered. He quickly inhaled at my use of his nickname. *Johns and Jules.* That's who we were once. He knew that I knew we weren't *those* people anymore, but maybe for that brief interaction, that brief moment, I allowed it to be just us again. The moment was officially over when I pulled away to face Brennan, the married man that I had started to fall in love with.

I walked out to the hall and paused when a familiar face flashed into my brain.

Professor Maxwell Hynes.

He was my gorgeous, charismatic, talented, music appreciation instructor at the University of Maryland.

As a brand new freshman, out in the world for the first time, I admired Professor Hynes' lips as he spoke about music being the soul of life. His sincere proclamation that each of us in the class was meant to use music as a way to purge our souls. His eyes were soft blue, but full of lust when he looked directly at me as he spoke those words to the class.

Unfortunately, his wedding band blazed far brighter than the sun, almost blinding the image I had of him naked. He became my whole world freshman year and I never missed his class. I hadn't met Dex or Johnny at that point, so my band couldn't even get him out of my mind. I was on my own, far enough away from my home town, to run from my reputation.

A couple of weeks into our first semester, Professor Hynes asked me to stay after class for one on one study sessions. I remember thinking that it was about time he had asked. I wanted those lips on me. I wanted those eyes to examine my naked body for hours. Professor Hynes, my first college sexual experience. In the back room of the choir auditorium, I gave Maxwell pleasure in a slow, methodical way, which made him beg me for release by the end. When he turned me around and slammed into me, I felt like I owned the college.

Our regular "sessions", as he called them, were experimental and amazing. It wasn't until I saw him and his beautiful brunette, and very pregnant, wife at a local coffee shop that I realized I was nothing more than his student slut of the semester. He didn't see my face when I watched in horror as they hugged lovingly. After that day, I ignored all of his attempts to continue his "sessions". I actually skipped classes and when I was there, I sat in the back and said nothing. The last day of class, he dropped a note on my desk along with my final paper. I will never forget what it said. *See me after class for an A. Leave and I hope you enjoy the C.*

I never worked so fast to pleasure a man. I imagined his wife. I saw her laughing and hugging him when he called out my name as he came. I wiped my mouth off, stood up, and waited for him to speak. His small smile told me I had gotten the A I deserved even without this act of bribery. As I walked out of the door, he called after me.

"Jules, I look forward to second part of Music Appreciation in the spring," he smirked. He was so beautiful, but so fucking ugly in that moment. I changed my course selections that same afternoon to avoid him at all costs.

Brennan tore me out of my memory with a light touch on my shoulder. I watched him in a daze, trying to find the similarities between him and Professor Hynes. What would Brennan hold over my head now? Why do married men cheat?

"Everything alright?" Brennan asked with concern etched on his face.

I nodded and put my hands in my pockets. Out of the corner of my eye, I saw Sean and Johnny speaking quietly in the corner.

"I'm tired. I want to go home," I said, a bit harsher than I should have. I didn't know what to do. Call him out here in front of everyone? Call him out when he tries to hold my hand, or even more, when he tries to kiss me? There were no grades involved here. I didn't need to save a mark in school or even my reputation. I didn't owe him anything, and that made me sad because I did want to owe him my heart.

Brennan, on the other hand, owed me everything.

He owed me an explanation and an excuse. Maybe
he even owed me a little groveling for forgiveness.
Despite how this was about to play out, Brennan
would be on his way back to Brooklyn by day's end. I
couldn't be with a married man. I had promised myself
back when I was only eighteen. Eleven years later, I
still felt so vulnerable.

I looked at Brennan's left ring finger on the hand
that was still pressed against my shoulder. There it
was. An indentation the size of a large man's ring.
How did I not notice it before? Hadn't I examined our
hands at length when he first held my hands in front of
the Prudential? I pushed passed him and out into the
fall day.

I could smell every colored leaf in the brisk fall air.
The contrast of the brown, the yellow, and the vibrant
red each had different smells, but together it reminded
me of pumpkin patches and hay rides in New
Hampshire. Hot apple cider at the end of the brisk ride
was nowhere in sight, as I stood on the bustling street
outside of the studio. I couldn't enjoy my favorite
season because I knew that going forward I would
associate the smells of fall with heartbreak. And fuck,

Dinosaur, Jr. He took that away from me, too. I tried to reign in my anger.

Johnny walked out with Sean, Brennan trailing behind. Sean cut me a look. He shook his head slightly, like I shouldn't say anything right then, but I needed to know more.

I cleared my throat. "Hey Sean, while I was in there, I realized there is one tattoo I might want. Can I talk to you for a moment in private?"

Johnny knew what I was doing. Brennan looked confused, or maybe he looked offended that I hadn't asked him for a design consultation. I briefly smiled at him as I took Sean's arm and walked down the street for a little while.

"What the mother fucking shit, Sean?" I asked, practically raging in righteousness red. "*Why* did you introduce us? Why in the *hell* did you send him to my hotel room when you knew he was married?"

"You have to know, I wanted to say something but he asked me not to. It isn't as simple as it looks, Jules. Amelia and Brennan are different. They are... open.

She knows he is here with you," he explained, almost defending Brennan.

"She knows?" I repeated with wide eyes and the ultimate look of disbelief.

He nodded his head.

"She is a really open-minded woman. *Very open.* Brennan explained he didn't like that part of their marriage and... well, until he met you."

"Oh, that is a fucking compliment if I've ever heard one," I guffawed. "So, what? They do threesomes? Is he here to scope me out for her?" I crossed my arms over my heart, which was slowly icing over, with tiny little icicles dangling from the edges.

"No way! They don't do it *together*. They are open with other people. Shit, the day of the convention, she left with one of the guys that had a booth right next to them. It was fucking bizarre to watch. I mean, I understand the whole open marriage thing in my head, I guess, but when you actually see it happening, ugh, it's just fucking weird," Sean said in disgust. "Brennan tried to show a brave face, but I could tell he was hella uncomfortable. So, when I told him about going to see you that next night, it was awesome to see him smile about meeting you. I didn't really think anything would come of it."

"Why was she even there? At the convention, I mean?" I asked. My hands were shaking, my heart pounding, but I was going to wrench out every detail about this disastrous set up that I could.

"Wait... he hasn't talked about his partner at all? Amelia is his business partner. ABC Designs," he said, rattling off the information in a professional tone. ABC. His tattoo. She designs his tattoos. Amelia Brennan Curtis.

I couldn't help it. I went to the brick covered trash receptacle and threw up the coffee that I had drunk that morning. It came out like acid. Acidic poison was my life. It didn't matter what I did, I would always find myself in these fucked up situations.

Brennan's voice boomed over me, as his hand moved up and down my back. "Julia, are you sick? You said you were tired? Maybe you are coming down with something?" he assumed. His voice made me want to burst out in tears. I loved his voice next to my ear, telling me we had something special. I hated his voice for tricking me into falling for it.

I turned my head slightly to see Sean walk off and catch up with Johnny. Johnny nodded at me once and he quickly turned to leave. I wiped the vomit off of my mouth and stood up, feeling woozy. Brennan wrapped his arm under mine to keep me up.

"I need you to get your fucking married arms off my person!" I spat out in his face. I heard the gasp from behind me.

Female. *Fuck*. Lizzie.

"What the fuck?" Lizzie yelled out. "You're fucking married? You son of a... " she was cut off by Nick picking her up and throwing her over his shoulder. I heard him say that it was none of their business, as she yelled out something about shitty creeps, and an apology to me. I didn't stop glaring at Brennan's pale and sickly face. Of course, he was still ridiculously gorgeous, but he wasn't mine. He belonged to another faceless and most likely, equally beautiful woman. Brennan withdrew his arms from me and backed away, slowly and steadily. He held up his hands in a defensive stance.

"Before you go off on me, *please* listen to me," he begged.

I shook my head, feeling like I was going to hurl again. Instead, I started walking towards my apartment. He just needed to leave. Leave me the hell alone. I wanted to cry but the son of a bitch didn't deserve one fucking tear.

He caught up to me, turned me around so fast, and my confused, aching head started to throb once again.

"What?" I screamed. "You came up here to what? You wanted me to fall in love with your touches, your laugh? You want me to love the way you look at me while I talk? Or was it that I offered you a blow job that first night and hadn't asked your wife for permission?"

Brennan was talking over me the entire time I was screaming at him. People stopped and watched. Cars slowed and looked out their windows at us. I heard Brennan say "no" and "stop" and "what?"

I shook my hands out, in a nervous, jumpy way. I needed to shake this off. I could no longer look him in the eyes. I darted my eyes everywhere, but into those dark, muddy eyes of ecstasy.

"Can I speak now?" he shouted. "Can we talk about this like adults, maybe somewhere a little more private? I am pretty sure all of your friends hate me now and I would like to be able to walk into this city again after today," he said, as he pushed his dark curls out of his face with force.

"Where's your wedding ring?" I asked in a lower voice, resigned to know that I had just fallen for a married man... again. A-fucking-gain.

"In my bag. I don't...," he sighed. "Neither of us wears it when we are with other people. It is one of our ground rules." Brennan's flurry of words was tossed up into the air for me to piece together and understand. Impossible. None of this would ever make any sense. Except, oh, I am the mistress... again.

It is one of our ground rules, I thought. I did get that.

I ended up scoffing at his blatant response, because while his casualness about the topic was quite fascinating, it was also so completely filthy. In all the years that I had slept with guys, I had never felt like as much of a slut as I did right now. The laughable part was that I didn't even have the pleasure of fucking him.

I closed my eyes and tried to compose myself. I needed a bottle of wine, a muscle relaxer, and a bubble bath. I needed *sex*. Yes, I needed casual, yet animalistic sex with a large penised, unmarried man. I needed to rid my brain of any topic regarding Brennan Curtis and fuck the daylights out of someone. Or *someones*. For a week. *Straight.*

"Amelia and I are in an open relationship. She is... she is a loving person. She would love you. In fact, when I told her I was coming to see you, she was happy. I mean, it has been a while since...," he trailed off.

"You fuck *women*? Without your wife?" I screeched my question with so much ugliness. My father and my step-monster's faces flashed through my mind. Cheating was cheating, open marriage or not.

"Okay, yeah. You are so upset, so please, let's go somewhere. We need to talk privately. I wanted to talk to you over the phone about it. You seemed so open, you know, the way you are with guys and your body. I thought you would be a perfect person to have more with," he admitted.

"But more isn't what I want, Julia. I don't even think about Amelia when I am with you. I don't want to leave. I want to be inside of you so bad, but I can't...," he said in a defeated tone. His eyes were tearing up and his lower lip started to shake.

"If I have sex with you, I want to make love to you, Julia, and that *will* be cheating on my wife. It wouldn't be the same as just having sex with someone, you know? You are not the same to me as the others. Hell, you aren't even my wife and I fell... I am so confused." Tears fell down his face and my whole body tensed up. I couldn't watch a guy cry because it made me uncomfortable. It went against human nature. Men crying meant they had feelings, and most of the ones I knew, besides my brother and Johnny, did not.

"Well, I am not confused. Everything is pretty fucking clear to me. It would be best for your safety if you walk away from me and to go back to her... now," I demanded. "Oh and thank you very fucking much for making me feel like a worthless piece of shit! God damn it! Another fucking married man! Jesus Christ. You started to mean something to me, too. That is what is most screwed up."

He put his palms on his eyes and nodded behind them. I felt kind of bad for him and I wanted to punch myself for feeling anything towards him. I should be able to just kick him to the curb like every other guy. I couldn't. He had made me feel compassion in the short time I had known him. I wasn't even upset with Johnny anymore. I wanted to forgive everyone that ever hurt me. But this admission of marriage proved one thing; I wasn't worthy enough for love. I was a slut, through and through.

Another man's face flashed through my head.

John Sands.

I took his virginity our junior year in college. He asked me to marry him the next day. We had been messing around for a few weeks. I liked him because he was pure and different. He was nice. I didn't hook up with nice. I had no idea I had taken his virginity until he was inside me; asking if he was doing it right. The broken look in his eyes when I told him I couldn't marry him made me hate myself every time I thought of him. I looked him up about a year ago. He is a Pastor at a small town church outside Philadelphia and happily married. *Thank God.*

I moved Brennan's hands from his face and placed a solid, warm kiss on his lips. My insides dropped into the pit of regret and poor circumstance, a place I had been in countless times. As I drew away, he wrapped his arms around me.

"I am afraid, Julia. Amelia has become the *other* woman to me and I am so scared. We have been married and happy for years. But happy is a meaningless word. I didn't know what true, deep hunger for another person felt like, until that night when I met *you*. It was instant. I had to see you again. I had to... " I cut him off by kissing his cheek.

"Goodbye, Brennan." I pulled out of his arms, and walked away.

He didn't follow me. He didn't call after me. I didn't dare turn around to look at him for fear that he would still be there.

That afternoon, in a bubble bath, with a bottle of wine, and as a muscle relaxer made its way through my blood lines, I cried like a little baby. I cried for Brennan. I cried for Johnny. I cried for Professor Hynes. I cried for John the Pastor. I cried for every time I let feelings get involved in my life. Feelings were stupid and I wasn't going to have them anymore. I was done.

I climbed into bed, hiccupping in the aftermath of my breakdown, and fell asleep. In dream after dream after dream–I dreamt about the summer when I turned thirteen. I tried to find the words on the board, as the pointer flew. I called out to Jason and told him that I loved him as he walked off with one of his older girls. I watched Grace get raped and strangled. Despite all of those horrible visions, I still couldn't get out of bed for days.

If it hadn't been for the recording contract and Dex's bucket of cold water, I may have stayed in bed until I became a leaf of a girl with hollowed out cheeks.

TWELVE

2010

Spring sprang up late in Boston. The cold wouldn't go away and the rain was driving the nails into my spirit's coffin. I wrote sad songs and took to my apartment most days. After the recording ended, I decided to stay in Boston. Johnny left for New York City and Dex went to Maryland to be with his on again girlfriend. To this day, I never even bothered to learn her name. He didn't share much either unless they were off again. Bitch was her name during those days.

I didn't want to go back to New Hampshire or New York. Both places made my heart hurt, so I took over the lease from Nick and waited for Love Sick Ponies' next tour dates. We were doing an East Coast run first thing in the summer. Our second part of the tour would be along the California coast line.

I looked forward to hitting the road. We would have various other bands open for us because Desired Pitch had already started a Spring Tour and we couldn't line up a date to play together. I was okay with it. I still felt uncomfortable when I thought about the day when Lizzie overheard that Brennan Curtis was married. She and I never spoke about it again. Ignorance is bliss and all that but I stayed away from the topic anyway.

I didn't stay away from thinking about Brennan though. I thought about him at least five times a day. I became obsessed with the term "Open Marriage." I read books. I read articles. I gaped at the famous people who were in them. I thought about what or who Brennan and Amelia were doing every day. It was pathetic. It was seriously destroying my game when it came to finding casual sex partners. I didn't want just anyone. I decided I could pretend it was him but I didn't have the energy to conquer some nights. It was so unlike me.

I made the local pub, Iron and Lime, my steady hang out because hot guys frequented there. It was close enough to Northeastern and Boston University to attract my type of guys. They distracted me from my rambling thoughts of Brennan. I allowed them attend to me just as much as I pleased them.

When the first guy after the clusterfuck with Brennan went down on me, it was instinctual to tell him not to bother because I didn't know if I could concentrate long enough for my body to build up. But when he held my legs down and pushed his mouth onto me, I shut the hell up. *Good God.* I fell in love with the feeling once again. Even so, every time I had sex with a guy, I closed my eyes and pretended it was Brennan. Since I never knew what it actually felt like to be with him, I became passionate and pleased him by proxy through those men. Then they got kicked out of bed, which either pissed them off or relieved them from having to stick around for cuddle time. Fuck cuddle time.

I did meet one guy regularly at the pub. Simon. He broke off our regular fuck dates after only three weeks because he *thought* I was in love with someone else. I couldn't help it that I cried out Brennan's name that one time. Okay, maybe it was a few times, but I told him that I really did mean to call out his name. That was something special, wasn't it? Guys that acted like chicks pissed me off.

Besides, Simon wanted more. Every guy did. I was, after all, Jules from LSP and they all knew it. If they didn't know, someone quickly made sure they knew who was hitting on them. I wasn't just a pretty face and an easy roll in the bed to these hot guys. I had fame and money. Guys could see the dollar signs just as much as the girls did with Johnny and Dex. Brennan didn't want me for my money or fame. He paid for my coffee. He bought me a hair clip I liked. I still couldn't put that black sparkly bow into my hair without wanting to cry. It had been almost six months and my feelings for him were so strong.

I faltered one Sunday afternoon. I picked up my phone and flipped through the contacts. I didn't delete his name because I knew one day I would do this. I pressed call as I started to sink in defeat. I held my breath.

"Julia?" His voice was sun shining through this rained out day. His voice was the first beat of a song that got my blood pumping. I felt alive. I was determined and hesitant at the same time. I couldn't speak.

"Julia," he breathed out my name. "I *never*... I didn't think you would ever call me. Julia. *Please*. Please let me hear your beautiful voice."

"What are your ground rules, Brennan?" I asked. It was the one question I had wanted to know the whole time we hadn't spoken.

His exhale was audible. "Our ground rules?" he asked. "I haven't seen or spoken to you in what feels like years and that is what you want to know?"

"Yes," I clipped.

"Well, when we met at a club, Amelia was already part of the lifestyle, but we felt a connection far more than sex. When we had been dating for a few weeks, she admitted that she was trying monogamy but needed to love other people. She goes both ways," he blabbered.

"Ground rules." I couldn't have been clearer. I didn't want the history of how they met. I wanted to know who he could or couldn't fuck.

"We both have to know of the other person we are going to... be with. We have to agree that the person isn't a threat to our marriage."

I half-snorted which turned into a full belly laugh. "A threat? How could you screw another person and not have it be a threat?"

"Do you want me to go on or can I just listen to you laugh because it is such a lovely sound?" he growled into the phone. My heart sputtered–I held in my next laugh with a quick intake of breath.

"We still have sex. That was one of the first rules we wrote out. Shit, I don't know how to explain it. The ground rules work for us. It helps to separate our desires from our emotional relationship to one another."

"Separate emotions from sex?" I asked.

"Yes," he answered quickly.

"You couldn't have picked a better lover than me then. What I don't understand is why you just didn't let it happen? I would have forgotten about you the first night. I am the best candidate for casual sex," I lied–maybe, I wasn't lying about my general nature but I was certainly lying about sex with him. I was *all* emotion with Brennan.

"Tell me about other women you have fucked, like the women that are on the so-called list." I held my breath–bracing myself. I was already jealous of those women.

Brennan didn't speak for a long time. It is obvious that he was uncomfortable by the frequent sighs I heard through the phone.

"Listen, I just want to know how it works–why you and your wife thought it was cool to add me to the list of yours. I want to know what other type of women you have had the pleasure of… " my words fall away as I realize how absolutely ridiculous I sound. I was a masochist–asking the man I couldn't stop thinking about, dreaming about, or touching myself for, to describe the explicit details of his sex life. This was low–even for me.

"There is one woman that I saw regularly… well, up until the night I met you," Brennan began.

"Wait, what? You stopped having sex after meeting me?"

"No, I have sex, Julia! Damn, this is fucking uncomfortable! I don't want to talk to you about this. Why can't we just talk about how you are, or how the record is coming along?"

"No." I want to know about the woman that he saw "regularly."

"Her name is Anne. She is a friend of Amelia's and has been since college. She was also part of her circle that swung. She is happily married with two kids and every week, she and I met." His long exhale doesn't go unnoticed. My hands were fisted so tight on the phone and the jealousy I had towards Anne was more acute than what I had felt about Amelia. Why was I jealous over her?

"More." I can't stop myself from choking out the word.

"What do you mean more?" Brennan sounded irritated. Good–we were both on the same page.

"I want to know how it works," I deadpanned.

"Okay." I hear the inhale through his nostrils. "Anne and I meet at her place every Saturday afternoon while her husband takes their kids out. She does the same for him on Sundays but I don't know who with–not Amelia. When I get to Anne's house, we normally talk for a little while–twenty minutes or so– over a glass of wine. Depending on our mood, either Anne or I will initiate foreplay. We never use her bed. We normally fuck on the pull out couch in the basement. Sometimes, we just do it once and other times, I stay for a few hours."

I knew that he wasn't going to say anymore because after a few beats, he cleared his throat and then went silent again.

"Why her?" My hands were trembling and my voice was small.

"She's cute. We like the same positions."

I couldn't hear anymore. I was starting to feel ill. And it had stopped after he had met me? What for? I wasn't around anymore.

"Jesus Christ, Julia. I just told you everything and that wasn't easy for me. Say something," he half-shouted into the phone.

"I miss you, Brennan." My voice was still small. I felt so incredibly small.

"I miss you so much. God, I miss your eyes, your lips, your hands and the feel of your breath on my neck." He continued to voice his thoughts without a filter. I held on to every word and was giggling by the end of the outpour.

"I missed that giggle, too. It is so much more beautiful than all of these worn out Love Sick Ponies CD's that I constantly listen to."

"Thank you for answering my questions... honestly," I concluded.

"Are you getting off the phone?" he asked, sounding startled.

"I am," I replied.

"Please let me see you," he breathed in a plea.

"I don't think I can, Bren," I whispered back.

"*Please*," he begged. A long moment passed as I thought about his smile, his long curls, and his conversation. I miss him as a friend just as much as I am in love with him. I could be friends with a married man, *couldn't I*?

"I will catch a flight to JFK and stay in Manhattan for a couple days," I say. His phone dropped and I heard him curse. I heard a couple of other things fall to the ground. He came back on the phone.

"Text me with the details and I will be there," he says sounding both relieved and excited.

The following morning, I stepped into the bathroom at JFK airport to freshen up my makeup and hair, *not* for the benefit for Brennan. I escaped from the bathroom when a few teenagers recognize me and I slipped on my sunglasses. I had the desire to throw on my Red Sox hat but my hair looked so damn good, I just couldn't do it.

The girls followed me out to the waiting car area where I became a frozen statue at the sight of Brennan. His pale green Henley was pulled up and a black beanie covered his dark locks. He wasn't wearing his glasses but his squinting eyes as he beamed at me made up for his deliciousness.

The girls threw papers at me and crowded me as they switched out to take individual photos with me. I scribbled my name and kept my eyes on Brennan as I smiled for the camera. These were rare photos. Jules Delaney from LSP smiling? Doesn't happen. Normally I made the rock and roll sign with my fingers. I never ever let my arm fall over the fan's shoulder but here I was, breaking the rules. *All of the rules.*

Brennan came up in between the crowd and made the girls automatically part. He brushed his thumb over my bottom lip before he took my face into his hands. His hard forced kiss made me moan and we immediately opened our mouths to let each other in. He smelled like cologne and male sex breath. I got lost in his groans and his hands in my hair. His hand moved down to my ass and squeezed as I tore my mouth through every inch of his.

Cameras clicked off as people started clapping. A guy called out for us to get a room while another man with a notepad asked what the name of the guy was. The paparazzi were here. *Fuck*. I begrudgingly slipped my tongue out of his mouth.

"Bren, we have to get out of here unless you want your photo on the cover of SS Weekly," I groaned.

"Doesn't this airport have a bed or even a table somewhere in this place?" he laughed back into my mouth.

I shook my head and took his hand. He grabbed my suitcase and as he did I noticed he had taken his ring off his left hand again. I felt a sudden pang of sadness. How long would he be mine this time?

155

As he opened the passenger door to his black Jetta, he answered "Brennan Curtis" to the annoying asshole that wouldn't stop asking his name. My mouth dropped open. He just "outted" himself to the world and he was *married*. Scandal was on our immediate horizon and I couldn't give a shit less. I made a mental note not to turn my cell phone back on. *Ever*.

I wanted him naked. I want him under me. I wanted him for days. I practically jumped on top of him as he pulled over on the road to kiss me.

"Julia. You are more perfect than I remember. More gorgeous than any photo can take," he groaned, as he open mouthed kissed my neck all the way down to my breasts.

"Brennan," I said for the lack of a better sex word. Brennan was sex. Synonymous.

"I had a plan, Julia. I didn't plan on wanting inside of you the moment I saw you." He quickly pulled away and I was left feeling bereft. "Let me do this right, okay?"

I rolled back over to my seat and exhaled loudly. He wasn't going to take me to bed right now and I needed to calm myself. He took my hand and kissed every finger.

"Please. I need to do this right. I need every moment. I want every second to be about you." His face was determined. He still felt guilty. I was just horny. I waved my hands for him to go. He chuckled as he put the car into drive and took us down to the Ritz where I had booked the penthouse suite, stocked with everything romantic.

We didn't make it to the bedroom before our pants were off. I felt him against me and I grew nervous. I stopped kissing him in a tizzy and he noticed me backing off.

"Julia, it's okay. We don't have to do this," he murmured into my ear.

"Does she know that you are here with me?" I asked, feeling small and somewhat dirty.

"She knows you were coming to see me," he said. His voice was tight like he didn't want to talk about Amelia. I couldn't help but move away. I left him standing there, a large tent of clothing protruding from his rigid body. God, his muscular, dark body was eye candy and I wanted to lick every inch of him. We stood quietly for a bit all the while enjoying our mental foreplay. We looked at every line, every curve, and every movement of our chests.

"You're the most gorgeous woman I have ever seen," he whispered.

That is all it took. The image of a faceless Amelia and the dirty feeling I had, went poof. Everything that held me back before fell away as we grabbed for each other. Brennan picked me up and carried me into the bedroom. All the while, he sucked through my tank top on what would become his favorite part of my body.

THIRTEEN

2010

New York City

The intensity of our love-making made the atmosphere in the hotel room electrify. The vivid colors of the room, the sun beams through the windows, and the sounds of pleasure between us were gorgeous and magical. Brennan tried to catch his breath while tugging on my breasts with his teeth. For hours we laid naked and twisted up in sexual perfection. His moans and grunts even after we had climaxed made me want to roll on top of him again. If only I could move my body. I never felt like a pile of blissful mush in my life. He had wrecked me. An inch of my body had not gone unnoticed and as I brushed his hair with my fingers, I closed my eyes, picturing every moment that led up to this one.

"What are you thinking about Julia?" Brennan quietly breathed out as he continued to pay close attention to my chest.

"After that? Not much. Bren, you fucked every thought out of me," I laughed. He froze. My eyebrows drew together at his reaction. What had I said?

"I didn't *fuck* you, Julia," he said, as he made his way up and brushed my hair out of my face. "I *worshipped* you."

"Worship away anytime," I smiled at him as I waved my hand towards my naked body. I was truly happy and excited for the next two days alone with Brennan. I wanted him to read to me again. I wanted him to hold my hand. I wanted to sing to him.

I took a deep breath and looked into his eyes.

My mind has a blank space where you belong

Lover.

You take up my heart in the wrong way

Baby.

But don't you know? Don't you know?

I can't not love you

I can't. I can't. I can't.

I ended the last word on a long, deep note. I had written the song for him in my spare time. I had written many songs that I wouldn't show to the guys. It felt too personal to share with them.

"Is that a new song?" he asked, completely engrossed in my eyes and lips as I finished singing.

I nodded. "It's not a LSP song. I wrote it on my own. It's too sultry for the band. It would kill my angst image," I sniggered.

"When did you write it?" he asked. He wanted me to say I wrote it for him. I shrugged.

"A few months ago. I have been writing a lot. Did you like it?" I asked, genuinely interested in what he thought.

"It was... Jesus, Julia. I have no words," he beamed as he shook his curls into my face.

"I wrote it for you," I whispered into his hair.

"Sing it again," he demanded as he looked into my eyes.

"No way. You get that one memory from me. No repeat performances."

"Tease," he laughed as he tickled my underarms. I instinctually shoved him off me and told him in every choice word there was to stop.

"Don't tickle me. *Ever*," I nearly yelled at him. Brennan held up his hands in surrender as he looked at me with sympathy. I felt like an asshole but Goddamn, I hate it when people tickle me. I put my hands over my eyes and his face flashed into my mind.

Jason #2.

I squashed that memory of losing my virginity down. I pulled my legs up to my chest as I felt the weight of the complicated thoughts that memory had just caused.

Brennan was laying quietly on the other side of the king sized bed. He was obviously afraid to touch the tiger that was me.

"I am sorry I yelled at you," I whispered with a grim smile. I looked over to him with a pleading expression. I wanted his arms around me. His touch lit a fire in me that I had never experienced before.

Brennan rolled over and placed his hand on my foot. He started to rub methodically as he looked up into my eyes.

"Why? Why did you yell at me?" he asked.

"I want to tell you because I don't like to be tickled but it's more than that. I guess it reminds me of the guy that I lost my virginity to," I shrugged.

Brennan popped up on one elbow with hardness in his look. "What it bad or something?"

I couldn't look in his eyes as I said, "I don't want to say bad. It just was. He was my brother's friend. He took my virginity. At the time, it made me feel so damn special. I mean what older guy wanted to be with a kid like me? I was awkward and hardly had friends. My two best friends and I grew distant that summer. I had just turned thirteen. They didn't come to my party but Jason made it *his* job to make me feel special," I admitted.

"Over that summer, we all changed. Emmy was kind of popular with the girls. She was still nice to me and said "hi", but we didn't hang out. Angie was distant. She kept to herself and shit, I don't even remember if she ran with a crowd. I was popular... in another way," I said quietly as I rolled my eyes over to Brennan. "I was the easy girl, the slut. I was just popular around the boys that wanted my body, you know?"

This was the most I had ever told anyone about my history and it pained me to think about that little girl. I felt like I was still that girl only being recognized for my big chest and plump lips.

"God, thirteen years old? So you... " he asked, looking like he couldn't find a politically correct word.

"I *am* a slut," I finished for him. He scoffed at me and I gave him the *bullshit* look. Didn't he hear Johnny back in the hotel room when we met? I didn't get the ultimate title by telling boys to keep their pants on.

"You are not a slut, Julia," he said adamantly. I smiled back at him. It was a genuine smile that probably made him think I believed him. Brennan was so very sweet and so very wrong.

An hour later, we had taken a sex fogged shower to a new level and were dressing in slick clothes to go out for dinner on the town. We were both giddy and just could not stop touching one another. If I were a spectator, I probably would have vomited at least three times by now. I made last minute reservations to a five star Italian restaurant that I wanted to try the last time I was in town. When I name dropped, I saw Brennan roll his eyes at me as he smirked. I stuck my tongue out at him and the make out session started yet again. Everything led to us kissing. Go ahead and vomit for that one, too.

For the first time in my life, I let another person spoon feed me. Brennan sat right next to me at our table so that he could treat me like a little child and make sure I tasted and enjoyed every part of our meal.

"Close your eyes, Baby," he said softly.

I drew back and opened my eyes a little larger. Baby? Where did that come from?

"Did you just call me baby because you are literally spoon feeding me this meal and now I kind of feel like one," I laughed hollowly.

"Did I just call you baby?" he asked, perplexed while he dabbed a napkin at the side of those appealing lips.

I nodded my head.

"I promise you, *Baby*," he emphasized, "that I only called you that as an endearment from my heart." Okay, he was smooth.

"Aw, Bren. You are melting my black heart," I cried out sarcastically. He chuckled along with me.

"Now close your eyes, Julia," he demanded. I saluted him and did as I was told. It was such a foreign feeling but I felt so damn safe with him.

"Open your mouth," he whispered.

The minute I did, a chocolate explosion took over and I moaned. I let the molten chocolate cake, which he must have been hiding up his ass, dissolve on my tongue. After a few beats, Brennan joined in on the chocolate and entered my mouth to enjoy the dessert, too. This was one of those moments I would never forget. His tongue and chocolate together was heavenly glorious. I heard him moan into my mouth and I snapped my fingers for the check. We made out through Brennan paying the check, Brennan putting on my coat, and all the way back to the hotel room.

The many explosions that followed the dessert decadence transpired while we were naked and in the king sized bed. We didn't sleep a wink and I had never been more content and satiated in my entire life.

FOURTEEN

"What do you feel like doing today?" I asked as I played with Brennan's locks that covered my whole stomach. I loved the feeling of him resting his head on my heart while looking up at me. It was so intimate. Cuddle time was awesome. With Brennan. Only Brennan.

"You," he laughed as he squeezed a very exposed breast. It hurt, but after the tickling incident, I was not going to complain about his administrations on my body. How odd. I was thinking of his feelings before mine. Was this what truly caring about someone really felt like?

"And? There must be something else you might want to do. Money is no issue," I stated as I tried to braid a few of the locks together. Damn curls were so silky that nothing stuck. My long, thick hair remained out of an elastic band and hung all over my face and shoulders just the way Brennan liked it. He played with my hair a lot, too, when we talked like this.

Brennan rolled his eyes. "I know you have money, Julia. That is not the point of us spending time together. I have money, too, you know. So... what would you like to do in New York City?" he asked, emphasizing New York City with a flourish.

"How about a really good cup of coffee first?" I nodded at him with a smile.

He smiled back at me as his palm when to my cheek. "Sounds perfect," he whispered.

"Umm... then maybe we could go out the Statue of Liberty?" I asked, covering my eyes and feeling like a total dork.

"The Statue of Liberty? Seriously?" he questioned in shock.

"I've never actually been out there," I admitted as he pulled my hands away from my eyes and started to stroke them gently. I moaned at the massage and closed my eyes anyways.

"I will take you anywhere and everywhere, Julia," he said. I opened my eyes to find his so firmly locked onto my face. He was memorizing everything. I saw the moments they flicked to a different part of my face where he would spend one, two, three, and four beats just staring.

Trying not to be so intense, I smirked at him and took a fistful of hair to pull him up to my lips. "Statue of Liberty." I stated with finality.

He kissed me soundly and from afar I heard his phone ring. He didn't even flinch. He just kept kissing me. Amelia. I had totally fucking forgotten that I was retreating to a private vacation for lovers with a married man. I felt the air leave my lungs and my lips stopped responding to his. The ringtone was the worst of it all. Out of all the millions of songs to have as a ringtone, that one had to be a sign. It had been days since I last had the nightmare and here I was, wide awake and living it all over again. Girls on the merry-go-round closing me into the middle. "Jules is a slut, slut, slut, slut. Jules is a slut, slut slut, slut," they sang out to me as the ringtone continued.

Brennan pulled back, clearly confused. "What is it, Baby?" he asked.

I shook my head in a daze. "Why is your phone playing *American Pie*?" I asked slowly and numbly.

He shrugged, not understanding the significance, but he didn't have to. He knew he had struck another chord with me and quickly popped off the bed to go shut it off. I watched his muscled, beautiful, tatted, and naked body reach for the phone and with strong forearms and fumbling fingers, he powered the phone completely off. He sighed at it and then looked up to me, his hair falling all over his face.

"Is it better now?" he whispered tentatively.

"Yes," I said confidently. And it was. Somehow, the sight of Brennan in all of his vulnerable glory shutting off a trigger of mine so I could be happy, made the girls' voices stop. I mentally told them to fuck off and got up to hug him. He wrapped me in his strong embrace, tight and safe.

"I am falling for you, Brennan," I said weakly. "I am so scared. I am doing everything I want for us. It feels so right to be in your arms right now. But then I remember that we aren't supposed to want or feel right for each other."

"No, no, no," he groaned. "This has been perfect. It has been the best time I have had in so damn long. Please don't ruin it now."

Moments passed as we slowly rubbed each other's nude backs and swayed to the music of Manhattan day life.

"What was so bad about that song, Julia?" he finally whispered in my ear.

This was him asking to know me. He wanted to get under the plastic wrap that held my true self firmly inside. *Tight and tucked in with no air to breath.* What good would come out of me telling Brennan about my dream? There was too much confusion, too much pain. Sometimes, I felt like I was the one raped and strangled.

Telling Brennan, in detail, about what I did to make myself feel normal after that summer, wouldn't change him being married or me being a slut. I didn't know how to trust anyone. I wasn't ready and maybe, I would never be. My mother and father certainly didn't show me how. My brother did, somewhat, and yet he still had no clue that his best friend took my virginity. I was fucking pissed that I couldn't trust Brennan. I just couldn't do it.

"It's nothing. Was that Amelia on the phone?" I questioned. He nodded slowly as he took in my reaction to his question about the song. I showed him nothing. He was so honest and yet I couldn't be. He didn't answer the phone because of me. Because of us. I was the woman he was taking into account. I wasn't his, we weren't a real couple, and he did not need to know anything about me. That was the cruel reality. We were lovers, off on a small, private getaway.

I had to take this thing between us at face value and find the normal Jules again. She didn't give a rat's ass about more with any guy. The faster, the better. To the point and jump ship. Coping mechanism or not, it worked.

Except, not when Brennan Curtis was looking at me the way he was. Nope, none of those shitty tactics worked when he grazed my stomach with his. It was devastating to watch myself getting caught up in him. It turned everything upside down and then fucked it sideways.

"I am going to take a shower. I would like to head out for the eleven o'clock boat ride," I stated nonchalantly. It was no matter that I just had the biggest revelation in my entire life.

"May I join you?" Brennan asked gently as he took my hand into his.

"Of course," I answered in the same gentle way. We silently turned the water on and got in. He took the soap from my hands and washed me. He washed under and over my breasts. He washed my belly button. He washed inside my thighs. He washed in between every single toe.

He proceeded to wash my hair. It was incredible. His strong fingers stroked and massaged in my earthy scented shampoo, which even my internal moans of pleasure, were covered up by the silence that we didn't want to break. But I felt every moan in my heart. I felt every word of endearment. He loved me in a way I had never experienced before. By the time he was done, I had tears in my eyes and so did he.

An hour later, we were on the boat to Ellis Island. We left our cell phones in our suite and held hands on the boat. I marveled at his presence. The beanie was back on, his glasses were getting a little fogged up, and I was soaking in his every movement. A woman from the other side of the boat was watching me. When I looked over at her small, older face, she gave me a knowing smile. *Yes, you love him*, she said without words.

We paid for the crown level tickets and found ourselves high up and looking onto Manhattan. A small man with a professional camera approached us for the photo bait shot everyone wanted to buy but cost way too much for the average tourist. People could easily ask for someone to shoot a photo with their own camera phones.

Since we didn't have ours and secretly, I did want the professional stamp from the Statue of Liberty, I bought four of the photos and gave Brennan two. We looked like an amazing couple. His arms went around my shoulders as he stood behind me. In one picture, he smelled my hair and I was laughing with a genuine smile. It had been years since I took a photo without the scowl on my face.

Brennan noticed that a couple of twenty-something girls recognized me, guarding me from their approach, we quickly made our way to the small museum before the boat headed back to Manhattan.

"Do you think you might be able to make it to Boston sometime soon?" I asked him on the short boat ride back.

"I want to. Would you have me for a few days? Am I allowed back into the lair of Julia Delaney?" He smirked at me and I gave him the stink eye.

"I would love it if you came to visit," I assured him. We kissed softly and that seemed to break the compounded ice that the morning had produced.

FIFTEEN

We took a cab to Fifth Avenue because I was in desperate need of new jeans. We decided on Saks and when we entered, Brennan went one way and I went the other. It was amusing and eye opening that we were comfortable enough to be independently together. I didn't like shopping big stores but the rocker clothes were staples of the outfits that showcased my image on stage and in front of media. After forty five minutes or so, I had acquired a couple pairs of awesome jeans and some rocking designer shirts for the upcoming tour.

Shit, I thought. *I had an upcoming tour without the possibility of seeing Brennan.*

In that moment, I was anxious to see him. Knowing I soon wouldn't even talk to him on the phone, I felt compelled to go to him and suck up every minute we had together. I combed through the expansive men's area and found him trying on a dark brown bomber jacket that Saks should have specifically asked him to model for their catalog.

"What do you think?" Brennan asked skeptically when he looked up to find me with my mouth agape. Did he think I hated it? Was my look not expressing how darn right sexy he was in that jacket?

"I think I want to fuck you in the dressing room," I laughed.

Brennan actually turned a slight shade of pink. He shook his head at me and gave me a disdainful look. "You and I don't fuck, Julia. We make love. How many times do I have to tell you that?"

So he was annoyed and grumpy about how I perceived our relationship. Interesting but not crucial. It didn't matter if I called it fucking or making love because either way, he would go home to his wife and I would hit the road. Couldn't he feel the end of our time together speeding up like a train that was just about to make its abrupt stop?

I felt it. I heard the damn train's whistles loud and clear.

"So you like it?" he muttered as he pulled it off and checked the label. Damn, he was in a crap ass mood.

We went from playfulness to quiet to irritation. The emotional roller coaster was making us both sick.

"If you don't buy that jacket, I will never make love to you again," I sassed him, trying to help him feel some sun rays of positivity. Wow, I did truly care about what Brennan felt. It was a first for me to actually want to see a man happy. So weird.

"Sold." He retorted. *Good, he's back.*

He pulled on a grey looking pea coat that closely resembled mine. *God damn.* I was going to rigorously have my way with him tonight and tomorrow morning. I yawned, remembering we didn't sleep a single minute the night before. That made me smile. It was a fucking fantastic feeling.

"So where are the dressing rooms in the men's department?" I asked as I started looking for the signs hanging from the ceiling.

"Really? This one, too?"

"Absolutely. Please. You must get them both." I begged. "Are you getting hungry? Should we do room service tonight or go out?"

"Let's do one more dinner out and then we can do room service for breakfast. Or... I could just eat you for breakfast," he smoothly said as he took my hands and wrapped them underneath the pea coat and around his waist. It... he smelled so delicious. The sexy new coat overwhelmed my senses and I about crawled up his body. I wanted in.

Brennan insisted on paying for our purchases while I hung back and pouted. I made all of this money and yet the guy had to be chivalrous. I was playing a part though. Secretly, it was absolutely foreign to me for a man to pay for everything so I quietly thanked him with a kiss. He beamed at me as he pulled his beanie back on to brave the cold once more.

With bags in hand, Brennan and I made our way back to the hotel. I collapsed on the couch and shucked off everything I could with the remaining energy I had. Brennan finished pulling off the rest as I gave him a deliriously happy smile. He gave one right back at me while he undressed down to his boxer briefs and crawled behind me to spoon. Spooning was awesome. *Wait. Did I just think that?*

"I agree," Brennan confirmed. No, I didn't just think that. I said it out loud to another person. Who was I and what happened to 'just sex' Jules? We fell asleep almost immediately to the late afternoon sounds of Manhattan.

A few hours later, I woke up to a hand slowly circling my stomach and going lower down into my panties. I let out an exhilarated sigh and hummed.

"Hi," I whispered.

"Hi," he softly said.

The rest of our communication involved hands and legs and circles and moans. He treated me like the dessert we had had the night before and I loved every moment of it. When we had regulated our breathing, I asked the first thought that came to my mind. I had zero filter with Brennan and I knew it would probably get me in deep.

"Do you and Amelia want children?" I inquired. I asked so casually that I even surprised myself. Everything about our situation was so surreal. I didn't know why I wasn't jumping up and down and whining for him to pick me.

Brennan stilled his lazy hand movement and I believed he began to hold his breath. I waited a while before I turned towards him for an answer.

"Bren? Kids?" I asked.

"I want children," he deadpanned.

"Ha! That wasn't my question and you know it," I teased.

"Julia, I don't want to talk about Amelia. Not when I am with you. Do I want kids? Yes. Does she? I think so. But we are far from that happening. Very, very far." His last words spoke volumes but I didn't dare to ask why. He said he didn't want to talk about her so I let it go. If I were Amelia, I never would have asked for an open relationship and I certainly would want his children. Again, another revelation. It was time to admit it. I was in love with Brennan. It killed me.

"Let's get ready for dinner," Brennan suggested. "I want to take you to this awesome Polish restaurant in Brooklyn."

"Alright but won't that be weird? I mean, you and your wife live there. What if you run into people you know?" I asked cautiously.

Brennan shrugged and started to pull us both up. He slapped my ass and told me to get moving. I kissed him one more time before finding my new clothes and making myself look hot just in case we did run into someone. Maybe even one someone.

Just as we were about to open the door, I heard Brennan's phone buzz from his jeans' pocket. I looked down at it and waited for him to pull it out to answer. He didn't move but opened the door for me, briefly kissing my temple as I walked through. The buzzing started again as we walked down the hall to the elevator. I stopped, leaned up against the wall, and crossed my arms.

"You need to answer your phone?" I asked.

"You haven't answered your phone so I won't answer mine," he retorted.

"I didn't turn mine back on. You did," I faintly accused him.

"Well, I meant to turn mine off after I checked my messages for work," he snapped back, looking more uncomfortable as we continued to banter about his phone buzzing. Just as I started to say that he didn't subconsciously ask for Amelia to call, the buzzing started again and he groaned. I was officially put off. He wanted to talk to her. This was turning into a fucking nightmare. Maybe one night, this situation would replace my age old nightmare about Grace.

He grabbed it out of his pocket and pushed a button.

"What?" he barked into the phone. I heard a female's voice through the other end. It was so damn quiet in the hall and I felt like I was a voyeur looking in on his phone call.

"Baby, slow down," Brennan said in a gentle voice. I sucked in my breath at the mention of him calling the woman his baby. *I* was his baby. Wasn't I?

"Ok," he said and started to pace up and down the hall, while I stood there like a fucking afterthought.

"So where are you now?" he asked with concern. He flashed his eyes over to me, as I bit my lip from yelling out that he should have never ever answered the phone. Or maybe I bit my lip to discourage the sob that my body needed to release. The shakes were coming back and I didn't want him to see. This was all wrong.

184

"Ok," he barked into the phone. "Yes, yes!"

He was leaving me. He was leaving me to go to *her*. His wife. I came all the way to New York City for him and now... I looked like the biggest fucking dumbass this side of the earth. He punched the off button and looked at me with resolve. Brennan shoved his hands into his pockets and then took them out again. I watched him do that and run his fingers through his hair several times.

"I guess we aren't going out for dinner?" I asked, inspecting a cuticle so that I appeared unfazed by the change in events.

"Julia. I am so, so sorry," he emphasized as he came over to crowd my space. I held up my hands so he didn't come any closer.

"Julia," he started. I shook my head in anger and disgust that cloaked over my whole body.

"I am not your baby, Brennan," I said so slowly that a two year old would be able to understand. "*She* is your baby. But I suppose you didn't notice that you just called her that?"

"Fucking wait a minute, okay? Amelia is sick. She needs me to go to the store." Brennan scrunches his face as he thinks.

"Oh! We can just stop on the way to dinner. It'll only delay us ten minutes, at most… " he surmised.

"Fuck that! Go home, Brennan. Take care of your wife. This was a mistake. A big fucking huge monumental fuck up. I have no idea what the hell I was thinking. You're married and I… " Damn myself for not being able to finish that sentence. I had the word permanently etched into my brain. I am the slut.

"Julia, listen. I didn't want to talk about her because she and I are taking a break. I wanted this time just to be about us. I don't know why she is calling me. I mean, she does have other people she can call but she sounds scared. I feel like I should just check. I honestly didn't mean to call her baby," he noted with a look that said he was being serious. But the truth was he did call her baby. That word was etched in *his* brain. For her.

"A break?" I asked. "What does that even mean?"

"Uh," he groaned as he cursed under his breath. "She has been fucking my friend and he wasn't on our safe list. Our ground rules were broken. I can't... I don't trust her and besides I can't even look at any woman, including my fucking wife! You have ruined me. Even for her, the one I thought was forever. And it is so fucking confusing, Julia."

My mouth dropped open in shock. I didn't know what to say. He was separated from his wife? Amelia slept with an *unapproved* person. He didn't trust her. He wanted only me and yet, he was running, no *sprinting* to help her now?

I couldn't get involved. I didn't want any part of their fucked up relationship. The more rules a relationship had, the more ridiculously confusing it was. Words were just words until you saw those words in action.

Right now, Brennan's actions said, "I'm sorry Jules. I want to fuck you all night long, but I need to go take care of the love of my life, who happens to be my wife."

I turned and walked back down to my door. I pulled the key card out of my back pocket and slipped it through the metal lock. I barely heard him calling my name as I continued to curse myself over and over again. When the door slammed shut behind me, I went to the bar and poured myself three shots of tequila and I took them one right after another.

I wondered who would come rescue me if I got sick. Oh, right.

No one.

SIXTEEN

I was officially the drunken door mat for men. I thought about creating a personal ad on craigslist, in case there were men out there that needed a woman to walk on. Brennan never came back to the room that night, or maybe he did and the loud music I blared while dancing to tequila, answered his knock. I switched on my cell phone and there it was. He had called or texted every ten minutes, begging me not to leave the city. A text came through as I was deleting my voicemails.

Brennan: Julia. Please. I haven't slept. You can't push me away. Please open your door.

I furrowed my brows and reread the text. Open the door? Open what door?

Me: What door?

Ten seconds later, as I watched my phone screen, there was a hard knocking on the suite door so loud, it had to be waking up the rest of the hotel guests. I threw off my covers and ran to the door.

189

I opened it and grabbed his jacket to pull him through the door.

"What the hell are you doing? You will wake up the entire hotel, if you haven't already," I scowled as I bore my eyes into his red, puffy ones. Had he... been crying?

"Brennan? What is wrong?" I asked, feeling a bit taken back by his visually emotional state.

"I left you. I have ached to hold you for months but the minute Amelia called, I left you to be with her. And after all of that? It was a fucking test," his voice started to grow in volume.

I shook my head in confusion. "I am not understanding, Brennan. What is a fucking test?"

"She *pretended* to be sick to see if I would leave you," he said slowly and with ultimate disgust. "We have never played games. She is playing games."

"Brennan. You are *supposed* to go to her. She is your wife," I said adamantly. "I may not know all of the rules of an open relationship, but I am pretty sure that your marriage *always* comes first. I knew what I was doing when I came to see you. I wanted you. I mean, I want you but now... I also feel... I mean, I have never felt more dirty or filthy than I do right now."

"You are not... " I cut him off by covering his mouth with my palm. He wasn't one to talk. In my eyes, he was just as fucked up as me. That's why I need to save us both and make him leave.

"I need you to leave now," I husked out in my tequila hangover morning breath.

"I can't. I need to be around you. I am not trying to hurt you. There is something between us and it has made me so unhappy these past months. I am so unhappy in my marriage. I think it is you, Julia. It has been you. Please. Just give me *today*. Just *friends*. You came all this way to see me and I fucked it up. Please. *Just* today and I turned off my phone," he said as he pulled it from his pocket to show me.

My heart wasn't in this anymore. I wanted to brood over my half ass life. Brennan wasn't worth all of this misery. He was a married man who was too complicated, too beautiful, and he brought out shit in my past that continually reminded me of my poor choices. Brennan was one more poor choice. I smiled sadly at him when I thought that.

My phone chirped. I looked down at it and saw Johnny's smiling face on my phone and a warm blanket wrapped around me as I looked at him. I clicked the button.

"Johnny?"

"Jules." His voice was resolute. He knew where I was. He sounded mad but was trying not to show it. I was the only one who could call him on his bullshit.

"Yes, Johnny. I am in the city. Where are you?" I asked as I started to walk back to my bedroom to put on pants. Brennan was following me. I could *feel* him seething... or sulking. He was a wreck but I couldn't find it in me to show him that I cared. When I turned to see how far into the room he was, he was leaning against the door jamb with a tight grip on it. *Johnny and Brennan officially want to murder one another and I need the hair of the dog.*

"Jules, have you looked outside your hotel this morning?" Johnny asked in his big brotherly voice that sometimes reminds me of Kent. Like right now actually.

"No, why would I?" I asked slowly.

"Um, maybe because you were sucking face with married douche at the Statue of Liberty on Madfame last night and the paparazzi followed you to your hotel?"

My breath stopped. I slowly dropped the cell phone on the bed and looked out the window. I noticed television vans but it was the front side of the hotel. I could get out the back. Up until now, our disguises, pseudo names, lay low public appearances, and limited video/photo shoots kept us out of the limelight. But now? This was the official start of a game on field day.

This was a monumental fuck up. They had been waiting to pounce on me like ketchup on French fries and then splatter their assumed, but correct, opinions of me being the world's biggest slut in the American rock scene today. Nick and Johnny protected my image. I practically made every guy swear on their lives. I took pictures of their dicks and kept them safe on a hard drive. I had not done this with Brennan. I hadn't done anything "just sex" Jules did with him.

LSP was a popular up and coming solid rock band but as individual members of the bigger umbrella of the rock world, we had decided that we would never become independently famous over lies and drama in the rock celebrity scene. We limited our appearances. Everything was handled through our tour manager, Danielle, who reported back to our distant manager in LA. I had never even met the guy, Bob something or another, but I think Danielle received a ton of pressure from him. She protected us as like she would her children. She was damn good at it.

But now?

I had blown our image–my image–and Danielle might not like me so much anymore. That would hurt. LSP always stated in interviews that it was about the music when asked about relationships and everyday life. *Always*. But we were fooling ourselves, especially now that we were hitting it real big. We couldn't walk around like other normal people and make out with married men in the airport waiting area. Those days of "Just Jules" were over. It made me despise the choice to follow my dreams of making it big. Shit would hit the fan and yes, our ratings would go up. But everyone who cared about the band's image would be crawling up my ass, too.

I returned to the bed and picked up the phone to Johnny still talking.

"Echo at nine o'clock. I don't want to wait that long to get you out of there though. Is he there right now?" he asked, venom spitting through the phone and poisoning my ear drum with every word. I nodded my head as I looked at Brennan. He had relaxed his stance. He walked to the window out of curiosity. If he had spent the night in the hotel hall, he had no idea either.

"Yes," I whispered. Johnny exhaled loudly. "Johns, I didn't know. I forgot. I missed him and when I saw him, I don't know. It was tunnel vision. I fucked up. I fucked up."

"No one ever even suspected us. No one ever knew I was in love with you. Even on stage. Why is that, Jules?" Johnny asked me in a softer tone. He was still hurt. I had still shoved Brennan in his face on fucking national television. I didn't have to say it was definitely over anymore. I went public with the man I wanted to love and hate. I was so fucked up.

"Get rid of him. I will be there in a little while. Danielle is freaking pissing her pants. Brennan said his fucking name on television. They are searching the whole state of New York for him. It didn't help that he picked you up in a Black Jetta with plate numbers in clear view," he said. He was mocking me now. I was a stupid whore and it hurt worse than if he had just come out and said it.

I pushed the off button and went to the bar. Half the tequila bottle was gone and I tipped it back twice to settle my hangover shakes and my publicity kill image nerves. Brennan walked to me. I handed him the bottle with a half-smile.

"Your life is about to change. For the ultimate worse. I hope last night was worth it for you," I said sarcastically.

"My marriage is in pieces and I don't give a fucking damn, so yes, it was worth it. She saw me and you on television. She saw the passion in the way we hugged. That's why she fucking tricked me. I was her dog with the bell last night and I am so very sorry," he earnestly apologized as he brushed his hand along the side of my face.

"Pavlov. He *always* goes to the food," I deadpanned. Brennan shook his head vigorously. I felt my sad but compassionate smile and watched him register my knowing look in a series of emotions.

"I am a tiny blip on your life map, Bren. *So tiny.* You married your wife for a reason and God help me for being a part in a cheating marriage because whether you have the rules or not, I would never ever be okay with sharing you as my husband. Those are *my* rules," I admitted. "So you need to find your way out of this hotel without being seen. You need to go home to your wife. Have a baby or buy a fucking house. Figure your marriage shit out but just... forget about me. I have a wonderful life. I have my brother, my mother, and my band. I am good."

He grabbed me and held me tight. I didn't cry although I really fucking needed to. I ran through all of the guys that led up to this one. The ones I let use me. The ones I used. The ones that felt dirty. The ones that wanted marriage. The one who stood by me through it all. Brennan was my biggest temptation that I couldn't refuse. He was the one who got away before I even met him.

SEVENTEEN

2 YEARS LATER

2012

Portland, Oregon

"Do you think I suck ass at that solo part?" I asked no one in particular. I had abruptly stopped my rendition of *It's Your Solid Rock* on stage at the MAX, one of the hottest venues in the Northwest. We would be playing the massive venue the following day and I was screwing around with the awesome acoustics. Situated in the Gorge and with a stunning view out the back of the auditorium, I was alone on stage, playing to no one. Johnny and Dex were somewhere in the building, working on some technical difficulties, and there was a handful of people setting up lights and equipment.

"Nah, you sounded perfect," a guy in a gray suit yelled out to me from behind the sound booth. "I was listening. Real good. You own that stage."

I bowed to him and then blew him a kiss, whoever he was. I started to strum again, trying to come up with our set list for the next night. The boys always left me in charge of it and I was trying to pick songs that mirrored this incredible place. After a few beats, Johnny came up behind me and kissed me on the cheek.

"You look beautiful today, sweets." His short buzzed cut hair and silver lip ring sparkled in the mixture of the stage light and the fresh natural light coming from the outside windows. I kissed him softly on the lips.

"You don't look so bad yourself, Johns," I said in my most seductive voice. "Maybe we should quit this whole band thing and make a living out of giving each other compliments all day."

Johnny went to the microphone. "My girlfriend says we can have sex all day instead of this shit. So, we quit. Consider *this* our last gig."

Dex rolled his eyes and muttered "Love Sick Ponies is a shit name anyway."

Johnny and I decided to go public with our rekindled relationship in an interview with K105.8FM BLISS radio in San Francisco less than two weeks ago. It was a fantastic day. I felt like I could breathe again. People knew my relationship status so they basically backed off of me for once.

The whole Brennan debacle blew up in our faces and Danielle had stuck James, who happened to be ex-marine on me for weeks. I was grounded to the tour bus and could only leave for food and water. Even then, shit, it was just depressing.

Johnny made it his business to be the entertainment segment of the treacherous time out. He built a puppet stage out of some milk crates and got costume designers at one show to help him make puppets of us, as ourselves. Mine was brooding and actually pretty fucking hot. He didn't hold out in the boob department. I also noticed that puppet Johnny had a bigger bulge in his pants than puppet Dex. *Poor Dex.* His girl broke up with him... again and he seemed fine most days. Beating the drums helped and well, watching the bullshit I was going through made him decide that he didn't want the drama of a girl after all.

The puppet shows and pizza parties, filled with loud My Little Pony themed cracker toys from children's party stores, made us bond over full bellies and cramped quarters. After weeks of writing songs and talking into the early hours of the morning on our tour bus, Johnny kissed me. It was nice and familiar. He was a new Johns. I didn't know what happened but the same funny guy that made me laugh until my stomach split in two was back. He never looked at women... ever. He only wanted me.

I kissed him back with hunger. Both of us realized, and talked persistently about how we didn't want the life of the after party, the after concert sex, or the pendulum of good and bad vibes between us. In short, we were meant to be best friends, lovers, and we believed we had a solid future together. We confessed to everything we had done while we were separated and he confessed to some things he had done while we were together. I knew that I felt something for him because knowing that the busty blonde that night wasn't his first misstep made me sad and angry. He apologized profusely and we worked it out, promising that we were starting a clean slate.

We both got tested and after we got our results, Johnny took me to a beautiful five star hotel overlooking Atlanta, Georgia. It was a beautiful night of both love making and full out ripping off clothes sex. We slept for the following two days on the bus, cuddled up in each other's arms.

I will never forget one important turning point night in our relationship. It was weeks after we had solidified our relationship in Atlanta. I expelled everything about Brennan because I knew it was eating at both of us. I told him the truth about how Brennan had made me remember and see how I had let men take advantage of me year after year. Brennan had expelled the bank of memory pushbacks. I think we both made peace with him that night, maybe even thanking him for showing me that I didn't want to be that girl anymore. It was, after all, just as much my fault as it was Brennan's, that we hooked up or maybe even, fell in love. The latter I would never say out loud to anyone ever again.

If Brennan had been honest with me from the get go about his marital status, I don't know if I would have turned him down or not. When I told Johnny this, he thanked me for being honest. Of course, he wanted to hunt down Jason #2 and the professor to bash them into pieces with a machete. *Is that even possible?* When I laughed, he gave me a sympathetic and loving look. A look that shattered another piece of the plastic confidence I showed the world. I will never forget how he said that those experiences were not my fault. He then cuddled me all night while I cried in his arms.

"What time do we head over to Kent's?" Johnny asked as he took my hand and played with the ring he had gotten me. It wasn't *the* ring. It sat on my right ring finger and it was a black diamond that matched both my hair and my heavy eye makeup.

Kent was living in Vancouver, Washington now with his wife, Chloe and their two little girls, Claire and Marina. They were close to teens now and it had been years since I had seen them. I was itching to hug them all and give them the largest of LSP swag bags. Kent had said that the girls were crooning that Johnny was "so hot". I was pretty sure they were only excited to see him.

"Let's go soon. We can grab dinner and spend a good amount of time with them before we have to head back tomorrow afternoon," I said, thinking about our timeline. Being on the road had been hard for all of us. It was our longest headline tour to date and I hadn't seen my mom, though she still didn't accept my career or fashion choices.

Johnny complained that he missed his babbling psychotherapist mother and younger sister, Tiffany, back in Baltimore. We were looking forward to seeing family and being a regular, normal couple. Dex had a friend in town, so he was going to hook up with her. Since he had been single, it seemed he had a "friend" in every city we played in.

Two hours later, we pulled up to Kent's large ranch style house on a big lawn. I saw two long dark haired girls running around with flowers and bubbles in hand, laughing at their dog. Kent opened the front screen door and I practically mangled Johnny to get to him. We hugged each other so tightly.

"I have missed you so much, Julia Child," he said into my hair. I couldn't help it. My eyes misted up and I wished for the days we were back in the Merrimack house playing guitar and laughing at each other's high pitched singing. But Kent's graying hair showed his years and as he took Johnny's hand, the girls came to the front stairs and stared at Johnny and me in awe. I turned slowly and smiled.

"My beautiful nieces. My goodness, you could be *my* babies," I said. Chloe came out of the screen door with a smile while wiping her hands on a hand towel.

"Didn't you know, Jules? They are yours. Time to take them back!" she said with excitement. Kent rolled his eyes and went to chase after the girls. Johnny and I both hugged Chloe at the same time. She was a little petite dark haired beauty. Kent wasn't worthy of her patience and generosity. When I had first met her, it was her that told him to mind his own business when it came to my seductive clothing and piercings. To prove that she was supportive, I took her to a tattoo salon one day and she had a nipple pierced. Kent never said a word again.

She eyed Johnny's new lip ring. "That's pretty hot, rock star."

He gave her his wide amused grin and put his arm around my shoulder. "This girl is the only hot rock star presently."

"Presently?" I asked facetiously.

"Yeah. Sometimes you are smoking or sexy. Beautiful or gorgeous. There is a plethora of words to describe you Jules," he said. Chloe watched us in amusement and then started to make the gagging noise.

"Well, let's get you to the guest room and settled. We are so happy you are in town for a show. We would bring the girls but the pot smoke and mosh pit wouldn't go over well with Big Daddy."

We walked into our guest room, laid our bags on the bed, and sighed in contentment. Johnny looked nervous all of a sudden and I watched him suspiciously.

"Johnny, what's wrong?" I asked.

"Nothing. Not a thing. Just... tired, I guess. What do we do now?" he asked. He looked lost. It had been so long since we had a house full of people to hang out with, that we were both a little wary of what was expected of us.

We went into the girl's playroom and handed over their presents. Johnny had picked up two Bratz dolls that looked like rock stars. I gave them pink tee shirts with the band's logo on it. On the back, we wrote

Delaney, Johnny and Dex, and we all signed the short sleeves. You'd think we had given them a million dollars.

After a while of playing with the dolls, Johnny got up and looked into the closet to inspect what other toys they had.

"Holy... cow," he said, stopping himself from swearing as he brought down a game board box. I watched as he placed it on the floor and my heart stopped. It was the OUIJA board. *The... my* OUIJA board. I knew it because I had written my initials on it the day after Krysta gave it to me so she wouldn't take it back.

"Mommy says we can't play that one yet. She says it is too scary and might give us nightmares," Claire said as she brushed her doll's hair. Johnny shot a quick smirk at me and stopped.

My face must have been ashen pale and dead looking. I was immediately transported back to the summer of 1993. Emmy. Angie. Grace. Murder. Dad. *Slut.* I was going to be a slut when I grew up. Slut, slut, slut. Johnny tried to pull me out of my trance but it didn't work. I wasn't there with Johnny and the girls. I was a twelve year old girl asking her older brother what slut meant.

"Do you want to play?" Johnny asked, tapping on my shoulder.

I shook my head. "I *can't* play that game." I looked at the board in horror and the words sounded like I was under water, sputtering for air.

I wanted to scream to everyone that would listen that the fucking game works, it tells the truth, and it *ruins* people. Johnny just stared at me in confusion. I was numb and yet somewhere in the back of my chest, I felt a pang of pain.

"Hey, where did you find that one?" Kent's voice boomed through the play room. Claire and Marina scrambled up to show Kent the dolls but his gaze locked on the box and then slowly moved up to my face. He saw my blank shock. He saw something that made him instantly tense. He muttered a word under his breath and looked back to me with resolve.

"Girls, I need your aunt for a little while. Johnny, can you watch over them?"

Johnny nodded, looking confused as he looked at Kent and my gaze on one another.

"Julia." He cleared his throat. "Jules? I need to speak with you for a minute," Kent asked or demanded, I didn't know. His words were fighting with his tone of voice. He looked at me, looked purposely at the box, and then back at me. He lifted his eyebrows and I knew. We both had a story to tell about that board. His stare told me he needed to know what it had done to me.

I stood up on shaking legs and Johnny tried to steady me from his sitting position. I pecked his lips as he searched my eyes with concern. He would know soon enough. But *I* needed to know first.

EIGHTEEN

Kent took my hand and tucked it underneath his elbow, as we walked down the long dirt driveway. I could see Mt. Hood and Mt. St. Helen's from the high elevated land that Kent's house laid on. It was breathtaking. The landscape was so unlike any horizon in the North East and I could see why Kent loved it here. I didn't think he would ever make his way back to New England for good. I felt a tinge of sadness at that thought. We all grew up and moved on from our little town.

"You really have a beautiful family and place here, big brother," I said, smiling at his success. He had taken to music in a different way. Still a musician at heart, Kent was working with a big software company in Oregon to produce music applications for phones and tablets.

"Thanks. I still can't believe my little sister is the lead singer in one of the hottest bands this year," he said, his eyes wide with amazement, as he shook his head slowly.

I pushed his shoulder and laughed at him.

"I owe it all to you, you goof. Well, you and Dinosaur Junior and Portishead and... "

"Yeah, whatever. I only taught you about hand placement and chords. Anyone could have done that," he said dismissively.

"But it *was you*," I declared, with admiration in my voice. "You, Kent, were the one that taught me that and much more. You taught me about patience. That was the biggest lesson. I don't know how many times I wanted to beat that guitar against the wall. Actually, I think I tried once but you grabbed me before it connected."

Kent laughed and nodded at me. He remembered, too and I smirked. I loved him like a brother and like a father. Maybe we had a bum deal with a full time working single mother but it didn't look so bad today as we walked together in healthy and happy contentment.

"The OUIJA board," Kent began. My whole body stiffened and I flicked my gaze up to his dark eyes, which were glued to mine.

"Shit," he groaned, stopping in place, and rubbing his hands over his face. "I knew that it happened to you, too. I just didn't want to believe it. I guess I just thought... *fuck*."

I whipped my head around and looked at Kent. What did he know?

"What do you mean by *too*?" I asked slowly and cautiously. Maybe I didn't want to know the answer. Wait. I *did* want to know the answer. I didn't want him to say the word I had stuck in my head. I wanted him to tell me it was all a mirage of shitty memories.

"You and your two friends did the board one day. I remember it because that night you asked me...," he coughed as he blushed a bit. "You asked what a slut was."

I nodded my head, eyes wide open, holding my breath like I was under water, and waited to see how long it would take for me to surface.

"You got slut right? From the board?" he asked. "Who got nice and who got crazy?" He was dead serious. He wasn't fucking with me and I started to tear up as I realized he knew what I had been for years.

212

"How do you know?" I whimpered.

"I was dating that girl. Krysta? You remember her, I am sure. She and I grabbed the box from your closet one night while you were sleeping. We decided to take it to a party. When we did the board, we got Grace," he said as he blew out a big breath and looked up at the wide, blue sky.

"We laughed it off until she started calling the girls who were doing the board names. One of them threw the board across the room and when I turned back around, it was back in place in front of them." Kent visibly shivered. I didn't. I knew what it felt like because I still had the dreams. They weren't every night but they happened enough that some nights I prayed that they didn't come.

"That sort of happened to us, too," I said, remembering how the pointer worked without us even touching it. Kent nodded and looked down at the ground, kicking a rock.

"Krysta cheated on me that next week. She got pregnant real early, like the day after graduation with some douchebag from Concord. The last time I saw

her, she was working at a diner and came on to me...
using her obvious boob job as the main attraction."

"No shit?" I laughed. I didn't know what else to do.
I probably would have gone that way, too, if I didn't
have my music.

"The other girls I don't know about but every time I
try to throw that damn box away, it shows back up. I
tossed it in the river one night with one of the Jasons,
and the next day, it showed up on my bed, completely
dry." Kent's piercing eyes didn't distract me from the
tremor in his voice. Had he been more affected by the
OUIJA board that I was?

"You have to keep it away from the girls," I said in
a panic.

"Well, that's just it. After several attempts to get rid
of the board, and I mean fire, trashing it with a
hammer, running over it with a car, I had no idea what
to do." Kent turned around and stood to look at the
volcanos with his hands in his pockets.

"I thought I was going to go crazy so I went to see
Grace's father in jail. I acted like I was doing a college
paper on murderers within the familial structure," he

laughed hollowly. "I asked him if he did he killed her, you know, just to act like I was genuinely interested in that aspect of the story. I asked him about Grace. He was awful, Julia." He shook his head and turned his head to look at me with a sad smile.

"He called her a nice little slut. A nice little slut. That poor little girl had to listen to him call her *that* for years while he... he hurt her. The day she finally fought back, she was on the way home from helping her cousin get to daycare. He pulled up in his truck and grabbed her. I guess he was drunk and she got tired of his shit. He said he drove them out to the woods and she tried really hard to claw at his eyes. That's when he called her a crazy slut. He explained the whole thing in detail, Julia. He strangled her until she couldn't scream anymore. *Then he... you know.*" Kent bent over, put his hands on his knees, and let out a few deep breaths.

I couldn't look away from him. I was sick. I felt sick for Grace, a poor little girl who couldn't defend herself. And if what Kent was telling me, Grace was just repeating what her father had called her over and over again, which meant...

I am *not* a slut.

I had a wonderful upbringing, despite my father abandoning us. I had a good mother and a very loving older brother. I had wonderful friends at one time but Grace's father, that fucking psychopath, ruined not only one little girl's life, but many others—including mine. He killed my self-esteem the day he murdered Grace. I believed in that board because Grace proved it to be true by telling us who killed her. But she never meant to make me think I was a slut. She was telling me that *she* was. My whole world tipped upside down and right side out. I had been betrayed since I was twelve. I believed. I was *wrong*.

If I could tell my twelve year old self that it was a bunch of fucking crap, would she have listened to me? How could I prove to her how I turned out? In that moment, I cared about what others thought of me. I had been so wrong all of my life and I had done so many despicable things. I thought that life was black and white. I am a rocker so I rock. I am a lover so I love. I was a slut so I fucked a married man... two married men. I broke hearts, left debris in my wake, and focused on one thing besides the stage. Penis.

I felt Kent wrap his arms around me. I wanted to tell him everything but it was too late. There wasn't anything good that would come out of me ridding myself of all of my sins to my brother. Plus, I had no doubt he would hunt Jason #2 down and kill him. I thought about Kent's family and how I suddenly longed to be back in our house, doing it all over again. He was such a great father. I still looked up to him.

Brennan's face flashed through my mind and I just about crawled up Kent's body for comfort. I needed to feel safe and I didn't want to let go. We hugged for what felt like hours. It was beautiful.

"So why do you want the girls to keep it?" I asked, finally drawing away from him.

"Oh hell, I don't. But one night, Chloe and I did it. When Grace came out and started saying the words, we just started to tell her we were sorry. We chanted it like we were in a fucking meditation or something," he laughed. "Chloe gets into that shit. She believes in tea leaves and tarot cards so I just went along with her hair brained idea."

Kent looked at me with a determined expression. "Then when we did it again the next week we got nothing. She wasn't there anymore. It's just a board game now that moves if you move it. As it *should* be. And to answer your next question? I haven't gotten rid of it because it is a reminder of the day I lost my Julia Child." A small tear fell from the side of his eye and he quickly wiped it away.

"You didn't lose me, Kent. I just got lost for a while. I have turned my life around, you know? With guys," I said, trying to smile. I wondered about Emily and Angela. How were they doing? Were they happy? Had they been affected by the board, too?

"So do you love him?" Kent asked. He didn't look convinced by the apprehensive expression on his face. Kent didn't know Johnny well enough. I knew Johnny would always be there for me. He was my safe place. We had grown up together in so many ways. I nodded with a small grin. Kent mirrored my nod but didn't return the grin.

"You are a passionate person. Any man who calls you his, is a very lucky guy," he said as he shoved his hand through his hair.

"Shut up," I laughed. "You are such a big sap." We stood and smiled at each other as the sun started to fall down in the sky.

That night, as Johnny and I lay in bed, I told him the whole story behind the OUIJA board. At first, he made fun of me and told me that I was ridiculous to believe in shit like that, but once I told him that Kent had not only experienced the same thing, but followed up on Grace's story, that seemed to shut him right up.

"I wish I could go back and do something different. Maybe if Emily, Angela, and I had stayed friends, I wouldn't have ended up the high school slut or worse..." I said on a sigh.

"We all end up where we are because of small little moments like those. Think of this," Johnny said, throwing his head up on his hand to look down at me. He was a pretty man. So fit and tatted and he had face that melted women's panties everywhere he went. "If you had stayed friends with those girls, you wouldn't have spent any time on singing and music. We *wouldn't* have met at college and you wouldn't be the hot rocker you are today," he smirked, as he pulled on my belly button ring.

His fingers walked up to my chest, underneath my shirt, and drew circles around my areolas. My nipples peaked and he leaned over to flick them with his tongue ring. I groaned.

"I do love sex," I moaned.

"God, Jules. I don't love anything more than having sex with you," Johnny murmured, whispering his tongue up my neck to my ear lobe. He hit the exact spot on my neck, I started to meow, and rub up against him like a cat in heat. The spot, which only two men knew about, made me say and do things out of my control. It was like... crackle, fizz alert, alert, shut down... Jules' brain is in shut down mode. Sex kitten Jules is present and accounted for. Keep licking that spot... and I am lost.

Johnny grabbed my hips and turned us around so I was on top of him. I stripped off my bedtime tank top and could feel his erection through my small thong. He sat up and continued to flick his tongue at my nipples. As I moved up to place them in his mouth better, he pulled off his boxers, my thong, and sat me back on top of him. Our collective sighs of relief made us look into each other's eyes. I pressed down while he pushed up and we both smiled at each other in enthusiasm.

"I love you," he moaned, as I started to set our pace. Johnny had started saying that to me since our interview, and I had yet to say it back. Of course I loved him. *Of course!* I just didn't know how... quite yet. Did I see a future with him? Yes. If our band split up tomorrow and we both had to find jobs at Walmart? That age old question of would you still love me if... That was the one that tripped me up because I am not sure I would still love him the way I do if we were anything but this.

Sometimes, I felt like I was cheating on Johnny because every so often, like *maybe* daily, Brennan's face flashed through my head during the hot sex we had. So, when I asked myself if I truly loved Johnny, I couldn't help but think about the fire that burned in my stomach when I thought of being in Brennan's arms. My mind wanted to tell my heart and stomach to shut the fuck right up. Brennan and his stupid wife were two sick sons of bitches. They had no consideration for people outside their loveless, sick, and twisted marriage of hokey pokey that never turns itself around. It all just falls.

And why am I thinking about the conscience of two people who are not in my life while Johnny is climaxing inside of me? Shit, I was thinking so much that I forgot to have an orgasm. I rolled off him and we both caught our breath. Johnny turned to me and cleared his throat.

"When are you gonna say it back?" he asked between his deep breaths. He looked hurt, and maybe slightly suspicious.

"You know I love you, Bren... " I quickly popped my hand over my mouth and my eyes widened as large as his did.

"Oh, you have got to fucking be kidding me," Johnny exclaimed, popping off the bed to retrieve his boxers.

"I'm sorry. It was the whole OUIJA board thing. I've been processing a lot of my sexual issues with Brennan," I lied.

"I am so, *so* sorry. I do love you. I love you so much that I can't even imagine what life would be like without you in it. Johns, you are everything, and I mean *fucking* everything to me."

I was panting, begging, almost tearing up, and he stared at me like I had never spoken before.

"You can't?" he whispered.

I am confused. "Can't what, Johnny?" I asked.

"You can't imagine life without me?" he asked.

I shook my head and put out my arms for him to come to me. He did and just as I started to nibble on his ear, he whispered, "Then marry me, Jules."

NINETEEN

New York City

The yellow princess cut diamond on my ring finger sparkled and made kaleidoscopes on the walls, as I ran through my guitar solo. We were at the Mix Max Convention Center in Brooklyn and nearing the end of our long three month tour. We were ready to return to Johnny's small apartment in Manhattan and sleep in, take walks, and plan our next recording.

Johnny had picked the ring out months ago in San Francisco and when he proposed in Vancouver, I couldn't say no. I didn't want to say yes. But I did anyway. We celebrated with my brother and his family the next day. Sometime during the middle of the night, after he had asked me to be his bride, he walked two miles to a nearby river and threw the OUIJA board away. I kept in contact with Kent and it had not reappeared. He knew it was gone for good.

I finally felt like that chapter of my life was over. I was a different person being Johnny's fiancé. There was no awkwardness. Well, when he talked about dates, I clammed up, but after a few steady breathing moments, I tried to come up with ideas. They were terrible ideas. So, our conversation moved on.

Johnny stood and watched my fingers in rapt attention. His blue eyes were fierce and protective. He walked over with his bass slung over his shoulder and started to nibble at my ear. The crowd went nuts. *Pure madness.* They were so responsive to our public relationship and the magazines were calling us American's Rocking Love Couple. I was just so glad they hadn't melded our names into Johnnia or Joonny. We made up those names one night and secretly waited for them to hit the news.

I giggled and dropped a few chords in with the public display of affection. He noticed and gave everyone an unapologetic shrug, as he walked back to his side of the stage. I looked back to see Dex in his ready stance and rolling his eyes dramatically.

When I turned my head back around to the crowd of ten thousand people, one lone and motionless male in the front of the pit, caught my attention. Long black locks, brown squared glasses, and one full tattooed sleeve mocked me, as my jaw clenched up. I slipped up on the transition, but I quickly recovered by turning my back on the crowd. I needed to slow my breathing. It had just gone up in rapid tempo. *Too fast for this song. Too fast for my body.*

I am pretty sure that is when I froze. For a few minutes, I heard, saw, felt, said, sang, and breathed nothing. How dare he show up at a LSP show and stand in the front so I could see him? He wants to throw me off? *He wants to ruin me.*

In that moment, I wanted to stomp off the stage and find the first airplane, train, bus, or bicycle out of this God forsaken place. Sure, I knew we were playing Brooklyn but never, ever did I think he would just show up like nothing happened. *Like I didn't make it perfectly fucking clear two years ago that he had to leave me alone.*

My thought process about what to do was wrecking me. I was struggling with my memory to grasp our last words to one another when I realized I had totally fucked up the song. My back was to the crowd, my head bent over the guitar that I was hardly strumming and I should have been at the microphone singing the second verse to *Live Free or Die*. Okay, that is a song.

Johnny and I wrote that song. Johnny was my fiancé. Yes, we wrote about my history in New Hampshire, and how I never understood the license plate motto. My head was officially back in the game as I listened to Dex do a slight Lars drum solo that was totally out of rhythm and foreign to this song in every way possible. I could only thank God that we hadn't released it yet. It was still a work in process.

Johnny cut me a look that practically brought me to my knees. He was pissed off. I was pissed, too. I was right damn pissed. I mouthed "I'm so sorry" to him but I wasn't exactly sure what I was sorry for. Sorry I fucked up the song? Sorry that Brennan Curtis made me falter both physically and mentally? Sorry that my heart was beating to a different tempo than it ever had with Johnny? I started to sing and closed my eyes to block out the crowd of people, or the crowd of one person.

I cut back a look at him and he was smiling again at me. *Panic attack.* That was a panic attack because of the heat and lights. He did not affect me anymore. He wasn't drop dead gorgeous in that fucking white tank top and low riding jeans. I couldn't breathe. By now, the song was winding down and I looked out into the crowd. He was still there with a disappointed expression on his face that made me want to crawl right to him.

Brennan mouthed, "I miss you." I grabbed the microphone stand to keep myself from falling over. Then I grabbed it with my left hand and flung my ring finger into the air, screaming "live free or die". It was the worst moment of irony I had ever experienced. He has just put me in a prison of want while I was living free on stage. So, to make it explicitly clear to him, I walked over to Johnny after the song ended and totally out of character, I whispered "Jules Lennox" and gave him an open mouthed kiss. He has been begging me to take his last name when we marry. But the fuck of it was I didn't say that for Johnny or myself. I said it because, by proxy, I was telling Brennan to suck it.

Johnny pinched my ass as I walked back to my spot. And... he was still there. Through my little show, through the brush off, through the fuck off, he stayed. *Content to be patient.* He wanted more reaction and I had nothing. I was a robot throughout the rest of the show. I wouldn't look his way. I really couldn't. It felt gross and wrong. It was like looking at a bloody mess that couldn't be unseen. But, Lord, I felt him. It was enough of a passionate exchange to sense the cloudy abyss on the horizon. The more I sang the bigger hole I dug. Depression was only one bed away.

It was the longest show I had ever experienced. It dragged on like the bus ride from Kansas to Colorado. I felt like I would never get there. On the outside, I played my part and luckily, after my total fuck up, Johnny, and Dex didn't seem to notice my inner turmoil. What had Brennan been doing to me by showing up?

Right before I left the stage, I looked up and he was gone. I felt both lighter than air and truly disappointed. I hated not knowing. I was always in control. I always called the shots, but Brennan made me fucking crazy and he didn't even know it. He looked so goddamn sexy with that leather band on his non tatted arm. I had bought that for him. It had the letter "J" on it. No beanie. No sweater. No holds barred. He was stripped of his extras, taunting me to see him as he was.

I walked into the backstage room to start signing and taking photos with fans. I waved Danielle over and told her that Brennan Curtis was on the no pass list from now on. Johnny came up right behind me as I finished my request.

"Why would Brennan come to a show?" he asked with concern.

"I saw him in the crowd tonight. That is why I fucked up that one song," I answered him. It felt good to tell the truth. Johnny wouldn't want lies and I didn't either. I needed to be straightforward or I would get myself into a shit heap of trouble.

"He was?" he asked incredulously. He started to look around the room and when I put my hand on his arm, he startled at my touch. I quickly pulled it away.

"Look. It means nothing, Johnny. He can come to a show *but* I don't want him anywhere near me." I answered with equal suspicion.

His eyes softened as he took in my face. I was telling the truth. However, the reason behind the truth wasn't the same truth he thought it was. I didn't *want* to get caught up in Brennan's stupid married web. I didn't *want* him to make me feel. But he did.

My phone vibrated in my bra. I clicked it on and saw the text on the locked screen and nearly died.

You were beautiful on stage. Congratulations on the engagement. I am glad that you're happy.–B

My hands shook as I stuck the phone back into my bra. I went to the bar and begged for three shots of whiskey. I threw them back and felt the weight of the phone, the weight of my lies, and the weight of what I was doing wrong in my life. I might not want to marry Johnny. I might not want this life anymore. I was exhausted.

I signed for about a half an hour, begged off a headache, and left Johnny and Dex to play nice, while I went to find that bed.

TWENTY

I stayed in bed for days, maybe even more than a week. At first, it was cramps. Then it was the stomach flu. Then I was just plain tired from touring. Johnny ran around the city, picking up medicine I wouldn't take and getting food I wouldn't eat.

I received a text message from James around noon one weekday. It was totally cryptic. I had to read it three times before I gave up and shook my head at the asinine text.

James: My dad is in town. Will you come down to meet him? He's a fan.

Me: WTF James? I am in bed.

James: Well, get out of bed dumbass.

Me: You're fired.

James: See you outside in twenty.

I looked over at Johnny, who had his earphones on and was playing his guitar to the music.

His lean back begged to be touched, but I couldn't put out my hand far enough to show him the love he had been begging for throughout my depression spell.

Yesterday, he had asked if my low had anything to do with Brennan. I didn't answer. He slammed the door, which didn't even make me flinch. He had every right to be pissed off. I hated myself as much as he probably did in that moment. When he came back to our bedroom, both of our eyes were red rimmed as we lay, staring at each other. Something was changing between us. God damn it, I didn't want it to.

I forced myself to move over and touched his back tentatively. He flinched and whirled around with wide eyes. He immediately threw the equipment down on the floor and scooped me up into his arms.

"Johnny. I am sad. I think I am lost," I whispered, touching his cheeks with my fingers.

"I know, Jules. I can't do anything to make it right. I am scared. I feel like I am losing you," he choked on the last two words.

I grabbed him and hugged him so tight. He whispered how much he loved me and I nodded into his shoulder. I knew I was losing him, too. Hell, I was losing myself. I didn't want music. I didn't want men. I didn't want me. I wanted to get rid of myself for one day. Just fucking one day that I didn't have to be in my own stupid, fucked up head.

I wished I had never met Brennan. I wished I could hug him instead in that moment. Two men, two nights, two separate future lives. I needed to be carried through this confusion and if no one could hold me, or if they didn't want to, I wouldn't say anything ever again. I would break.

"James wants me to go down and meet his dad," I said. I twisted my face up in disgust.

Johnny pulled back and smiled. "That sounds like a great idea, baby." I cringed inwardly at that endearment. Baby, I was not. Not to anyone. Especially not Brennan. Amelia was his baby.

"Do you think so? I don't know why he wants me to go. I mean, James never acts like a fan boy," I said, twisting my lips into contemplation.

"Just go. See about riding along, maybe. Get out of bed and have a day out. I want to hook up with Dex and some other guys on this new song," he said. He sounded more and more excited about me leaving by the minute. That's when I realized this was, in fact, Johnny's apartment. Not mine. I had moved in. I was encroaching on his bed, his space. Fiancé or not, I was cramping his style to some degree. *I had to be.*

"Yeah, alright. I will get a quick shower and go," I conceded, moving out of his arms sluggishly. I didn't wash my hair. I threw it up in a messy bun on top of my head. I threw on an old Depeche Mode tee shirt and jeans. They were loose. Depression was good for weight loss. There was something.

My head already hurt from the activity and I went into the bedroom, where Johnny was stripping the sheets, and replacing them with new ones. He had his ear plugs in and didn't see my embarrassed look of shame. After a few moments, I waved my hand and then smiled faintly when he looked up. He took out the plugs and came over to me.

"You look gorgeous." He hugged me and I could feel excitement radiating off his body. I suppose I did look good. It was a far cry from the bleak tank and panties that I had been wearing for days. The makeup probably helped my outward appearance, too.

"Thanks. Are there any photogs out there? Should I do the sunglasses?" I asked on a heavy exhale. Talking was so much fucking work. I felt light headed.

"I didn't see any when I went out for coffee, but bring them just in case. Text me later, okay?" He kissed my nose. "Oh, and Jules? Enjoy your day."

I nodded as I grabbed my bag and headed down to the street.

The black town car was waiting on the curb. I opened the back door. James normally did that for me, but this whole ordeal was already bizarre as fuck, so I just went with it. The first thing I noticed was that the partition was up between James and me. I saw the back of an older man's head in the front seat with him. They were talking about something but of course, I couldn't hear them. I knocked on the window and asked him what the hell was going on.

"Put this thing down, James. We never use this," I demanded. "Are you and your dad going somewhere because Johnny said I should tag along, okay?"

No answer. Nothing. I plastered my face against the partition to get any idea of what the hell was going on but I couldn't make out anything they were doing.

Then, we pulled out into traffic and I started to panic. Had I gotten into the wrong car? I banged on the partition and nothing happened. Was this a fucking joke? We made it two streets away from Johnny's apartment when I heard a loud laugh. It wasn't James' laugh. Holy shit, I had just been kidnapped. I panicked.

"You are not James, you bastard! Where the hell is he?" I looked around the town car. This wasn't even his town car. Holy fucking hell, I was abducted.

"I am calling 911 right now. It's a life sentence in the slammer for kidnappers," I yelled. The partition rolled down just as we hit the Williamsburg Bridge. The Williamsburg Bridge? Why were we leaving Manhattan? I was totally fucking creeped out now and I shuddered in fear.

Brennan turned to face me first and I gasped. I looked to the passenger and swore. My deadbeat father didn't look back at me. Both of their eyes faced forward, as they expected that I was taking in the crime scene.

"What. The. Fuck?" I was hysterical. I started to hold my head in between my hands and rocked back and forth.

"Keep calm, Julia Child," Dad said. *Julia Child?* He was using my nickname? Did he think we were best buds and were just meeting up for a daily outing? I hadn't seen this guy in years and I mean years. He didn't even look like my dad anymore. The picture I had in my head was a far cry from who was sitting in the front seat of this car. He still dressed like he was in the 1970's but his receding hair line had turned into just plain bald. And he was chubby. I didn't know *this* man at all. So, I played along.

"You want calm, daddy dearest? Fine. How about fuck you and you," I said, pointing to both of them. "How about pulling over and letting me out of this... this awful car. I am not a child, I am not interested in having a little outing, and I want nothing to do with either of you." I toggled my accusations back and forth between Brennan and my father, not exactly sure who I was most pissed at. Dad kept a straight face, amused even. Brennan winced when I said the last bit about wanting nothing to do with him. *I lied, Brennan. God,*

I am so close to you right now. Why are you taunting me like this?

"Wow, she's got a mouth on her, huh?" My dad asked Brennan. Brennan smirked.

"It's part of her gloriously, beautiful charm," he replied. His eyes met mine in the rear view mirror and I gaped.

"Is this a joke? Why is it that I am sitting in a car with the two specific men that totally fucked my life?" I was beyond livid. I crossed my arms and started to find a way to get out of the car. *Nothing* good would come out of this.

"Johnny called me," Brennan stated. He didn't look at me in the rear view mirror this time.

Sure, he did, I thought.

"Johnny Lennox, my fiancé, wouldn't call you even if he had a gun pointed to his head. Put the fucking partition back up, please." I said. I was deadly. I was about to add murder to my long list of accomplishments.

Brennan was obviously fucking with me. They were the devil to my mental wellbeing and Johnny would never just throw me into the fire. He would never do this to me, I thought to myself, as I pressed the number one on my phone.

"Jules." I heard the fear in his voice. Johnny *did* do this.

"Why?" I croaked out. "You are fucking me over. You are fucking with us."

"Jules. You weren't the same after you saw Brennan at the show. You haven't been the same woman I fell in love with... both times. You need to figure out your shit. Your father has been contacting me for years and I told him not to contact you. When he called a few days ago, I don't know... " he sighed.

"Maybe... maybe now it is time to figure out what he wants from you after all these years. As far as Brennan goes, I am not happy you are with him. But before you walk down that aisle to marry me, you need to be sure that I am the one you want." He forced out those last few words through a fake confident tone. He was sad. I could hear his choked up throat. What did this mean? Was he letting me go?

"Are we breaking up, Johnny?" I asked softly, almost on the verge of tears myself.

The headache I had at the apartment had grown into a gigantic living monster. I was shredded. A long pause on his end made me start to tear up. It became clear to me then. He had no idea. Sure, I didn't either but Johnny had always wanted me. He had sweated over me for years. I finally gave him another chance and it was ending like this?

This time it hurt. The last time? I didn't have any feelings. This time, I knew I wasn't a slutty bitch that he could mess with. I was Julia fucking Delaney. I deserved good people in my life. I deserved a man who wouldn't just throw me to the wolves after a few dump days in bed.

"You know, when I threw that OUIJA board in the river at your brother's house, remember that?" I nodded, even though he obviously couldn't see me.

"I wanted to rid you of all your problems all at once. Even the ones you had when you were a little girl. I want to protect you and keep you safe, but I think that is my problem. I want you to be and feel happy. I mean, not all the time. I love fighting with you over stupid shit and I love your boobs," he snorted. "Shit, I guess that doesn't really have anything to do with it. But Jules, your boobs are killer."

I could hear his humor, and maybe even a little heat, as he was clearly thinking about me naked. Johnny's moment of truth was almost heart wrenching. He didn't do serious conversation very well, so the boob comment cover up told me he didn't have a fucking clue how to be my man.

Johnny and I loved each other enough to tell the truth. Nonetheless, I fake giggled at his boob comment. It was sad. I was sad. And I was in a car with two men that also made me sad. Not only was I dizzy from depression, but I was floundering in the house of bewilderment. All I needed were the fucked up mirrors that distorted my shape to finish me off.

"What now, Johnny?" I asked with seriousness back in my tone.

"You tell me. Go and be with them, I guess. They have the answers your questions," he admitted. "Then, I guess you decide what you want because I want the old Jules back. I want the girl that loves *My Little*

Pony, puppet shows, and laughs because of nothing all through the night. *This* new Julia scares me," he admitted, lowering his voice at the end.

"Okay," I whispered.

"Okay." His voice was stronger.

"Okay," I replied.

"Bye, Jules."

It seemed like the click was louder than usual when Johnny hung up. I watched the 'call ended' on my screen until it stopped, shoved my hand in my messed up bun, and looked out the window. I had no idea where we were going and it didn't matter anymore.

TWENTY-ONE

The car stopped in front of a deli. I didn't recognize the name of it but as I turned my head, I saw the signs for McGolrick Park in Brooklyn. As I was about to ask what we were doing there, Brennan opened my door and tipped his chauffeur hat at me. His eyes locked onto mine and the sizzle was there once again. I moved to get out of the car but he wouldn't back up.

"You need to step away," I said.

"No, I am good here," he responded. He took my left hand, raised it to his mouth, and kissed my engagement ring. It was *so* fucked up. He was so completely deranged.

I pulled my hand away like I had been burned. I started to rub my finger as I looked at him for what he wanted from me. Was he mocking me? My father came up behind him with a manila folder in his hand and waited patiently for us to finish our interaction.

"That's not your finger to kiss, Brennan," I scowled.

He beamed at me and nodded. "I know, Julia," he whispered. He looked down at the ground, laughed a bit, and then peered up to my face through his black locks. Holy hell, I needed to touch them and I did.

Very gently, I took a black lock between my index finger and thumb and rubbed. I closed my eyes to all of the memories of doing this before. I never thought I would be this close to him and I never wanted to be... until now. I felt him stare at me while I breathed in his masculine love laced scent. I opened my eyes to find that his were watering slightly.

"I never thought I would be this close to you again," he whispered closer to my face. He put his hand on the small of my back and led me away from the door so he could shut it.

Dad took my arm and interlocked it into his, while Brennan walked a few feet behind us. I looked around at the beautiful park marked with an overwhelmingly amount of tags. Graffiti lined every wall on the pavilion, every bench constructed throughout the walkways, and every blank space in between. I admired a few older gentlemen playing cards and keeping to their intense game. It was a normal occurrence. That much I knew for sure about this park. It was home to many people. Was it Brennan's home? Was I on his turf?

"Do you live around here?" I turned to ask Brennan, my steely resolve slowly melting away. His smile was breathtaking as he nodded in confirmation. He was sharing himself. He wanted me to know his life. But why now?

"Dad, why did Johnny do this? What questions am I supposed to ask you?" I pointedly asked him, both a little irritated and apprehensive. I rubbed circles on my temples. How should I be treating a man that I hadn't seen in almost ten years and was supposed to call my father?

Dad found the next open bench and sat down. He patted the open spot next to him and I sat like a little puppy wanting that treat. Damn men, starting with this one.

Brennan held back but examined me like he was trying to soak all of me in. I understood the feeling. Every chance I could, trying to be less obvious; I admired his corduroy pants, Adidas sneakers, and white Henley under a forest green cardigan. How can a guy pull off a cardigan so beautifully? I looked to his hands that were shaking a bit. That was a sure sign that he was nervous.

No wedding ring.

That wasn't a surprise. Take off the ring when the wife isn't around, Bren. Good move. *Solid.* And while I am thinking about it, why does he even bother? I know the bloody truth. That immediately pissed me off and I wanted this rendezvous over. I gave my father all of my attention.

"So?" I asked him pointedly. He looked at me and shook his head.

"Did your mother teach you any manners? How about, "Hey dad, what's up?" he said.

"Hey Dad, what's up? So?" I deadpanned, crossing my arms. I heard Brennan chuckle and it took everything I had in me not to look at that stunning smile. I didn't even have to look at him to see the creases in the skin by his eyes when he smiled, the dimples, and the look of pure amusement when I was topless and straddling on top of him. Dear Lord Baby Jesus in the Manger.

Dad pulled out some photos.

"This is the summer I met your mother," he said as he handed it over to me. He was laughing with a golf club in his hand. Her hand was on his arm as she looked up at him adoringly. She looked awestruck.

"Nice." What the fuck? So, let's get this straight. My fiancé tricked me into going with my absent father and my former lover so we could look at photos in a park? I didn't get it. And the questions? What did I need to know that I didn't already? I wondered if Kent knew about this.

"And, this is a picture of me and your... what do you and Kent call her? Step-monster?" He asked with a grimace.

He handed me a photo of her laughing at him and he looking at her like she was the only woman in the world. His eyes were captivated by her. I couldn't tell what he was looking at. Her teeth? Her smile? Her eyes?

"Julia, put the photos side by side and tell me what you see," my dad said.

I put the photo side by side with the one of my mother. She wasn't looking at anything specific either. It was like they were not necessarily looking at the person but the spirit in which the body took over. They were looking right through them with love and wonderment. It was like they were asking themselves, how did I get so lucky to love this person?

"The picture of your mother and I was taken during a golf tournament obviously. She hated golf. Probably still does. Someone had made a joke about me keeping the ball out of the water hazard so I laughed. She wouldn't have found that funny at all, which puzzled me when I first saw this photo," he said, rubbing his thumb nail on his forehead.

"When I saw the picture of me and Carrie, I remembered we were at a local church benefit and someone had said something funny about baking. I like to eat cookies but baking jokes? Really? But I smiled right along with Carrie. I smiled because she was. I am a part of her soul. I have other pictures at home where her expression is the same as mine or your mother's in these photos," he finished.

"You weren't in love with mom," I whispered. "You couldn't stay. Even though leaving your kids was an ass hat shit move, it wasn't Mom you needed to be with."

Dad remained silent as he handed me two more photos.

"When I saw how you looked at this young man," Dad said as he pointed to Brennan. "I knew you were in love with him. You look so much like your mother. I..."

I cut him off. "He's married, Dad. I won't fucking break up a marriage and an engagement for the purposes of a look in a photo."

Dad cleared his throat. "Yes, well. I figured you would say that, but I had to come see you. You know, I follow your band. I pay attention. When I saw this photo of you and Mr. Curtis, I needed to find you. You finally looked happy. I got in touch with Kent. He gave me nothing. I contacted your agent. Nothing. But Brennan here. He said he would find a way. I wanted to tell you how I am so proud of you," he said. Tears started to well up in his eyes. "But, Julia? I don't see that same happiness in that photo."

Dad pointed at the latest photo of Johnny and me. We were smiling at each other but there wasn't any spark. We looked like we could be brother and sister, just looking at one another with appreciation. The photo of Brennan and me outside the airport the day we made love for the first time, we looked like we had just won the lottery. Our hands were all over each other. It was night and day. Dad pulled me out of my latest revelation, but I think I already knew. I was in love with Brennan. But I still couldn't have him.

"You were and always will be my Julia Child," he said. He patted my leg twice and got up. I watched him walk towards the Town Car. He got in and drove away and I never saw the man again.

TWENTY-TWO

"It feels like the circus just came to town. Johnny is the Magician, Dad is the Clown, and you... who the hell are you?" I asked Brennan.

"I'm that guy on the tight rope, offering you a hand to do a double twist jump down to the next rope," he proposed, as he took a seat next to me on the bench.

I smiled down at the picture of me and Johnny. God, I did love Johnny, though. Why the hell would he want me to come see my Dad? A little fucking too late, I might add. Yeah. Too late for lots of things. And Brennan? What was Johnny thinking?

"Why would Johnny want me to hang out with *you*?" I looked at him.

Brennan shrugged his shoulders and put his hands on the back of his neck as he crossed his feet, lounging out on the bench like we were going to be there a while. Maybe we would be. Dad had just taken our transportation back to the city. How was I going to get back to Johnny's?

"Johnny did not want me to be here. I told him that I was coming here only as a friend, which I am," he said, looking over at me. Was that a flash of pain in his eyes?

"No, Johnny and I are engaged. We are forever. He knows what happened between us and we could never be friends. Why would he want me to see you, knowing how I felt about you?"

"How *did* you feel about me?" he asked in earnest.

"Let's not go there, Brennan," I quickly retorted. I needed a nap and I certainly did not want to spend more time going over what Brennan and I had or didn't have in the past. I had made my decision and the new Julia did not fuck around. I was with Johnny, whether I had a powerful attraction to Brennan or not. Trusting, honest, loving, and kick ass Johnny would have my back for the rest of my life. And yet, in this moment, I was actually becoming comfortable, just sitting here with Brennan. I had absolutely no desire to go back to Johnny's apartment. I considered the idea that he didn't want me there either.

I took my cell out of my back pocket and pressed the button to call him. It rang and rang. Then it rang again. Voicemail never picked up. That must mean he was calling out. Or something funky like that.

I hit call again.

"Hello?" a women's whiny voice came over the line. I heard Johnny's bass and Dex drumming in the background.

"Whom am I speaking to?" I asked professionally and slightly irritated. Why wasn't I at the jam session and why on earth was there a woman answering Johnny's phone?

"Amber. Who's this?"

"Jules Delaney. I need to speak with Johnny please."

The phone sounded like it fell to the floor and then I heard Amber calling out to Johnny. The bass stopped first. The drums a few beats later.

"Come on dude. Let's finish this shit up so we can party," Dex called out to someone in particular.

The phone was muffled and I heard nothing until I heard a door shut and Johnny came on the phone.

"Jules?" he asked, sounding out of breath.

"Johnny?" I asked.

"What's up?" He sounded disinterested. I looked down at the photo and bit my lower lip. I looked over at Brennan who was looking straight ahead, expressionless.

"Why?" I asked.

"Why, what?" he sounded annoyed. Was I annoying him? How? Why? I wasn't even there. He was my frigging fiancé and he was acting so weird. This was all so surreal.

"Why did you arrange this day? Why are you jamming without your lead singer? Why was that girl Amber answering your phone? Why are you acting like we aren't engaged?" I felt my heart starting to pound. I didn't realize how much I had to be pissed about until I listed them off to him. I had more but I thought four questions hammered at him were enough for the time being. "Go ahead, Johnny. Tell me what this is all about."

Johnny exhaled loudly. "Listen. We needed a break today. The depression was getting too intense, you know."

I sucked in a breath. Johnny wants a break from me? The guy that day in and day out begged me back into his life? *Fuck this.*

"You have been a zombie, Jules," he continued. "You see Brennan one night and you go to bed for days. It fucking hurt. Like really fucking hurt. And, maybe I deserve that after what I did to you when we first broke up, but right now you need to figure out your shit and I want to have fun. I don't want to watch my girl lay in bed all day long, probably thinking about another guy. I don't want to deal. I can't make anything better for you. I tried. You know?"

"So, to answer your questions, I wasn't thinking about Brennan in bed. Second, are you having fun with Amber?" I asked with a bloody dagger in my voice.

"No, Jules. It isn't about that. She is just here. Don't you see? This is more than that. This is about our love. It is about our future and right now, it has to be about you facing your demons. Brennan, who promised he would not fucking lay a hand on you, by the way, is one of those demons. Face him. Talk to him. Do what you need to do. Then, we can talk."

"This is what you really want, Johnny?" I asked.

"No." He almost shouted his answer and then reeled it back in. "Hell, no. I want you to be here, sucking on my ear lobe, and talking about a dance party later. I miss that life. This new Julia isn't fun. You just aren't you anymore."

"I get it," I said. And, I did but damn it, Johnny wasn't supposed to be the smart one here. I should have known all by myself. I didn't know who I was, now that I was acting like the person that didn't need sex and booze to be happy. Everything changed after we had gone to see Kent and he told me the real story behind Grace's murder. I hadn't had the dream since that night.

I did, however, continue to have dreams about that weekend with Brennan. I was lying to myself. I couldn't click a button and become a non-slutty, married, and devoted life partner Julia Delaney Lennox.

"I know you do. So now you have to stop thinking about me. Do what you need to do to get back to that girl I fell in love with because she is gone. And I think it has to do with that guy sitting next to you." His words cut deep. He wasn't giving up on me but he wasn't fighting for me either. He was letting go and giving me the power to determine our future. Johnny was trying to see the real picture. He wanted the old girl back but I didn't want to be that girl again. I didn't think I could go back to her and that was who he wanted? I was so damn confused. Johnny was confused, and by the expression on Brennan's face, he was confused, too.

Hence, the bed.

For days.

And I would do it all over again.

In fact, I was tired. I wanted my... wait, shit... *his* bed. Didn't I?

I said nothing. He said nothing. Long moments passed and I sighed. There wasn't anything else to say. I needed to get this conversation over with Brennan and then decide what I needed to do for myself.

"Bye, Johnny."

"Bye, Jules."

I stuck the phone in my back pocket and stood up, rocked on my heels, and looked down at Brennan.

"Apparently, you and I have something between us that needs to be resolved," I said, pointing in between us.

Brennan looked up and with a perplexed expression, he asked, "Resolved?"

"Yes. I need to figure out why seeing you that night and that fucking text you sent me made me go to bed for a week. Then, I need to get back to my life with Johnny."

"Hmmm," Brennan hummed as he stood. He towered over me and with that painful flash once again, he took my hand, and we began to walk the pathway in the park.

"So how is engaged life?" Brennan asked casually. I glared at him. The universe had officially turned on its axis.

"How's open marriage life?" I snorted.

"Touché."

"What are we doing here, Brennan?" I asked, totally exhausted already. Was this some sort of intervention by all the men in my life that fucked me over? The father I never had, the best friend and former cheater I was about to marry, and the man that could never be mine because he was married.

The only person I was missing was Kent, but then I thought that Kent didn't fit the mold. He was always good and consistent with me. We loved one another unconditionally. There were a lot of conditions between me and *these* three men. Tons maybe. I was so fucked. If I could somehow morph myself into an old Polish male who looked forward to cards at the park every day, I would be good. Yeah. I would be stellar. And where the hell was James in all of this? *Oh hell.* Obviously, this was a well thought out plan from all parties involved. I dusted off my dignity and stood a little straighter. I didn't need any pity about my depression. It fucking happens.

"What *did* you feel for me, Jules?" Brennan asked.

If I was going to rid myself of my demons, like Johnny had requested, this was the next spot on the board game. I was the pee green, jealous, and scorned pawn and I landed on 'Tell Brennan the truth or go directly to bed.'

"Brennan. I fell in love with you. I fell in love with who I *was* when I was with you. I didn't want you to be married. I didn't want to share you. You brought out memories and feelings that I forgot existed, and I... you totally rocked my world," I looked at him with raised eyebrows, "No one ever rocked me both mentally and sexually. Just you."

"I fell in love with you, too. I *am* in love with you," he said. It was so casual, so strange, and he didn't look torn at all.

This was not working for me. This actually sucked ass. Demons be damned. Can demons be damned? Aren't they already? I needed out of here. This, all of a sudden, was too damn intense.

"So, what does Amelia think about you being in *love* with another woman?" I asked with contempt. "She must be furious. Damn, I bet she went out and fucked a bunch of people off the list, huh?" I jabbed him hard. Did he just tense against my finger or my words? I couldn't tell but I clearly hit a sensitive area for him. Physically or emotionally?

I wasn't interested in niceties. He and I weren't pole liners in the circus. He and Amelia were the fucking gypsies outside the tent. They stole the money and faith of all the hopeful people, who only wished for someone to tell them that they would have a harmonious and successful future. He stole *my* harmony. The night he chose Amelia over me, the morning I told him to go back to her, and the moment I saw him in the crowd at the show. He was not a fan boy. He was the best and worst choice I ever made.

"What the fuck do you want from me?" I tore my hand out of his and starting pushing on his rock hard chest. He had been working out more. He didn't even budge against my hard pushes. And I was strong. You can't be a rocker and not have upper body strength.

He pulled me to his chest and groaned. His head fell to mine and he inhaled the scent of my hair through his nose. I subtlety relaxed into him. It was like all time stopped, and we weren't there to talk. I allowed my eyes to close and I thought, *"I will give you everything you want right now."* I would do anything to keep this moment frozen in a photograph that I could pull out again and again to feel better when I got sad.

Johnny's voice about finding the answers echoed through my thoughts and I leaned back to find that Brennan's eyes were full of passion. He was just as affected by the closeness as I was. He didn't want our bodies to break apart. I didn't either so I let him hold me while he searched my face for what to say next.

"I want all of you. I have wanted all of you since the moment I saw you on stage for the first time. You know it. I know it. Amelia knows it. And, I would imagine that after listening to your end of the conversation, your fiancé knows it, too." He was so matter of fact about the bomb of words he just dropped into my heart. Chaos ensued and recovery in the near future was necessary. Please call the medics now. I started to shake.

"Johnny said that I needed answers," I suggested, in case he knew what he was talking about.

Brennan nodded and looked pained as he heaved a sigh. "Did your father tell you everything you needed to know?"

"My father will never be able to fully explain why he left. I will never understand because I was on the receiving end of his disastrous choice. He taught me that men leave." A small knot formed in the bottom of my throat. I suddenly wanted to cry. My father was never really a father. No, he was the first disappointment in my life.

But today, when he came with the only words of wisdom he knew how to share, I listened. He believed that I was fucking my life up by marrying Johnny. He didn't realize that I was fucking up my life way before I even made the scandalous magazines. Did he know that I was a complete slut when I was a teenager? In fact, did he even care that I gave it up to any guy who I thought was worthy? Well... up until now.

TWENTY-THREE

I twisted my body out of Brennan's arms and started to walk down the pathway again. A pathway to total confusion. I had to get my facts straight. Brennan didn't allow me to though. He pulled me to the side of a large oak tree and put his hands on the sides of my face.

"What I am about to tell you, Julia, is very difficult for me," he said, as he searched my eyes.

"What the fuck are you talking about?" I screamed at him.

"Julia, I need you to calm down and listen to me. The night I went to your concert here in Brooklyn? I didn't go alone. Amelia wanted to come and see you. She had been so damn jealous of you. I followed you on the internet, in magazines, everywhere I could. I had been so obsessed that I started to question my own sanity. I missed you so fucking much. I felt injured all day, every day." His hands were shaking on my face... hard.

"Amelia was at the concert?" I whispered. Brennan nodded slowly, still piercing me with his eyes.

"So when I told her I needed to see you in person, she begged to go with me. I didn't care at that point. I was just going. She could watch me drool or whatever. I didn't feel anything, you know. I didn't feel bad for hurting her or making her mad. My marriage didn't matter. I knew you were going to be so close to me. That was all that mattered," he stated. His eyes closed briefly. He looked so pained.

"It was hard seeing you, Brennan. I... I... " I started but Brennan cut me off by shaking my head forcefully.

"No, I am not done. I texted you when you went out back. I walked outside for a while. Amelia and I fought about my feelings for you. When I finally decided to come find you, Dex said that you had already left. I went backstage anyway. Johnny was there and he looked tanked already. When Dex let me in, I didn't realize Amelia was right on my heels, so she got backstage, too." His lips twisted in disgust and he looked away from me.

"So?" I asked.

"So, this fucking blows." His hands pushed through his hair and he growled as he fisted his hands at his sides. He was physically angry. I just stood there, waiting. He started to chuckle. "You know what is so fucked up, Julia? Your fiancé, Johnny, was so fucking quick to call me out on being married. So fucking quick. Yes, I should have said something but nonetheless, I should have been the one to tell you. Just like that fucking bastard should be the one to tell you his fucking secrets." He was seething. His jaw worked hard and his eyes didn't have passion anymore. He looked like he wanted to strangle someone. I hadn't seen him like this before, but hell, I had only spent a weekend with him. I just never knew he could... wait, Johnny has secrets?

"Go on, Brennan," I demanded.

"So... when Dex told me you weren't there, I got pissed and took off to find you. I couldn't. I didn't know where you went. But Amelia... she stayed behind. Julia, she and Johnny, they fucked that night. I am not just saying they had sex. They fucked each other in our living room... while I listened." His eyes were dead on me. I looked back into them in horror.

"Wh... what?" I whimpered as I started to fall. My knees fell out from under me and I couldn't breathe.

"She told him that you and I are in love. She told him that if he fucked her, you would choose the right person. He would tell you and you would finally choose who you wanted. It was so sick. She is so ill. Jealous, I don't know," he said as he backed off from me and he ran his hands over his face.

"She fucked it all up!" He screamed. I started to crumble. I fell to the ground and started to cry. Small tears at first, then hot streams of pain fell down my face, over my shirt. It came out of my nose and my ears were muted to the outside world.

Brennan tried to hug me on the ground but I shoved him off.
"Get the fuck away from me. Is this some fucking joke on me? Some fucking ploy to get me?"

Brennan shook his head harder than before. "I *left* her, Julia. I packed my shit right after Johnny left our place and told her I wanted a divorce. I couldn't be with anyone that would want to hurt you. She hurt the only woman I have ever been flat out on my ass in love with," he begged.

"So now? I have to choose which fucking loser I should love?" I yelled at him.

He shook his head again. "No. You don't get to choose. You get to know the whole truth and do whatever the fuck you want to do. Julia, I gave up on having you a long time ago. I knew we were done. Our love was real. It was real but the trust was totally gone. I know firsthand that trust is what you need in a relationship. Open relationships teach you all about that," he said, trying to smirk. His wounded face wouldn't allow any smile to push through.

I laughed through the mask of wetness. Open relationships... ha. No relationship was ever really open... not fully. The monogamous ones were just as fucked, too. I tore my engagement ring off my finger and threw it out on to the lawn. I started to get up from my seat on the dirt.

I was done with Johnny once and for all. I wasn't choosing him. And I certainly wasn't choosing Brennan. He broke my heart already. He was right. I didn't trust him. From the look of my scorecard, he would do it again. I didn't need to choose because I didn't need anyone.

That was my answer. Maybe that is what Johnny wanted me to figure out. Did I truly want him? Did I *need* him to make me feel like a complete person? No.

Actually, hell no. He just did to me what every man I trusted in my life had ever done. He hurt me, he left me, and he killed my spirit once again. I decided in that moment underneath the branches of the large oak tree that I didn't need sex or love or even a bed for depression. I didn't *need* anyone but me. I needed my self-worth and pride, something I never had before. It was robbed from me so early in my life. None of this would have happened if I had those two core qualities from the start.

Brennan left me to search for the engagement ring in the lawn. I dried the tears from my face and looked around, confused as to where to go next. I needed to get my shit out of Johnny's apartment. I needed to find a place to crash. I slowly turned around and looked at the expansive park, all the people going on with life while mine just took a nosedive into a volcano. *Fuck them all.*

Brennan came back and took my right hand. He placed the ring into my palm.

"You can't be a little girl anymore, Julia. You have to face him like an adult. It is your choice to listen to him. It is your choice to forgive him. I don't think he really knew what he was doing. Amelia can be very convincing so give him a chance," he said earnestly.

"Are you fucking kidding me?" I laughed and balked at him. "That man has cheated on me. Multiple times, Brennan. Do I look like that much of an idiot to you?"

"No. You are beautiful. Even when you are in pain, you take all the air out of my lungs. I feel alive when I am with you so no... never an idiot. An amazing woman with a heart of gold." His hand went up to my face and I automatically turned into it. I couldn't deny that our sexual attraction was ever in question. He may have been the only lover I felt safe and cared for with.

"I need to find a place to stay until I am calmer. I want to be able to tell Johnny the things I need to say," I said softly into his hand.

"I understand," he smiled at me. "I know this shouldn't have come from me. I am so so sorry."

I nodded because if I spoke, I would choke on another sob. I pushed that shit back down into my stomach.

"Where can I take you?" he asked.

"I have no clue. I want to be somewhere comfortable and far away. I need to be alone so I can find my real voice. Not the plastic one I have used for so damn long." I replied.

"My friends are out of town and are letting me use their place. I can take you there and then go to work," he offered. He was nervous. He didn't want me to shut him down. He wanted to help. Then it dawned on me. I was so stupid. This guy just left his wife because my fiancé deceived me. He wants me to feel safe. He wants to give me what I need.

"Okay," I choked. He took my hand and we walked several blocks past a few bakeries, a tattoo shop, and a couple Polish restaurants. We didn't say anything. His grip on my hand was firm but warm. He was so steady, holding me up as we walked.

We went down a side street and he opened a tall fence door. It led to a small white house. It looked totally out of place in Brooklyn. It felt far away from the city. From an airplane, you probably couldn't even see it with all of the tall buildings towering around it.

He unlocked the door and I was met with the scent of coffee and home. It was cozy and I fell into the fuzzy sofa couch without any warning. He chuckled a bit at me and moved to get me the remote control to the television that was opposite me.

"I don't want to watch TV," I snapped out.

"Okay. Well, if you do, just hit this button and then this one for the cable," he said as he pointed down to it.

I didn't even look at what he was showing me. I didn't hear the words coming out of his mouth. I watched his face. The dark black hair, curly and soft surrounded his eyes as he looked down at the remote. His forearms looked so strong, almost like he could pick up a brick house with no problem. His beautiful tattoo that was on display for the world, yet just for me in this moment. When he was done talking, he looked up to find me staring at him. He placed the remote on the couch softly and then he sat on the coffee table opposite me and we sat there–staring at each other for long moments.

Very slowly, very deliberately, we both moved our faces towards each other at the same time. The moment our lips met, we both moaned in relief. Only our lips and our noses were touching and yet I felt enveloped in his whole being. I parted my lips and his head turned to the side to kiss me deeper. It was intimate and sensual. He was lovely. His curls brushed against my eyebrows and my hand went up to feel the back of his head. I played with the curls and with my feather light touches, I allowed him to relax into me.

TWENTY-FOUR

Brennan carefully took my hand from his hair and placed it over his heart, where I could feel the bass sound of his body playing steady. When he placed his hand over my heart, I became flustered with desire. It was an intimate move that I wasn't ready for. I could feel both of our hearts kick up in tempo and I began to feel nervous. It was too challenging to keep myself from kissing him. I slowly leaned back on the couch as he sat beside me, our hands stayed connected to each other's rhythmic energy.

"I wish our story had been different," I quietly offered.

"Me, too," he agreed with a small smile.

"We would have been perfect for one another, you know?" I said as casual as my tightened chest would allow. I still wanted Brennan but right now, I also wanted to vomit. The idea of being with Brennan from the very beginning without the open marriage, the lies, and Johnny's impure actions, sent the little hope I had before this day into an inferno. Too much history

275

destroyed our chances and we were ruined before we ever met. I wish that Brennan never met Sean at that convention so long ago. I don't know where I would be if I hadn't met him, but I would like to think that I wouldn't have this sick feeling. I wouldn't know that everything in my life, up until right now, has been for nothing.

"We still could be." His eyes are downcast and his words are too late.

I didn't say anything. I didn't need to. I was too damaged to make any decisions about anything. I was essentially homeless. It didn't matter whether I had money in the bank or not, I still didn't have a place to run to. I was sick of it all. One moment I wanted to find the solutions to everything and the next I pressed my lips onto Brennan's and urged him back on top of me. He groaned into my mouth and with impatient need, he started to undress me.

He was so rushed and it felt wonderful. As he took of my shirt, he kissed my collarbone. When he unhooked my bra, he kissed the center of my chest. His hot, heavy breaths tickled the skin on my breasts right before he licked my nipples one at a time.

I helped Brennan remove his shirt and as he sat back up to work off the sleeves, I gazed at his beautiful chest. He was so fucking beautiful. His body was strong and rich. His skin was warm and begged for my touch. His body belonged to no one but me.

"You are breathtaking," I whispered as my fingers found the ridges around his pectorals.

He smiled radiantly at me and it set my heart, my tummy, and my insides on fire. It was a slow comfortable burn, the way I desired him so acutely. I craved Brennan. I always had. I wanted for us to be together again, even if it was just this once. His hastiness from just moments ago came to an abrupt halt while we watched each other with admiration, wonder, and love. This time, I was fully present. I was all of me. I was both the reckless girl and the mature woman in our final glorious moment together as one.

That afternoon, on the couch of strangers, in the middle of no place in Brooklyn, Brennan Curtis and I made sweet, uninhibited love. We devoured every inch of every part of each other's bodies. It was perfection. Finally, I had made the right choice. I giggled at his dimples and touched him in places I never had. I traced his ears, flicked his nipples, massaged his legs, and smiled more in that afternoon than I had in a year.

Later, while Brennan went to get us food, I laid on the couch and flipped through the channels on the television and landed on two girls fighting over one guy in a reality show. It wasn't amusing. It made me sick. I switched it over to Mega-fan Tonight and saw familiar faces on the television. Johnny and Dex were leaving their practice studio in Manhattan, while girls were trailing after them like little swooning ducks. I sat up straight and listened to the host say that 'there was trouble in paradise for Lennox and Delaney'.

"Will they make it down the aisle?" the host asked. Pictures of us kissing on tour filled the screen right when Brennan walked in with takeout Italian food. I clicked off the television and grinned up at the bag.

"Hungry?" he asked with a deliberate smirk.

"I am positive I burned off every calorie I had left in my body. It's exhausting just to talk," I said as I grabbed for my foiled plate. I looked down at the manicotti and sighed in wonderment. God love food. God love food after sex. God love good food after fabulous sex.

Brennan laughed at my merriment and we sat side by side on the couch to eat.

"What were you watching that you didn't want me to see?" he asked. He wasn't upset or suspicious. He was just Brennan asking a question that probably didn't need an answer either way.

"Just crap about Johnny and me splitting up," I said as I took a humongous bite of cheese and sauce.

"Yeah? You guys breaking up?" he asked with a mouthful of chicken parmesan.

I nodded. "Yep. I am leaving the band, too."

Brennan nearly choked. He started coughing and I rubbed his back while he put the food on the coffee table and reached for the glass of water.

It took a long time for the coughing fit to subside and I felt bad. But it was the truth. I was leaving the band. I couldn't see a way to have a future with Johnny in any capacity. It felt over, too. I felt the finality of it in my chest and it didn't hurt. It felt right. I didn't know what my next step was or where I would go but I was done with Love Sick Ponies. Ironically, I was sick of love and all its repercussions.

"You can't leave the band, can you? I mean, aren't you under contract?" Brennan looked astounded. I giggled at his face and gave him a kiss on his soft dimpled cheek.

"I can do whatever I want." I shrugged. "I am under contract, but that doesn't mean I can't get out anyways. I will just have to pay a lot of money to a lawyer. No matter what, I will receive royalties on the albums I have done with the band."

I thought about it for a minute. In fact, if I didn't sing one more song for the rest of my life, even my children's kids would be financially set. So why was I homeless? Oh yeah, I was living with my rock star fiancé. *Jackass.*

"So, you want out? For real?" Brennan was truly surprised at my decision.

"For real."

"What will you do?" he questioned. It was a damn good question. I thought about it for a long while until I realized I had no idea.

"You don't know, do you?" He shook his head and I waited for his next question.

"You won't leave the band, Julia. It is your passion. Everyone sees it on stage."

I nodded my head in agreement. It *was* my passion. I did feel it on stage. It was such a fucking rush but then I thought about turning my head to the right and seeing Johnny's face. I would see him fucking girl after girl after girl and I wouldn't be numb towards it anymore. This time it hurt. This time I wouldn't be able to watch.

Brennan and I watched television long after dinner. We didn't have sex again and when I saw that he was sleeping peacefully, I got up quietly. I went to the kitchen of this total stranger's house in search of a pen. I found an envelope and a sharpie. I wrote the letter I dreaded but it was the final message that had to be shared between us. Dropping Johnny and running into Brennan's arms was foolish. This girl needed to find and love herself for a while. I was scared to death but I wrote it anyway.

Bren,

Making love to you again was exactly what I needed. You are probably the love of my life and yet, it would never work. I hope you find true happiness. XOXO–Your Julia.

One down, one to go.

TWENTY-FIVE

When I got back into the city, I made sure to get a coffee from the convenient store before I headed back to Johnny's apartment. It was nearly one in the morning and I knew that I wouldn't sleep tonight. I didn't even know where I would go after I left Johnny's. I cursed him again for being a fucking asshole but somewhere inside me I felt the pain start to creep up. I had a few more moments until one part of my life is over and the next part begins. I was dizzy. I couldn't make sense out of what I wanted to say. I thought about the ways it would go down. I thought about the ways it wouldn't go down.

Both ways, we were over and that recognition was mere moments away. Anxiety ripped up my body and I swerved a little again. I was really doing this. I was really fucking leaving after all these years. *All this time.* Tears came to my eyes and stung the shit out of them. I shook my head and yelled, "No!" at myself. Luckily only a few people on the streets turned their heads so I was quick to grab my phone and act like I was really talking to someone other than myself.

I walked up the four flights of stairs instead of taking the elevator. I needed the physical build up. With a coffee in hand and being slightly out of breath, I used my key to open the apartment door. I heard soft music playing in the bedroom. I shut the door with the normal force I always used and put the coffee and keys down on the living room table.

When I looked up to head to his bedroom, he was standing there, shirtless and weary. He wasn't drunk. He hadn't been partying. He was waiting for me. I fucking loved this man and I fucking hated him for what I was about to do.

"You came back," he stated in a monotone voice.

"Yep."

"Didn't think you would," he said a bit more cautiously.

"Why is that?"

"Because I... "

"Because you what?" I snapped. My heart was beating so hard. I wanted to lunge at him and beat the fucking crap out of him. I took a deep breath. No ass kicking, Jules. Just a quiet conversation that ends in me packing my shit and never seeing my best friend again.

"I... ah... Jules, I slept with Amelia," he stated. He held out his hands like he was handing me a tray. A tray of heartbreak and distrust.

"I know."

"You know?" he asked perplexed. "How?"

"Brennan told me. I am just as confused about what today was supposed to be about. My father? Brennan? Two men that hurt me? You wanted me to get answers? Why? Did you want me to remember that I have been screwed by every man I ever loved so this... this thing you did with her would be okay?" I was shaking so bad. My voice, my knees, my heart, my hands.

"No. No, Jules. No, I didn't send you with them because of that. Shit, I didn't know what was going on. I wasn't sure if Amelia told him or not," he started. "Then Kent called and said I had to let you go with your Dad and... "

"Kent? Why the fuck would Kent know about any of this?" I asked incredulously.

"I honestly don't know."

"So, Brennan was in the next frigging room when you fucked her. The. Next. Room. He left her," I said, flipping my wrist out at him.

Johnny threaded his fingers into his hair and stood flabbergasted with both hands on top of his head. "You have got to fucking be kidding me?"

"Why did you do it?" I whispered. I heard a little pain come through my tone but it wasn't totally apparent.

"Jules, I was so hammered and you... You were looking so beautiful that night and I wanted you and you were watching him. You were watching him the whole fucking show! You didn't think I noticed but I did. It was unbearable. I started to drink... "

I held up my hand. "I know the rest. You can stop there."

"Jules, please. Jules." He started towards me. I held up my hands again and shoved my body back into the

286

sofa, so he knew I wanted to be as far away from him as possible.

"Where is your ring?" he snapped out. His eyes on my hand were murderous and his jaw tightened.

I said nothing. My face said nothing. Moments passed.

I saw the moment he registered that we were over. His body sagged and his knees hit the floor.

"Oh my God," he cried. "In my mind, in my thoughts, it didn't feel like this. I knew I would lose you but not with piercing pain like this, oh God," he moaned as he rubbed his chest.

I took in everything he said, everything he said he felt with a wide eyes and a closed off heart.

"But this isn't... no, this isn't fucking right. I fucked up, okay? God, Jules, I fucking love you. I love you. I *love* you. Please. I will stop drinking. I will do whatever you want, whatever you need. I will do it all for you. Just please, please put that ring back on. Tell me it's not over. Tell me it is all okay. Tell me you love me. *Please*... tell me you love me."

I watched my best friend of ten years fold into a fetal position and beg like a child. I watched him moan and swear. In a million years, I never imagined that it would go down like this. I could feel his hurt because I knew what betrayal felt like. It was so fucking palpable I couldn't feel anything else in the room. I swallowed a few times. I cleared my throat of the moisture as one single tear continually streamed down my face.

"We have been friends for many, many years, Johnny. I have loved you. I have despised you. I have watched you with women. I can't figure out if I was just numb then and pretended I didn't care. Now that I am aware or maybe because I fell in love with you a bit more, I do care. What you did. That... that wasn't okay," I said. "It wasn't okay then and it isn't okay now."

"I know. I know. It was the devil. The drinking and being pissed off at you but I never wanted to hurt you. Never that," he pleaded.

"What you have for me is called artificial love. It isn't real. It looks like love, it acts like love, but when it comes down to all of this?" I motioned my hands like I was making an imaginary circle to encompass us. "This isn't real. We are not true love."

Johnny was on his knees and I stunned him silent with my last words. No more begging. No more asking for the words. He was completely checked out. I took the ring out of my jeans pocket and placed it on the side table next to the couch. I turned back to him.

"I am quitting LSP. I am leaving you. I need you to acknowledge what I am saying," I said to him slowly and shakily. "I am going to pack a few things and you can toss the rest. I am leaving tonight and I don't ever want to see you again. Do you understand me?"

We stared at each other. I was so amped on anxiety to get the fuck out of there that I didn't notice the tears were still falling down my chin on to my hands and onto the floor.

Finally, I think he nodded through his wet eyes. His closed his eyes and the tears fell down his face. Eyes closed, he nodded again and said, "I understand."

I started to hiccup on every breath I took while getting my clothes together. I grabbed what I could from the bathroom and made sure I had my guitar and my favorite LSP shirt. One day I would wear it again or maybe I would burn it. Either way, I needed it with me.

With the duffel bag, my guitar, and my new sense of pride, I turned to him after I put my hand on the door.

"You are a beautiful musician. It has been a pleasure playing with you. I wish you the best. And *please* tell Dex I am sorry. I know you will be great without me. I know it," I said ardently.

A small smile found its way to my face. Who the fuck knows where it came from. I just had to smile. It would be the last thing I ever did as Johnny's bandmate and his fiancé. I closed the door quietly and let my head fall back as I started to walk to the elevator.

The booming smash of objects started within one minute. Heavy items, dishware, and the lamps maybe. I walked into the elevator to the sound of Johnny's world crashing down all around him.

TWENTY-SIX

2 YEARS LATER

MARTHA'S VINEYARD, MASSACHUSETTS

2014

The summer flowers were definitely in full bloom. The huge inhale of ocean, fish, and flowers made me smile bright as I rode my bike down into the small town of Tinsbury, Massachusetts. It was called Vineyard Haven to most tourists that made it to Martha's Vineyard. It was such a beautiful place that I about pinched myself every morning as I took in the magnificent view from my extremely pretentious mansion off of the main road. Ha, one main road on the island could mean anything.

I loved my Schwinn bike. I loved to coast down the road with my hands behind my head. When I was a kid, I had a Schwinn. Best bike ever. I was on my way to meet Pierre, a guy I met when I had taken my small sailboat out one day and went aground. I was scared to death but Pierre, in his small kayak, calmed me down with his Parisian accent and gorgeous blue eyes. His tanned muscles made me drool as he used them to tow me and the boat to land.

That whole incident was a little embarrassing. I tucked my baseball hat a little lower over my face while he took me into the slip and docked it for me. I became fast, but just friends with Pierre. Although there were times that I swear he had just walked off a modeling shoot and I wanted to lick his neck. He was so drop dead sexy. I bought Pierre a cup of coffee after my disastrous boat shit storm and it was then that I promised him I would go to Paris. I decided to plan to go that fall, after the leaves fell on the island.

Every Saturday morning we went to the Big Bagel on Main Street where he would teach me to speak French. Well, he spoke French and I just got frustrated. It was never assumed that he would go with me but he did make references to "what he would show me." I just smiled and knew the day would come when I said I was going on my own. I was on my own. It had been almost two years that I was just Julia.

After shit went down with Johnny and Brennan, I fled to my mother's house. Surprised didn't even begin to describe her face when I showed up at six in the morning. I was exhausted. I gave her a huge hug and fell into bed for a couple days. She was dating a guy seriously and he was thinking of moving in, so she made it clear that as much as she loved having me, I needed to figure out my next step in life.

So I started from square one. I decided one night to think like I was twelve again. I wrote out a bucket list as I listened to my mother answering the phone on my behalf.

"Listen, if I hear from Julia, I will let everyone know. I am just as worried as everyone else," my mother would say.

God bless that woman. There were at least twenty calls a day. Even though it wasn't on my bucket list, I had to contact a lawyer, who could make sure that I signed and paid for whatever I needed to, to leave the band. My lawyer also fought for royalties on the new songs I had written right before I left. Those songs hadn't been recorded yet, so it was a fucking mess trying to figure out my percentages. I left it up to my lawyer. I wanted a drama free life but that didn't happen for a while.

The media went fucking bonkers. I died my hair to a very dark red, took out my piercings, and wore moderately conservative clothing. Red Sox hats were bountiful. I did all of my shopping on line and my mom helped me buy a bad ass Jeep, in her name, before I took off to Martha's Vineyard with my bucket list. The list actually included learning to speak French, so it was funny that I met Pierre the following summer. However, the list included a lot of things. Learn to sail a boat. Check. Some of the things on the list were small. Bike more. Laugh more. Other things were harder to obtain and/or sustain. Find friends that were girls. Learn to cook. Write a book. Abstinence. So far, I was doing incredibly well at letting men down gently. The rest? It was a daily work in progress.

I didn't have to let Pierre down... yet. I have been waiting for the day. Pierre's a funny guy and has made me laugh at some of the simplest things in life. He tries to impress me with little things. He picked me some Hydrangea wildflowers once and I had to tell him I couldn't keep them in the house because Loves, my dog, eats everything. After explaining that the flowers were poisonous if eaten, he came back with red roses the following day. I thanked him, of course, but that was an awkward fifteen minutes, arranging them while he watched. Red roses? Really?

Then Pierre got me a card that said, "I'm thanking you." He meant to get one that said, "I am thinking of you." I actually cried from laughing so hard. He was a good sport and laughed alongside me. I thought, maybe he knew who I was but I never confirmed it with him. He was just a nice guy.

He always insisted on paying, which is comical, because I am pretty wealthy. Pierre asked me to dinner frequently but that was a tricky situation due to my no men rule. I really loved him, as a friend, and I wanted to *stay* friends. I knew Pierre wanted more and I just... didn't. I didn't feel the sparkle.

The Brennan Sparkle. That is what my girlfriends, Kelly and Joanie, called it. When I first moved to Martha's Vineyard, I stayed at their bed and breakfast for a month while I looked for a home to buy. They were an awesome couple. They were supportive of my new love for cooking and yes, they most definitely knew who I was. One drunken night Kelly confessed that she didn't really care for my former band. I about peed my pants, I was laughing so hard. Their apologetic looks were hysterical and I ended up confessing that I didn't really care for it anymore, either.

That was the night that my friendship with Kelly and Joanie solidified. They fell in love and approved of my new, five thousand square foot home. It had six bedrooms, a sauna, a huge yard, and a portion of the house overlooked the ocean. I put in a bid at for asking price and we all went to town with decorating the massive home. They were awesome, so check that off the list. Girlfriends were back in my life.

Although the house was huge and I hardly saw certain rooms for days, I thought "*what the hell.*" Kent and his family would visit. Maybe Mom and her new boyfriend would come at the same time. In the two years I had been on the island, they made plans once, but it never worked out. I understood they all had lives. I did, too, for many years. Now that my life was in slow motion, I guess I thought everyone else's was, too.

Van Morrison sang in my earphones about how we were born before the wind as I glided my bike into the parking lot for my Saturday rendezvous with Pierre. I felt so calm and free. I felt so complete. That night, the girls and I planned to hit the one and only club to dance. I loved to dance with them. They always included me in their seductive ass wiggling. I smiled to myself as I pulled out the earphones and put them in my backpack. I had a Trapper Keeper in my bag for French class with Pierre. He had eyed it suspiciously at our first meeting in which I responded with a shrug.

I was a kid again; growing up all over again. I felt like I was becoming a real woman, taking care of my house and I started a small garden. Loves, my golden retriever, was my *best* friend during the winter months. We took lots of snowy walks together. He was a bit upset when I left him to roam the gated yard. When I took off on my red bike, I could hear him whine for a few minutes, hence the earphones. He had a fantastic way of knowing that I would be gone for hours, *poor boy*. He also had a great method of making me feel bad.

I walked in and my eyes instantly fell on Pierre. He smiled his delicious smile at me. Okay, I was a woman. The abstinence thing was starting to make me question my sanity. Let's just say I had ordered a lot of battery operated boyfriends over the past six months. He waved down at the table, showing he already had my cinnamon raisin bagel and mocha latte waiting. *God love him.*

"Hey Pierre," I said with a dramatic flourish. I hugged him sideways and kissed him on the cheek.

"Français uniquement," he responded in his flawless and heart stopping accent.

I nodded and took out my Trapper Keeper.

"What did you do last night?" I asked just excited to see him. He gave me the stink eye.

"Pierre, désolé," I answered. I just wasn't up for the French lesson today. I wanted to play. I noticed we were both wearing cable knit sweaters and I giggled a bit.

"Belle... um... sweater?" I asked. We hadn't gotten to clothes yet.

"Pullover," he smirked and took a bite of his bagel. He got busy pulling out sheets of information and I sighed.

"Do we have to do this today?" I asked.

"What would you like to do, belle fille?" he questioned. I blushed at his use of calling me beautiful. Seriously, I knew it was just a word but the guy made it sound so seductive.

"Take a bike ride? Go out in the kayaks? It is such a gorgeous day," I said, getting more and more excited with each idea.

"Ah. Well, my bicycle tire is... uh... flat? My boat, someone is using today," he said, pushing out his lips in contemplation.

I've Been Loving You by Otis Redding started to play over the sound system and I sat back in my seat and closed my eyes. I got lost in the long notes and felt my head swaying. When the song ended, I opened my eyes to find Pierre and several other customers close by with shocked looks on their faces. A roar of applause started and I covered my ears. It had been so long since I had heard that noise that I forgot how deafening it was.

Confused, I looked to Pierre who was beaming at me.

"Jules, you never sang for me before."

"Was I just singing?" I asked mortified as I ducked my head. "Oh God. Please. We need to leave." The sudden rush that someone would recognize me had me storing all of my stuff in quick succession. French lesson officially over.

Pierre grabbed my bagel and coffee and followed me out of the door. Patrons had gone back to their business but I took a deep inhale of the ocean air and let it out purposely timed.

"I am so sorry," I begged Pierre. "I just don't sing in public."

He nodded in understanding. "Let's walk down to the ferry landing and watch the tourists for a bit. Maybe that will calm you."

He handed me my coffee and I slipped my arm through his. We were always walking arm in arm around town. The girls had a bet going on when we would eventually have sex but it wasn't going to happen. I loved Pierre but never in that way. He had saved me, literally. Figuratively, he showed me that a guy could be a friend without expectations. He never tried to kiss me. He was never pushy about getting together and, more than anything, I loved to listen to him talk in that French accent. I lived on a beautiful island with a Frenchman teaching me to speak French. I had to pinch myself to be sure it was my life after everything I had been through.

We sat on the platform and watched as the next ferry was set to arrive. I finished off my bagel and he got up to toss our trash in the can nearby. I put my hand over my eyes to see how full the ferry was. It looked horrendously packed. How all those boatloads of people actually fit on the island, I would never know.

"It's busy, yes?" Pierre asked as he sat down next to me.

"It's wedding season. The girls are totally booked for the summer." I shot him a sideways glance and he was staring at my profile.

"What?" I nudged him.

"I want you to sing for me like that again," he said softly. I shook my head.

"I got carried away. I love Otis Redding." I looked back to the boat that was just about to dock. The workers all started with their ropes and the people that worked the automatic ramp from the boat to the land called out instructions efficiently. What a boring job that would be. Roping and un-roping all day long? Yeah, no thanks.

"You have a magnificent voice."

"Pierre," I growled out.

"Well? You do," he exclaimed with his hands out in surrender. I smiled and nodded politely at him.

"Thank you, Pierre," I said with sincerity.

"Sing for me again?"

"What? Now... no! No way!" I stumbled through my words.

"Oh come on," he insisted. I was getting really annoyed now and thought Loves maybe wanted to play ball on the beach.

I started to get up and he groaned. "Okay, I am sorry. It just... made me feel something. You are talented."

I put my backpack on and he stood up to start walking back with me just as the tourists started to unload from the ferry. He wrapped his arm around my shoulder and told me he wouldn't mention it again. We got mixed up in the crowd and as we walked side by side, we got lost in our own observations of the other people.

And that's when I saw him. I stopped in my tracks and the people behind us bumped against us. Brennan's hair was longer. He wore a black V-neck tee and khaki shorts. Black flip flops and a gorgeous leggy blonde at his side completed his magazine good looks. I started to shake a bit. I wasn't ready to see him again.

Sure, I had thought about an email to his company or maybe a phone call over the last two years but as time passed it just seemed pointless. Now, it was apparent that I was right. People move on. *Other People.* But, not me. The colors, the sounds, the world was a blur and Brennan became the focal point. He was vivid and lovely in the way he walked and how he ran his fingers through his long, dark locks. I had cherished him with everything I was that last night together. I hadn't remembered the feeling of passionate love until now. It still hurt like hell.

I craved him but I couldn't be his. It wasn't practical two years ago. And time was always our problem. Tactless, poor timing ruined us then and the adequate stretch of time apart ruined us now. Deep, frantic longing that I once felt for only him was back with ferocity. It made me want to drop to my knees, sob in every foreign language, while pleading with the Goddesses for reprieve from my heart ache. He was the only one I had ever longed for and that much was perfectly clear. My feelings for Brennan hadn't and would never go away.

Pierre rightfully looked puzzled at my expression and then turned to see who I was looking at. He must not have seen anyone because he nudged me to keep walking with the masses of people departing the ferry. I followed the herd, but sluggishly. I watched the blond beauty wrap her arms around Brennan and beam brightly up to him. His dimpled smile blindsided me. I caught my gasp on some spit and I forced back the tears, but tried to muster up some composure. I needed to act like my whole world didn't just do a back hand spring. It would be alright. Brennan wouldn't see me in this dense crowd and I knew our love affair belonged in the past forever. I would not find a bed.

All those thoughts seemed to calm me until the blond woman with Brennan dropped her sunglasses and they both stopped to make sure they weren't broken. We walked slowly by and I looked straight ahead, pretending the love of my life wasn't mere inches away from me.

"What do you want to do now, Jules?" Pierre asked, rather loudly. My heart sped up and so did my steps. He tried to keep up but he was falling behind. A large hand landed on my shoulder.

"Pierre, I... " I said as I turned to look directly into Brennan's beautiful, dark brown eyes, mixed with a little green from the blue sky. His eyes were just as wide as mine were.

"Julia?" he asked in bewilderment.

"Oh...Brennan... hello," I said as casually as I could. I sounded like a twelve year old. I probably looked like one, too, with my Trapper Keeper in hand.

"How is it going? Long time no see!" I continued to say as I bounced a bit on my heels.

He looked at me and then shook his long dark curls in bewilderment. Blondie came up next to him, as I felt Pierre close in on me.

"What brings you... uh... two," I said as I looked at Blondie's arm wrapped around Brennan's side. "... to the island?" I laughed nervously. What brings you to the island? Jesus. How fucking cliché.

"Hi," Blondie drawled and put her hand out to me. "I'm Sasha. And you are?"

I took her hand in mine and smiled at her warmly and it was genuine. "I am Jules."

I looked over at Pierre, "and this is my good friend, Pierre." Pierre shook Sasha's hand politely and Brennan stood there, white as a ghost. When his eyes flicked to Pierre, there was a flash of something awkward. Abort. Abort. Abort.

"Well, we won't keep you two. It is such a beautiful day here." I said. I was smiling so hard it made my fucking cheeks hurt.

"You look so different," Brennan said in a hushed voice. He was still in stunned mode.

"Aw, I hope that's a compliment," I laughed as I poked his arm. He flinched at my physical touch. That was maybe a little too forward on my part, I guessed.

"Wait a fucking minute," Sasha snapped her fingers and shouted. "You... you are Jules Delaney, the lead singer from the Love Sick Ponies."

I cringed inward, outward, and all over the island. I did a quick scan to see if anyone noticed her outing me. I looked over at Pierre who was grinning widely and rocking back on his heels with his arms crossed. I shot him a deadly look.

"Beautiful Julia is more than just some lead singer," Pierre said. Brennan came out of his trance fast and his sudden, glaring look almost killed Pierre.

"Wow, can I like, get your autograph?" Sasha asked as she started looking through her enormous bag.

"Sorry," I said with a tight smile. "I don't give out autographs anymore and I am just Jules around these parts."

"Oh. That is too bad," Sasha whined. She gave up looking. "Well, Brennan, we should head up to the bed and breakfast. The wedding starts in like three hours and I have to get to work on my makeup."

I squinted at her face. Her makeup was flawless already and I felt Pierre laugh a little behind my back. I put my hand behind me to grab his. I needed solid. He was my solid. He would help me see the funny stupid shit in this dreadful reunion. Or maybe I would just take Loves on that walk and sob across the beach.

Either way, I was done with this fucking conversation.

"Well, it was nice to see you again, Brennan. You two kids have a great time," I smiled and waved as I started to walk away. Pierre helped me adjust my backpack strap as I let the shakes overtake my body. I was *not* good. I was *far* from good. I wasn't sure my awesome muscular biking legs could take one more step.

I quickly looked back over my shoulder. I couldn't help it. One last look. I saw Brennan standing where I left him. He looked like a statue as Sasha was talking up to him, waving her hand in front of his face, looking quite irritated.

I gave him a small wave, a small smile, and I locked my arm through Pierre's once again. We walked back to my bike and I told him that I forgot to leave food for Loves. He understood something just had gone down and tried to come along.

"Listen, I just need to go take care of my dog right now... alone. Okay?" I didn't really ask, as I was already on my bike and he didn't have one. As he kissed me on both cheeks, he reminded me of our appointment the following Saturday. As I took off, I yelled back that I wouldn't miss it. Paris sounded really fucking good. Like right now. I could catch the next ferry, get on the plane, and be speaking French in less than twenty four hours.

I decided holing up in my monstrous house was better. It was just one weekend, I hoped.

TWENTY-SEVEN

So I was a chicken shit. I called Kelly and Joanie right when I got back to house and canceled on dancing Saturday night. They asked why, of course.

"Brennan is on the island" was met with complete silence. We didn't say very much after that. The rest of Saturday I spent on the beach with Loves. He and I played ball and then stick for hours. My skin and mouth felt totally dried out by the time we made it back to the house. I wasn't in the mood to cook so I threw in a frozen pizza and settled down with a cheap romance novel. That was absolutely not helpful in any way.

The heroine was a slut and fell in love with a married man. Fantastic. The End.

I didn't sleep very well both Saturday and Sunday nights. I had to squeeze my eyes against Sasha wrapping her arms around Brennan and the look he gave her before he had seen me.

By Monday, I felt so much better knowing that the last ferry to the mainland had left at midnight. I breathed easier because *he* wasn't on my island anymore. Yes, it was my island. I found it first, I thought, as I dug in the dirt of my small garden. I was sticky with sweat and even though I had gardener gloves on, I still felt the dirt under my fingertips. I didn't care. Maybe I would take a dip in my small spa and let the stress of the weekend soothe my worries away. I was on the right track in life. I was checking off my bucket list items left and right. Sometimes I wondered what I would do when I finished the list, so every once in a while I added one more item. Just one. No biggie.

Loves came up and started licking my face telling me he was hungry. Again?

"Dude, I just fed you an hour ago. How can you be hungry again?" I laughed as we rolled on the lawn. Loves jumped off me and started barking at the tall, dark, and fucking sexy man heading up the lawn. Brennan. All the air in my lungs left me. *My island*, I thought.

Brennan stooped down to scratch Loves. I could hear him murmuring something to the dog but I didn't make it out totally. "Good" and maybe "Boy" but "mother" definitely stood out.

I took off my gloves and started walking down to meet him.

"Hey!" I exclaimed a little bit too enthusiastically. Maybe a little forcefully fake. My throat was clogged and I am sure I squawked rather than any other sound. Fucking throat.

"Hello Julia," he said as he looked up to me from petting Loves. "Nice dog. He's yours?"

"Yep, that's Loves," I replied, smiling at how stupid happy Loves got at new people's attention.

"Loves, huh?" He asked as if it was a piece of information that he was locking away in the mental safe.

I shrugged. "He loves me when the snow keeps us inside for days. Or when the storms are so bad and I can't sleep."

Brennan abruptly stopped scratching Loves and he stood. Loves came to sit at my side.

"You look so different," he said. What did he mean by that? What was he thinking? Why do I want to know every detail and observance he has about how I look different?

"Wow, Brennan, is it me or has your conversational skills become limited? You said that the other day." I slapped the gloves together to get rid of the excess dirt. "What do you mean by different?"

"You look really happy. Free. Your face glows like... like you are in love," he said cautiously.

I laughed. "Well, hell, Brennan! I am in love! Look at my house and my island. Look at my fucking fantastic dog!"

He smiled at me. His dimples were out to kill and I shifted a little to rid myself of the extremely foreign horny feeling.

"What are you doing here? Who was the little snitch on the island?" I laughed.

He laughed. "They told me I wasn't allowed to say."

"Oh God. Kelly and Joanie sent you?" I groaned. I would never forgive them. Our friendship was finished. I frowned at that thought. No, telling Brennan where I lived didn't mean I was going to break up with my two besties. I wouldn't be able to make it on the island year round without them.

He watched me as I went through the mental processing and finally his words took me out of my thoughts.

"What happened to you?" He was quiet when he inquired about this but it sounded like a painful plea.

"That's a question for the masses, my old friend," I said on a chuckle.

"I am not an old friend," he snapped back. "I was the love of your life. You were mine. You just took off and I called everyone. Your family didn't know where you were. You just dropped off the face of the Earth. The only way I knew you weren't dead was because in my total desperate measures, I contacted Johnny. He said you had hired a lawyer but that it was confidential as to who it was. Even to the band. Damn, you just quit it all."

"I *told* you I was going to. Our last night together? I *told* you I was done," I replied a little softer. I did not want to argue with Brennan. I wasn't that person anymore. I didn't feel hatred. I felt empathy and compassion for the man in front of me.

"I am *so* sorry I hurt you, Brennan. I did hurt a lot of people when I left but it wasn't because I didn't care. I *had* to leave for myself. I needed to get to know myself."

"So *where* did you go?" he asked. He really needed these answers. And for fuck's sake, it was a long ass story. I looked at him thoughtfully.

"How much time do you have?" I asked with a smart grin. "It's kind of a long story."

He threw his head back and fingered his hair through, letting out a large exhale. I took in his low riding jeans and a grey tee shirt with Desired Pitch written across it. I smiled at the thought of Lizzie and Nick. I wondered how their babies were. Was that band even still together? I had stopped listening to normal radio the day I left Manhattan. I made playlists and listened to only certain XM stations where I knew there was no way any of my old music would haunt me.

"I have a bit of time," he answered, nodding his head.

"Yeah," I drew out. "Shouldn't you be with... Sasha?" I asked like I wasn't saying her name in my head the whole fucking weekend.

"No." He firmly stated.

"Well, then, follow me and Loves. I need to get cleaned up a bit. I have some freshly squeezed lemonade or coffee," I said. When and how did I become such a hostess? All those small dinner parties with the girls trained me well, I thought. It obviously threw Brennan off because he looked at me like he didn't even know who I was.

I laughed.

"Or a fucking beer. It's got to be five o'clock somewhere on God's green Earth." I said, motioning him into the side door to the open windowed kitchen. I loved my kitchen. It was so New England but modern.

I didn't have to deal with hundred year old pipes but it still had the old island feeling. I noticed the tension in Brennan's body eased as he put his hands in his pockets to follow me.

Lucky pockets.

TWENTY-EIGHT

I opened the refrigerator and pointed to a bottle of Shipyard. Brennan shook his head as his eyes darted around my place.

"Coffee, then?" I asked. I was trying so damn hard to keep my cool. This was just like having Pierre over. Just a guy having a drink in my kitchen. Just that.

"Yeah, that would be perfect," he said as he scrubbed the five o'clock shadow on his chin.

I started the French Press and his eyebrows lifted. I giggled.

"When you live on an island, you have the time to do the extra steps. You take those few extra moments to enjoy what you would normally miss. No more tunnel vision." I pulled out two ceramic mugs that I made at a local pottery store that gave out lessons. Make pottery on bucket list–check.

"How long have you lived on Martha's Vineyard?" he asked. It was a thoughtful question, very casual but

I knew... I knew he was drawing a timeline in his head. The clock would start when I began to talk.

"It will be two years this October," I said. "Well, I moved in here then. I moved to the island in September just as the summer peeps left. I actually stayed with Kelly and Joanie," I confessed. I smiled to the memories of us down in the sitting area, playing Scrabble. I was so lost. I had no idea which way was up. I had my list and hope.

"So you just picked Vineyard Haven, what? Like on a map?" he asked with a queer expression on his face.

I shook my head as I started to pour the press over one mug and then the other.
"No, as a child, I had visited here once with a friend. We were ten. I remember thinking that this place was so magical, all surrounded by water. Comforting. It was so beautiful in my memories so when I left my mother's house, I came directly here."

"Wait. Back up! You were at your mother's?" he asked. Anger edged the sides of the words but he wasn't fuming.

"I take it you called there?" I asked as I slid the mug and condiments to him. I rested my forearms on the breakfast nook.

"Um... like twice a day for three months. She was your mother. How could she not know where her daughter was?"

I nodded. "You and about twenty five other people a day," I said, taking a cautious sip of my coffee. I winced at how hot it was. I went to the freezer and pulled out ice cubes, threw them in my huge insolated mug and poured the coffee over the ice.

He watched me in fascination. "You really look amazing." I could tell he hadn't wanted to let those words slip out because he went a little flush and looked down at his full cup of steaming coffee like it held all the answers to life.

"Did you miss me?" he asked the cup quietly.

I didn't say anything. I thought about it. I mean, I really thought about it. It was a very important question and yes, it had been asked many times by both the girls and me.

"Yes." I stated the word with firm deliverance, annunciating the "S" in case there was any confusion.

He looked up at me. "Then why have you stayed away for so long?" His voice was choked and I felt my own throat close up at the sight of him grasping for any semblance of calm.

We were not calm. This had disaster written all over it.

"Story goes like this," I said very matter of fact. It was the only way to blow through this very uncomfortable situation. "I went to my mom's after I told Johnny to go to hell. I stayed there for a month. I hired a lawyer to handle the band exiting shit. I made a bucket list. I wrote all of the things I always wanted to do as a child and never did."

I pointed at a coffee stained, worn down piece of paper in the middle of the refrigerator. It was the only thing on it. He examined the paper as I continued.

"So I made the list. First off was to buy a Jeep. Always wanted one of those," I laughed at myself. "The second was take residence on an island. I really thought it would be tropical when I first wrote it down.

But here I am!" I looked back to see the list and the first two things were most definitely checked off. More power to me.

"I moved down here. Found this palace. I learned to cook, garden, make coffee mugs," I said pointing to his coffee mug.

"The rest, well, I guess I don't really have any answers. I am officially an island girl year round. I am writing a lot. A memoir about a little girl I once knew and that takes me out of my head. Loves and I play a lot on the beach. Oh and Pierre is teaching me French for a trip to Paris after the leaves fall. I can't stand it when I miss the foliage," I said. That was it. That was my story. I suddenly felt bad for inviting him in. I could have easily just said all that shit back out on the lawn.

He stood up and walked over to the list. At first, I didn't show it to anyone. I was self-conscious about it. It was the only thing that was truly all me. After a few months, I showed it to the girls and now I am pretty sure it is a running joke with the locals. Every time I go into the hardware store or buy something different for the yard, bucket list is said somewhere in the store. The old hags. I let them have their fun.

"Abstinence," he stated. His eyes slowly moved to me. The question was in his eyes. I shrugged.

"Masturbation is quite effective, my friend," I said as I tipped my mug in his direction as to say cheers.

"I. Am. Not. Your. Friend." Brennan's low growl made my heart stop and then it picked up beating faster and faster.

"What about Pierre?" he asked, turning back to the sheet. I rolled my eyes behind him.

"What about Sasha?"

"Hey, I didn't write a bucket list that said I wouldn't have sex for an indefinite amount of time. So, Julia? What about Pierre?" he probed as he moved back to his seat and took a large sip off of his coffee.

"Pierre is Pierre," I said as I lifted one shoulder. "He teaches me French. Oh, and he saved me from the sharks one day. I was trying to teach myself to sail with one of those dummies books."

Brennan started laughing hard as I watched in amusement. I loved to make people happy in my new life. I started to laugh along with him.

"I know, right?" I laughed. "I was such a dumbass that day." I looked up for his response, quickly turning to my left to find him starting to put out his hand to touch my waist. I could see that he wasn't sure that he wanted to touch me. He watched his hand as it was outstretched to me. Would he get stung? Shocked? Would we both explode?

I stepped away. "So, Brennan Curtis. Did I answer all of your questions? See? Jules Delaney, rock goddess, is now a lowly island girl who likes to cook and garden."

I crossed my arms over my tank top, suddenly feeling very naked and violated. Why did he just try to do that? Why would he even think that I would consider it was okay? Why didn't I think it was okay? It actually sounded like a fabulous idea now that I was steps away from him, staring into his soul filled eyes of love, lust, and total pain.

"Do you want me to leave now, Julia?"

The air between us was thick. I could already feel his lips devouring mine. His soft words that I was his and he would only ever love me. He would pick me up and make sweet love to me on this striking Monday morning in my beautiful house.

"I don't think I do. No." I was confused and sad and terrified but I didn't want him to leave me.

"Good. I wouldn't have listened anyway."

His response sent chills up my thighs and I rubbed them hard to get rid of the goose bumps. He watched me. Brennan perused my breasts in my braless tank. He studied my muscular legs. He caught his breath when his eyes found my lips parted as I watched him inspecting me.

He came so close that I could smell the familiar scent. *Him*. It sparked everything. It made me think home and run and love and off limits and love. His chin went to the side of my throat and he tickled my earlobe with his breath.

"I am going to fight for you. *Hard*. I am going to fight to get back in your life so hard that you won't know what hit you. You wrecked me when you walked off two years ago. But I am here. My two arms are going to hold you and they won't let go until one of us is dead." His words were slow and they were beautiful. When he finished, he stayed right next to my ear like he was going to say more. I waited. He didn't say anything so I nodded my head.

"I believe you," I said quietly.

He moved back from me with purpose.

"Well, now that we understand that. I have to get a move on back to Brooklyn. I have lots to do. I will be back in a few days," he said as he went to my cell phone on the nook and typed in a number which turned out to be his from the sudden ringing from his shorts.

I was jumpy so when he moved about the kitchen collecting the mug and putting it in the sink, I followed him on red alert. When he turned back to me, he placed his beautiful soft lips onto my cheek for a long moment. While he kissed me, I felt our sensual passion for one another. It was an incredible kiss.

"I will call you but if I don't, it isn't because I am not thinking of you. It is because I can't stop thinking about you and I will be getting things tied up to come home here to you," he admitted. "I am so in love with you, Julia Delaney. I always will be."

I nodded, totally speechless. When he walked out the door, he gave Loves a quick scratch and told him he would see him soon. My hand went to my cheek and I watched him walk down my lawn and out of sight from my kitchen window.

And, I missed him already.

TWENTY-NINE

I remember as a kid being so excited when I knew someone was coming to visit. I would clean my room so prettily and get out the nice stuffed animals to show off. My aunts, uncles, and their kids were so much fun to have around the house. The silence that took up most nights with just Mom was unbearable sometimes. Our visitors made our house hop. It was fantastic. The crazy critters in my stomach would make me speak in a high pitched voice. I would giggle more. I would jump around the house. When it was time for them to arrive, I would wait outside in the driveway cross legged. I watched every single car drive by.

All those memories of having a visitor rushed back to me as I waited for Brennan to reappear on the island. We got a good amount of rain on Tuesday and Wednesday but I hauled my ass down to the ferry landing anyway in the hopes that I would catch that gorgeous head of black curls.

I imagined the moment he would see me and we would rush into each other's arms. I would show him how I redecorated the kitchen just a little and make something scrumptious to eat. I had lobsters but with each day that went by, I decided to give them to the girls so that they could have a feast.

Joanie opened the door and took in my pitiful look. I hadn't showered that day and I knew I smelled. Joanie and Kelly were slightly hyper-neurotic at self-care. Hell, probably everyone was but these girls had the island capris and polo shirt look down. They always looked so put together. Compared to them, I felt like the homeless little girl begging for food at their door tonight.

"He hasn't called?" she asked me.

I shook my head. "He told me it was because he was getting his life in order to come be with me but what does that even mean? Is he moving here? Is he just fucking with me and letting me hang out to dry like I did to him?" I was whiny. Joanie and Kelly didn't deserve that. They loved me when I was strong. I had to pretend I was strong.

Fuck that.

"You know, I used to call my confidence 'plastic'," I admitted with air quotes around the word plastic.

"I believed that I was a fake. What people saw on the outside was so far from my true inner self. I had such poor self-esteem," I said on a sigh.

"Now? I feel like my confidence is made of thin glass. Thanks so fucking much to Brennan Curtis. He made my confidence turn from steel to glass in one conversation. If I don't get to have him, my glass confidence will shatter and it will make bloody wounds for us all."

Kelly started clapping as she walked down the hall to meet us. She was mocking me for my dramatic soliloquy. She took me in her arms and we hugged for a long while.

"Oh sweetie," she cooed in a comforting way. "That man adores you. He was practically falling over himself when he checked out. He left a suit behind in the room and when I called him, he said to hold on to it. He would be back for it." She gave me a bigger squeeze to reassure me that he will be back.

"I love him, Kel," I whimpered. I don't know why I had the urge to tell them. I just needed them to know that my heart was on the line and I needed them now more than ever.

Joanie was behind her and she nodded with a pouty sad look on her face.

"We know. And we also know you brought us yummy lobsters!" Kelly did a little happy dance as I handed the paper bags over to her.

"They were supposed to be for us," I pouted as I cross my arms over my chest.

"You were going to cook lobsters on his first night back?" Joanie looked horrified. Kelly tapped Joanie on the shoulder before she kissed her cheek.

"Poor girl doesn't know romance, sweetheart," she taunted.

An hour and two bottles of Pink Moscato later, the three of us were doing really good work at cracking into the shells, sucking the juice, and picking meat out of every little piece.

I wiped my hands on a towel when I was done and took a long sip of wine.

"So? I should just chill?" I rhetorically asked the girls.

"You could call him," Joanie said as she lifted one shoulder.

I shook my head vigorously. "If I am totally right about him punking me, I am going to stay far away from a situation that could make me feel worse. Jesus, I could call and Sasha might answer the phone," I groaned.

"Sasha is the blond girl he was with, right?" Kelly asked with a smile.

"Yep, long beautiful legs," I answered, staring out into space as I took another sip from the wine glass. All I got was air. Joanie was right there with a refill.

"Darling, that girl was no one. She was here for some wedding and he was her date. When she checked out Sunday morning, she didn't look very pleased that he wasn't going with her." Joanie looked at me and her eyebrows lifted in a knowing expression.

"He dumped her?" I asked belligerently.

"Who says dumped anymore? What are you? Twelve?" Kelly scoffed.

"Ok, ok. He broke it off then?" I asked seriously.

Both nodded, looked at each other, looked back at me and nodded again.

"Oh yeah. She told us to put the bill on the ass face that she came with. Five minutes later he came down to ask if he could have the room for another night." Kelly was near doubling over as Joanie was stone cold serious. It was obvious who wore the pants. Joanie was stoic, broad, and had an edge. Kelly was all flair and emotions.

"Holy shit," I muttered. "He didn't even know where I lived yet." I looked down at my flip flops and wondered when he came out and asked.

"Well, not until I told him about thirty five seconds later. That was the next question out of his mouth," Kelly laughingly replied.

"Ugh," I groaned as I put my head in my hands. I was hopeless. This whole waiting around bullshit was for the birds. Immediately, I knew what it felt like to know nothing.

Oh. My. God. Two years of feeling like this? How could he ever forgive me? I promised myself then and there that I would contact people I really, truly cared about in the future. I would be a better communicator or whatever. I would keep in touch.

'*Ok, promise done. Brennan, come back to me,*' I thought.

I left the girls' bed and breakfast with a little drunk on. I sang Coldplay's *Speed of Sound* in a deep, raspy voice, which didn't match Chris Martin's version at all. I still tried all the way back to my house. When I got there, Loves wasn't barking. That was not like him. I called out his name but still nothing.

I went up through the back door and started flipping on lights everywhere. When I made to the great room, there were piles of boxes and shit everywhere. In the middle of that was the couch. On the couch was Brennan and Loves cuddled up with one another, sleeping. My heart dropped to the floor. He moved in with me. He was here. This was *really* happening.

I walked quietly out of the room to try to catch my breath because I seriously was going to start bawling.

"Julia?" Brennan called out to me. Loves lifted his head, sighed, and put it back down on Brennan's thigh. "Was that you I heard singing? What was it? Coldplay?"

"Hey you," I said with a grin. "I was trying my vocals out on the road. It's been a while. Better than that, it looks like someone moved in?" I took a look at all of the boxes again and looked back at him with a smile.

"You okay with that?" he asked. He didn't sound too concerned. He just sounded tired. "Will you be singing again sometime soon? I miss your voice."

"I am going to say yes and tell the rest of my doubts to go to hell," I replied with a smile. "It was nice to come home and find you here."

Brennan chuckled. He turned totally over on the couch and put his hands under his cheek to look at me. I sat down on the floor right in front of him and took a lock of his hair and pushed it back. It fell right back so I did it again. And again.

He watched me as I played against the hair odds and smiled. He was happy.

"I missed you," I whispered as I leaned in. I brushed my lips against his. He didn't move at all. He just let me kiss his lips, his cheek, and his forehead. After a while, I just leaned my forehead on his and sighed.

"You are here," I whispered, one small tear coming out of my eye.

"Nowhere else," he whispered back.

THIRTY

Loves did not like to be kicked off the couch or my bed. It was actually unheard of since we were the only duo. When Brennan pulled me up on to the couch so that I could lay across his body, Loves got pissed when I kicked him in the face. He nearly growled at me when he refused to move so I could straddle Brennan. It took a lot of coaxing to get him off the couch and when he finally did get down, he just laid at our feet on the floor.

"Loves is the best dog. It makes me happy that he was here with you this whole time," Brennan said as he started to rub my back.

"He really is the best dog," I replied. I couldn't move. I was glued to Brennan Curtis for always. I didn't want to change this position forever. And ever.

"Where were you tonight?" he asked as he started to play with the end of my ponytail.

"At Kelly and Joanie's. I bought lobster. For us. I mean I bought lobster to eat with you but I didn't know when you'd get here. I think they were on their last leg outside of a tank," I said.

"I'm sorry I didn't get here yesterday. I was all set to go and then my mover flaked out so I had to hire someone else and pay out the ass for the short notice."

"Was it very much? I can pay," I said worriedly. This was all so bizarre. I felt like a totally different woman from when I saw him last. I was concerned that the guy that just ambushed my living space didn't have to pay for his own moving costs. I let out a loud laugh and it startled both Brennan and Loves.

"Julia, you are not paying for one thing. I have money and I am here now. I feel absolutely complete."

The left side of my mouth came up in a smile and he gazed at it for a long moment. I could definitely get used to this.

"Which room is mine? I was going to just start loading my stuff into the room all the way in the second back hallway but it looked like you have a project going on in there," he asked, drawing me out of my love sick haze.

Uh... huh? Was he serious? What room? He wanted his own room? Why?

"Um... my bedroom is the second door in the first hallway. The one with the master suite bathroom?"

"Yes," he said slowly. "But I thought we would take this whole abstinence thing to the next level, maybe live together, and date for a while before I take your virginity all over again." He was laughing underneath me but I wasn't. I felt depraved and sad. I didn't know where that was coming from. It felt like he was dismissing the fact that I had waited because I wanted to be in love. He already had that. My love could be written out in the sky at no embarrassment to me and he wanted to sleep in separate beds. I felt like a child.

I got up quickly and started towards the kitchen for a drink of water. He was here. The wait was over and God, I was deflated. I was officially a fizzled out balloon.

"Julia? Julia. What's up? Did I say something? I wasn't trying to make fun of you being abstinent. I think it is very honorable and very unlike the Julia I knew. Shit... that came out wrong, too. See? I don't know who you are. I just upended my whole life to be with the woman I can't get out of my soul and I am verbally vomiting all over her," he said as he threaded his hands through his hair.

I looked at him over the top of my water glass and thought, *"Damn you can verbally vomit on any body part of me you want to."*

"It's okay," I assured him with a small smile. "I am just tired. Sure, you can take whatever room you want. I have questions about the life you..." I stopped when I noticed his other arm had something written on it. He had gotten another tattoo. It was inside his forearm so there was no way I could see it if he had it tucked in or under a long shirt.

I saw the letter J and my heart skipped. I walked over and grabbed his arm. My whole chest caved in when I read the words, "My Julia" in beautiful scrolled ink. He had them work lace into the edges of my name. Some letters were bleeding, some had stiches added to it, and the others were hollowed out like it wasn't finished. I knew it was. He was describing me. How he saw me. Nonetheless, the word "my" was so strong and fierce. He would take ownership of the whole girl, bruised, bleeding, hollowed out, and sewn up to heal.

I didn't realize I was full out crying until he reached under my arms and lifted me onto the breakfast nook. "It's okay, love. It's okay. I needed to get this. I needed you so badly after you left and as I went through the divorce and selling off my share of the business to my ex, I felt so alone. This was something I did to keep my mind off of everything I lost."

"But I am the one broken and bleeding on your arm," I retorted trying to stop crying.

"No. I couldn't even say your fucking name. It hurt that much. I had them portray what I felt about you. Seeing your name there, it helped me to move on, I guess. Shit, I don't know. We were always so fucked up. Our timing. Everything. I thought that if I read your name enough, the pain of saying it wouldn't hurt as bad."

"Did it work?" I looked up at him.

"It didn't work until three days ago, when I said it in this kitchen. It was a beautiful sound. Julia. *My Julia*," he said with a sheepish smile.

"You left that in your letter. You ended it with 'Your Julia'."

I remembered that I wrote that because I knew he was the one, but not the one I could have. I would always be his but I didn't know if he would always be mine.

"So no more wife? No more business?" I asked, trying to seriously tamp down the tears. Moving on to the facts.

I watched the tattoo with rapt attention as he told me that Amelia got most of everything in the divorce but he didn't care. He had started a new graphics company and was using his studio apartment as a work office.

"Can you work from here?" I asked.

He nodded. "Hopefully in a room separate from where my bed is so I can actually separate the two. Work is all I do. I met Sasha when she had me create a logo for her salon," he laughed. "She is a trip."

"Yeah? She is beautiful." I couldn't be jealous. I couldn't be unfair.

"Yes. She is, but not as stunningly, sexy, and gorgeous as you," he said, as he watched my eyes flick his down to his lips. He wrapped his arms around my waist more and tilted his head in to kiss my neck. He suckled and licked. He teased my earlobe the way I loved. He remembered how to hold my thighs and rub his thumbs up and down. I always went a little crazy at that small gesture.

When his lips finally found mine, I moved with force. I wrapped my arms, legs, and being all around Brennan. I pulled him closer. I needed him as close as possible. I felt his response to me as he rubbed up and down my body with his. Our tongues were so entangled I wasn't sure how they would ever come apart.

But they did.

And our heaving bodies separated, too. It was too fast, he said with his eyes. I told him that is was okay back with mine. We smiled at our nonverbal communication and he reached out his hand to grab mine.

"Show us to our bedroom, Baby. I want to cuddle," he said.

I stopped short of his use of the word baby, remembering the hotel hall and how he had called *her* baby.

"What is it?" he asked, looking alarmed.

"You called me baby," I said. "If you call me baby, you never ever call another woman baby ever again. Do you understand me?"

He closed his eyes and I saw the moment he remembered that night. He looked at me wide eyed.

"Julia. *Baby.* You were the *only* one. *All along.* I was too stupid and I kick myself every day. I kick myself for falling asleep on you that night. If I had stayed awake, you wouldn't have disappeared. You will always be the only one. The next time I call anyone else baby, it will be because an actual baby will be growing in that beautiful stomach of yours."

"Uh... what?" I asked, totally mind fucked.

He laughed so hard that he doubled over and I smiled at his lightheartedness. He was so endearing and so fucking sexy. And he wanted to have babies with me? It sent a warm flush through my face. Instead of reacting outwardly, I just pretended he didn't say anything about babies because, yeah, that was taking things way too fast for night one.

THIRTY-ONE

<u>BRENNAN</u>

I never thought I would see Julia again. When I saw her on the ferry landing, I couldn't believe my eyes. She looked ten years younger than she did the last time I saw her–the night that I made sweet love to her and mentally begged her to be with me forever. She wasn't wearing her signature eyeliner. She didn't have that permanent scowl on her face. God knows I loved that scowl but the serene look on her was so much more... it was just so much more. I was star struck and it wasn't because she was a rock star legend. Yes, the music community has paid special homage to her since she disappeared.

No, I was star struck because she was the famous person in *my* life. She was the woman I looked for in every crowd, every magazine, and any time I was on the internet. I tried typing in any name possible that she could have used as an alias. All that time I was looking diligently and she was within a fucking car and ferry ride away. I wanted to kneel at her feet. I wanted to ask to kiss her. It wasn't until Sasha brought me out of my reverie that I realized that I also had anger. I was so terribly pissed at her. And who the hell was the guy? Sure I had moved on to a point but I never thought she would trust another man... *ever*.

We were lying in bed with Loves at our feet and I kissed her hair. I sent up a grateful prayer to the universe. I had my girl back and I was never letting her go.

"Can I ask you some questions?" I asked into her hair.

She was so damn warm. Even though we did nothing but kiss last night, I knew that I was going to marry this girl and fill her tummy with babies. She was mine. I heard a muffled agreement into my bare chest. I knew she was just as overwhelmed as I was. We were soaking in each other.

"What happened with Johnny and the band?"

"Hmm... well, I hired that lawyer and told my family if anyone ever said where I was, I would disown them. They took that threat pretty seriously. I really haven't watched what happened. I know they have a new lead singer and he is amazing. I never talked to Johnny after that night," she said. I could hear a tint of sadness in her words. She missed it.

"Do you miss the stage?" I asked as I rubbed my hand along her bare back.

"I do, sometimes. But Bren, I love island life. It is so simple. I feel alive again. I am having so much fun. I don't have to work but when I get the need to be productive, I will either work on the house, or go help the girls, or hang out with Pierre." She started to get up off my chest and I pulled her back down.

"Don't you dare separate your amazing body from mine right now," I scolded.

"Do you miss open marriages and Anne?" Her tone was serious–her body stiff as a board. Oh hell. I knew she would say something about Anne. I did have it coming to me.

"No. That life style is not for me and Anne never, ever crosses my mind unless my girl brings her up to taunt me." I smiled wide at Julia and pinched her unbelievably, sexy ass.

She laughed as she put her lips on to mine. We were instantly in a teenage make out session. I felt her beautiful breasts and loved that she was squirming for me to get closer. She was ready but I knew her bucket list got her to where she was today and I wasn't going to be the one fucking with that.

Three hours later, we headed to the kitchen. Although it was three in the afternoon, Julia made us a big breakfast with the best coffee ever. A loud knock came to the side door and I inched my eyebrows over my coffee mug to her.

Julia shrugged and yelled, "Come in!"

Pierre walked into the kitchen with a bright smile until he took in our half naked selves. Julia was wearing my tee shirt from last night and maybe panties? I was bare-chested.

"Jules. I am so sorry. I didn't know you had company. I can come back later?" Pierre said in a Parisian accent. *Poor guy. I got her, dude. She is all mine.*

"Don't be silly, Pierre. Brennan is living with me, well I guess we live together," she looked over to me perplexed.

"Yes, this is our place," I concurred. I got up and handed out my hand. "Hey, I am Brennan. I hear you have been giving my girl some French lessons." That sounded really bad but whatever.

Julia laughed. "Sit down, Pierre. We have more waffles and coffee."

Dammit, no. I wanted her all by myself today.

"Okay. I can stay for a little bit. It smells so good, as usual." Pierre's dig did not go unnoticed by me.

Julia simply smiled at him with a knowing look. "You working on the docks today?" she asked as she started his plate.

"Yes. I wanted you to come down and help. I know how much you love to scrub boats." Another dig. Good one dude but I have licked every inch of her body. No one has shit on that.

"Oh that does sound like fun. Brennan, do you want to set up your office while I go work down on the boats?" She looked so fucking adorable. I just wanted to take her back to bed and... what was she asking me?

No. Fuck no! I didn't want her to leave. That was a craptastic idea. Stupid. I barely made out a forced smile before she noticed I had stiffened. She understood.

"Pierre, Brennan and I have a lot of house shit to do today. Désolé, Pierre," she said with a sad smile.

"Julia, don't be silly. Go. Have fun." I was not going to keep her from friends. This was her world and I was not going to interrupt it. I would just find a way in to be a part of all. "Leave Loves with me. We will go explore the beach when I am done setting up the desk."

She came over and kissed me soundly on the lips. As she pulled away I heard her say thank you. I shook my head and gave her an adoring smile.

"Is there an extra desk around?" I asked.

"Yes," she replied enthusiastically. "It's a good one for your business. I will leave a list of all of our information so you can update everything. And you can explore the rooms to find it and your new office," she said with a smirk. "Be right back. I am going to put on some clothes." She squeezed my shoulder on her way out. We couldn't keep our hands off of each other.

Pierre and I stared at each other like two little kids that were set up on a playdate without our permission. It was like a visual swordfight at dawn. Thankfully, he broke the silence first.

"I haven't known Jules for very long. I suppose I have a bit of a crush on her but she has never wanted anything from me. I see now that it was because of you? I didn't even know a man existed in her life?" He inquired. The guy seemed sincere and damn, he was honest about his feelings towards her. I imagined French people were just straight shooters. Nothing was getting past this guy.

I nodded firmly. What else could I do? I was her man. I was in her life. She was mine.

"Well, I know that she is a very talented and beautiful woman. If you break her heart, I can't beat the shit out of you because of this... that is not in my nature. But I assure you, Mr. Curtis that I will be there to pick up the pieces." His words were not delivered with a threatening tone but a promising one. He was telling me that he was remaining in Julia's life and that he would even wait for me to fuck up. Poor guy didn't even know that I had fucked up in all definitions of the words.

What I wanted to say was that he had no clue, that we had a long and seriously heart gripping past that had us both doubt ourselves, other people, and essentially the meaning of life itself. I wished to admit to this shithead that I saw a therapist for weeks just to figure out how I had gone wrong with Julia. I went to Mr. Grimes every single day for an hour to yell, cry, fight, and some days just numb out. I came out of those sessions admitting that Julia hadn't left me per se but that Julia left to take care of Julia.

I respected her choice and that outcome until I saw her again. In that moment, I respected nothing. All those sessions were for nothing. I would not let her go ever again. *Never.* I was in her home now. I was taking care of Julia in life, in her heart, and her bed. I wanted to tell him I prayed to see her gorgeous face in real life every night for nearly two years. I wanted to say that I was mind fucked numb for days after I finally saw her again.

"Thank you for being such a good friend, Pierre. I hope I have the chance to know you, as well. You are obviously very special to Julia," I admitted instead.

He curtly nodded his head and his smile widened as he looked behind me. I turned to find Julia in pig tails, a tank top with Vineyard written across it, and the shortest jean shorts in the history of short jean shorts. I could probably see her vagina if I looked close enough.

I cleared my throat. "A bit short on the shorts?" I probed before I could stop myself. The girl had to know that they were highly inappropriate for a friend outing. Julia giggled at me good naturedly. Yes, she was definitely a new girl. Before she would have scowled and told me to shut the fuck up. Instead, she came and wrapped her arms around me.

"Yes and when I get back, they are coming off, too," she whispered in my ear. I went instantly hard. Damn. I mentally told her that what she just did was so not cool, as I flicked my eyes over to the list on the refrigerator.

Abstinence. Julia understood and sighed as she warmly placed her lips onto mine for a quick smooch.

Smooching with Julia was like catching a falling star. It still felt surreal and I rejoiced in each and every one.

When Pierre and Julia left, I took a hot shower and thought about that what she had whispered in my ear until I was relieved of the tension she had left me with.

I spent a solid hour in my new spacious office. Julia wasn't kidding when she said the desk would be perfect. It was a designer's dream desk. I laid out all of my work stuff and hung a calendar with my upcoming projects. I set up my computer and my laptop. I took out a picture of me and my parents and thought about when I would be able to place a framed photo of Julia and me on my desk. I remembered her laughing face as she goaded me and I missed her already. *Damn Pierre. Cock blocker.*

To excuse myself from those thoughts, I sent a mass email out to everyone with my change of address and new phone number. Once I felt like all the emails and current office was in good shape, I nudged Loves, who had propped himself under my desk.

"Let's go the beach, buddy," I said.

Loves was in the kitchen, waiting with a stick and a tennis ball in his mouth when I made it out there five minutes later. Julia and Loves. They knew what they wanted and they weren't afraid to ask for it.

I laughed as I opened the door to the glorious island day.

THIRTY-TWO

<u>JULES</u>

Pierre totally surprised me when he came into the kitchen and saw us half naked. I thought he would run out screaming and/or crying but he remained pretty cool. He took in Brennan's and my appearance with grace. I identified that Brennan was uncomfortable with me leaving. He wanted me to stay and play house and so did I. Conversely, I felt gratitude for the man that had been clearly pining for me since the day he rescued me from my wrecked sailboat.

"No French today, ok?" I stated rather than asked. The only thing French I wanted was a kiss from Brennan. It was official. I was a sappy cheese ball.

Pierre laughed. "OK, no French. Let's just wash the boats and you can tell me about Brennan. He is... a surprise, no?"

That seemed like a fair enough lead in. It was probably killing him since he walked in to the house. Pierre probably wanted to know if Brennan was a full time live in lover or if he would be booted out the next day. His reappearance in my life was out of the blue for me, as well.

Maybe talking to him would firm up what I was feeling which was terribly nervous. Brennan and I did not have a good track record and our past pulled me into thinking that this may not work out... *again*. Maybe talking to someone about where we were headed would help me figure it out, too. I started to explain how we met and our instant attraction. I talked about the open marriage and Johnny. I talked about poor timing and his way of shattering something in me that I hadn't felt with anyone... ever. I saw him flinch when I said that and mentally kicked myself for being such a heartless bitch.

"Yes, I admit I did know who you were, Jules," he stated. That was so far from what I cared about in that moment that I just nodded. I already knew I was the lead singer of Love Sick Ponies. It was how he responded to it that made me like him more. I wasn't a celebrity. Pierre liked me for the girl that I had become on the island. The girl with the bucket list.

"That's cool. I figured you did but it was so nice of you not to say anything. You made it feel... I felt normal for once," I appreciatively responded as I grinned at him. His answering smile was so heartwarming but it wasn't all there. He was hiding something from me. Perhaps I had really hurt him with Brennan being there but he had to understand that I had never felt anything for anyone like I did for Brennan. I truly believed, especially after vomiting out the whole story that he was meant for me.

It was a slightly windy day on the island which made the docks a bit harder to walk on. My sea legs instantly found the board of the dock and I watched the sailboats and motor boats start to head out for the day. I needed to buy another boat. How I would love to lay on the bow and sip wine with Brennan on a stunning day like today.

When we were down at the docks, he showed me the two boats that needed the most cleaning. I noticed that a lot of people were off their boats. They were most likely perusing the town. It was a beautiful day. I took his bucket of water and the hose. Someone called Pierre's name from down the dock and he excused himself while I got to work on the first boat.

Pierre took care of most boats as they came in to dock. I was pretty sure that was how he made money to stay here. I had never visited his place and that was my choice. He had asked me several times but I never felt comfortable enough to go. Call it instinct or just call it that I didn't want to give off "love vibes."

I was just about to start with the hose on the bow of the boat that I had already soaped up when a loud song started to play. I froze. I hadn't heard that song in years. *I Sang for You* was taunting me in a boat not far from me. Did someone recognize me and they were playing some kind of joke? My heart restarted when I noticed that it abruptly stopped. I started the hose and tried to focus on my task when that fucking song started again. This time my feet were on fire. I needed to go shut the fucking music off. It wasn't until I followed the music that I noticed that the song skipped a few verses. It was someone's ring tone on their cell. I followed it three boats down from where I was working and realized that it had stopped again.

I ducked my head into the cabin and yelled out for permission to come aboard, something that Pierre insisted I use anytime I was on the docks. With no answer, I heard the Love Sick Ponies and my voice start to ring through again. I stumbled in towards the kitchen table and found the sickening culprit. I nearly lost my balance when I saw that the display read "Johnny Lennox". Who's fucking boat was this? *Holy shit.* What the fuck was going on? Johnny. Johnny was this one phone call away. He was calling this boat on this dock in this town on my island. How?

With shaking fingers, I pressed answer.

"Hello Johnny," I said in a surprising solid and cool voice.

"Who is this? I need Mark." His reply was irritated and unpleasant. I cringed at his brazenness and tried to figure out who the fuck Mark was. I mentally went through all the people I had met this summer and Mark was not a name I remembered.

"Mark who?" I questioned in a crossed tone.

"Wait, who the fuck is this?" Johnny spat out.

"Oh you would probably remember me as your ticket to fame," I answered in a taunting asshole voice.

The phone went dead. He fucking hung up on me. Coward.

I looked around the area for any clue who the person was that owned this boat when I saw it. I stopped still and my heart was dying. I was dying. This was it.

The OUIJA Board. *THE* very one with my initials lay out on the boat couch. It was in perfect shape. I went to touch it when a male cleared his voice behind me. I slowly turned around to see Pierre looking back at me. He looked at the OUIJA board with a smile.

"Do you know whose boat this is?" I asked in a scattered rush of words.

Pierre's perplexed look told me he didn't. He shrugged it off. He was casual but something was definitely off with him. He wasn't giving me the adoring looks I had grown accustomed to.

"Jules, you have to ask for permission to come aboard." His voice was fatherly, scolding the little child that had trudged mud into the house from the outside. Or that was what I imagined a father would sound like. I never allowed anyone to speak to me in that tone of voice.

Not since Johnny.

"I know, I know. But I heard the phone... and... " I stopped myself. That is when it hit me. Pierre was Mark. This boat was his. That phone was his. He was friends with Johnny.

"Are you Mark?" I accused him. I watched his eyes for any hint of fallacies. His body tensed just the tiniest bit as his eyes shifted to the cell phone on the kitchen table.

"No, I am Pierre," he said with his normal sexy smile. I would have believed him except his fucking French accent was gone. He didn't even notice since he started to grab my hand to bring me back out to the docks. I flinched away from him.

"Where is your fake fucking accent, Pierre? And while we are at it, how long have you been working for Johnny?" I demanded.

I was shaking now. I needed Brennan. Why the fuck had I come with Pierre? I should have stayed with him and now... Oh my God, Johnny knows where I live. He will know everything. He probably already knows everything. I was duped.

"Mr. Lennox is a client of mine. I was sent here to watch over you. He was just making sure you were doing okay since you left without word," he answered in a tone meant to calm an agitated animal. Again, Pierre... Mark started to move closer to me. I backed up and tried to find anyway to escape his grasp.

"Bullshit!" I spat out. "Johnny is completely aware that I left *with* word. I believe my last words to him were fuck and off."

"Okay then, Jules. His other message is that he would like you to know that Grace came back to him while you have been gone. He says that you really are a slut and that board doesn't lie. I even tried it out," he confirmed with an adoring look at the board. "No matter who you have fooled here on this island, you can't untie yourself from that little wonderful quality of yours."

The fucker was on top of me in two seconds. I actually had counted them as it was my new method of calming my body and brain in tricky situations. This qualified as a fucking tricky and freaky and fucking awful situation. His hands went straight to the short shorts that Brennan had told me not to wear and where he started to assault me with vigor. His hands and fingers gave new meaning to grabby hands. It was disgusting and repulsive.

I screamed... loud. He blanched at me before he slapped me clear across the face.

"Come on Julia, you know you want it. You want me. Johnny tells me you are an easy lay but you have made me work for it," Pierre... *fuck*, Mark hissed out. His hot breath on my upper chest made me cringe. If he kept up with the French accent, I may have been a little nicer to the guy but I was one hundred shades of pissed off.

I let him do his thing for a few moments while I thought of the moves I had learned in self-defense class. Bucket list. Check. I wondered if he had been following me back then, too. Fuck it. I was doing this and getting the hell off of this boat, away from Pierre, that stupid OUIJA board and the song that started to play on the cell phone once again. Johnny. I needed to run far from Johnny.

With a two finger jab at his eyes and a swift kick to his nuts, I watched Pierre or Mark or whoever the fuck he was fall down in one swift thud. I high tailed it out of there but not before grabbing his phone. I got to the end of the dock before I called the Island Police and told them Pierre had attempted rape. I told the woman as I started to cry that I needed to go home. They could and would find Mark on his boat or near the docks by either land or water. The female police officer was blatantly adamant that I was to go directly to the station or find a safe place nearby for the police to question me. I snapped that I was going home and again told her that they could find me there. I needed Brennan. As I hung up I realized that there wasn't any DNA to make the accusation stick but at least we would all find out what Pierre's real identity was.

When I got to the house, Brennan and Loves were both gone. Fuck, he said he was going to the beach. I went to the last back bedroom and locked the door. I sat in the corner and went through Mark's phone. There were thousands of pictures of me. I was eating at my kitchen nook. I was smiling with Kelly. I was tossing the ball at Loves on the beach. I was taking a shower? I immediately went to hit delete but thought better of it. The more sick photos on his phone, the easier a restraining order would be made on him.

Emails and texts sent back and forth to Johnny showed that Johnny was planning his trip to the Vineyard within the very next week. He was obviously livid that Brennan was back in town. There were even photos of Brennan at that wedding with Sasha. She was looking up at him. He was wearing a suit. He looked stunning but his face? He was obviously lost and not returning any of Sasha's smiles. He looked downright miserable and a small smile crept on to my face. Brennan loved me.

Pictures don't lie. That was the only lesson that my absent father ever taught me. I will never forget that day. The one day that my father gave five solid minutes to me and me alone. I snapped out of my reverie about my father and looked at the next fifty photos of Brennan. Why the hell were there photos of him, too?

I thought about the OUIJA Board. Johnny had claimed that he had gone out that night at my brother's and tossed it. I never did see the board again but he could have hidden it in his bag or his suitcase that weekend. Why would he have kept it? Why did he lie to both Kent and me that it was gone for good? Was it the OUIJA board that finally brought him to the realization to monitor me? Why did Johnny want me followed? What did he have to gain from doing this to me?

I heard the loud obnoxious knocking on my front door. It was the tell-tale signal of a police officer. I swear they had a class about how loud to pound on people's doors.

I jumped up, unlocked the door, and rushed down the hallway to look out the window. I saw the three island cruisers in my driveway and sighed a breath of relief. I opened the door to my preferred policeman, Officer McMains.

Mitchell McMains and I got to know each other over coffee down at the landing one morning last winter. I remembered it was freezing and he asked if I wanted to watch the water from inside the cruiser. Winter views of the ocean are extraordinary. Two hours later and we were best pals. I went to him whenever I had an issue with people not picking up their dog's shit on the beach. He would laugh and hand me a donut to appease me. It always worked.

"Jules, you poor girl. We got Mark Drury down at the docks. He was trying to untie the ropes when we got to him. He is not a happy camper right now. Did you know that he is a private investigator?" the older white haired man remarked. I hugged against his tensed up frame and brought him to the kitchen. I dished out a piece of banana bread and poured him some coffee.

"Not a Frenchman, I take it?" I scowled. Officer McMains chuckled around the bread. He shook his head and rolled his eyes.

"When they are done processing him and getting his statement, he will be escorted off the island with a 'no return' invitation." His stern voice was nice but it didn't convince me in the slightest.

I sighed. "Is that enough? I mean I don't want to press charges but what if he comes back?" I objected. A bunch of crackling and thrashing came from the side door and I looked away from McMains to see what the commotion was about.

Loves and Brennan broke through the screen door with enthusiasm and Officer McMains' hand went to his gun. When he saw Loves, he instantly set his hand away and went back to eating his bread unaffected.

"Julia, what is going on?" Brennan came over to me and inspected my body.

"Pierre is not Pierre. He is a fucking PI for douchebag Johnny. He has been following me for months. Brennan, Johnny knows exactly where I am and he is... like I think he is psychotic," I said a little more panicked as each word came out.

Brennan's jaw had dropped very low. He pulled me in for a hug. "We will do whatever it takes to fix this. You are not in harm's way. You are protected here with me. I will not let anything happen to you, Julia."

"That's right," Officer McMains said as he stood up from his plate and grabbed his police hat. "We have video surveillance on the Ferry landing. We will put his and this Johnny person's face on the monitors with the others that are not welcome."

Brennan and Officer McMains spoke more about what they could do while I spaced out. I was as flabbergasted as to why Johnny cared so much. He did sound like he was on something again. Maybe drugs and the tour pressure were getting to him. Did he really miss me that much to hire Mr. French Creeper? Why did it matter if Brennan was here? Why did Johnny still care after all of this time? No matter the answers, he was acting extreme and for the first time in years, I didn't feel safe and it didn't matter how much security there was.

I didn't realize how much time had passed until McMains and Brennan shook hands and promised to be in touch with each other the next day to work on their idea for more security. Brennan folded two pages of notes that he had been writing while talking to the officer. I looked down at my hands and noticed they were shaking. I hardly heard my voice when I said goodbye to my favorite police officer.

THIRTY-THREE

BRENNAN

Julia and I didn't sleep much that night. I felt her shaking and Loves could tell she wasn't good either. I tried to get her to talk but I think she just wanted time to think. I rubbed her back and her shoulders for hours. I told her how much I loved her and I would protect her forever.

Sometime during the night, she left the bedroom with Loves on her heels. I didn't follow. She hadn't asked but, God damn, I wanted to know what was going through that beautiful brain of hers. Minutes later, she came back with two sheets of paper and two pens. I noticed one of them was her bucket list.

I sat up and turned on the side light.

"What is it?" I asked.

She scratched out one thing on her bucket list and I watched as she wrote "finished" across the list. She handed it to me with the most amazing smile I had ever seen. My anxiety dissolved and I looked down at the sheet. She had crossed abstinence off of her list. Did this mean? Was she? I looked up to her and she nodded in confirmation.

There were still items on the list that obviously weren't done. Go to Paris. Write a book. Learn to make dough boys. I pointed to them and raised my eyebrows in question.

"This is a new bucket list. This is Jules and Brennan's bucket list. We are one now. Let's make a list. It really helps keep your mind off the stupid shit in the world," she said as she started to write out the title and the date.

I laughed when I saw she had written "Have loads of orgasms together".

"This is really one that will never be checked off," she laughed the sweetest belly laugh.

She handed me the pen and as I took it, I started to feel uneasy. Would she like what I really desired to put on the list? I was terrified but if we were going to be one now, she had to see my expectations.

I carved "#2: Get Married" on the paper. I made it clearly confirmed so that if people found it in a hundred years, they would consider it factual evidence that we were in love. I didn't look at her while I handed back the very special document. I could feel the blast of warmth in my face and my heart was pounding so hard. She didn't gasp or yell but started to write hers. She passed it back to me with just as much special caution.

She squiggled a smiley face next to my number two and then wrote "#3: Have a baby or two?" I was so thankful and felt the immense smile on my face. Yes. We were there. We were doing this. We were in this together. I regarded her and her eyes were bursting with tears. God, in that moment, I would do anything to take any disbelief out of her mind. So I pacified the moment the greatest way I could.

I crossed out her "two" and "the question mark" and changed it to "three" so it read "Have a baby or three." I followed up with "#4: Julia will publish book"

"Hell yeah!" she exclaimed as she read my bucket list item. Loves considered Julia and then sighed. I was getting the impression that he dealt with her outbursts frequently.

We continued our bucket list for an hour before she took it, dropped it on the floor, and then threw her whole body on mine. We were naked in record time. She played with me while I stroked her. When I finally pushed into her without any protection, both of our eyes went wide as we melted into each other.

"We love each other," I said. I then yelled it. I yelled so loud and she joined in. It was so fucking liberating. I pumped into her and we moaned together over and over.

We had number one checked off... for that night anyway.

The next morning, I went to my office and started to make calls about our own personal security cameras. I wanted the shots of the Ferry landing, too. I wasn't letting anything happen to my new family. Julia wandered in and I minimized the screen.

"No lies, Bren," she said. "No secrets."

"I want cameras," I said firmly.

She nodded and came over to sit on my lap. She had a mug of coffee that I immediately rescued from her hands. I kissed her on the cheek as she clicked the browser back on.

"Where we get to watch the fun from? Shit, now I don't have to go down there to make fun of people," she said. She was smiling and laughing until she thought of something and her face went slack.

"What is it?" I asked.

"Pierre... Mark... Whoever he was. That's what we used to do. We would go to the landing and make fun. He was such a great friend. I just can't believe it. I can't believe I won't see him. He never existed. It is so fucking weird. Creeps me out," she said on a shiver.

"Well, I like making fun of people. I will be your new French tutor," I taunted with my eyebrows waggling.

She pushed the curls out of my face. She grabbed the beanie off my desk and put it on her head.

"Nah, I am going to cancel Paris. I really liked the idea of publishing that book. It is going to be about the murder of that girl that came through the OUIJA board," she said out into space.

"Whatever you want. I will do whatever you want. I do have some jobs to get through this summer but the fall looks open. Let's plan a trip somewhere, okay?" I asked with hope.

She nodded and slowly kissed my lips. I put my hand on the back of her head where my beanie met her hair and got aroused all over again. She placed the coffee onto the desk and then straddled me in the chair. Within minutes we were panting out each other's names and I screamed so loud. It felt so good to love this woman in my office in our home. It was one of those moments that I realized that despite the past and its awful, painful memories, I was content. We were moving forward. Julia amazed me more now than ever before.

When she got up and off of me, she slithered her panties back on and declared more coffee. I sat there in paradise long after she left the room. I went back to looking for camera systems while I kept myself out in case of a repeat performance.

She didn't come back. An hour later, I found her out in the garden. She was humming and Loves was lying in the sun next to her. I got down on my knees and pulled her to my body.

"Well, hello there my beautiful man," she said.

I was so God damn lucky. Yes, Julia, I am *your* man.

"Hey," I said, a little hoarse. "I am going into town for some things. How about I make you dinner tonight?"

She gave me a look that said I didn't know how to cook and my look back said you want to make a bet?

"Ten dollars," she stated without emotion.

"You are on," I retorted and kissed her nose as I got up to head into town.

I went to the only jeweler in town. A nice looking woman saw me come in and I noticed her once over of my body. Sure, I might be a bit on the good looking side but my days of entertaining women were over. Open relationships were a joke. I had learned in therapy that Amelia had done a number on me. Several numbers, actually. She ran my life and the moment I caught a whiff of the air outside of her imprisoned walls, I started to see more clearly.

"Hello, what can I help you with today?" she asked in a seductively low voice. I smiled at her. Dimples and all. I wanted a good deal.

"Engagement ring, please. Large," I said, pointing down at the glass cases of jewelry. It took her a moment for my words to register but she recovered quickly. I wondered if she knew Julia. She would be laughing her ass of at this woman right now.

"Of course. We have sets over here and we also have an onsite custom jeweler if you want to go with something of your own design," she said, much more professional now.

I shook my head. The engagement ring was for the moment I asked Julia to be my wife and my only lover forever. However, our rings would be permanently inked onto our fingers on the day of our wedding. It would most likely be her first and last tattoo. I laughed at the look she probably would have sitting in the chair. Poor girl and it was going to hurt like a bitch.

"Just your largest square cut," I said in a decided tone.

"Largest?" she questioned in amazement.

I nodded and started to pull out my credit card. Money was no object when it came to Julia. I would offer to buy half the house that I knew she already owned out right but it would all become ours anyway.

"Is eight carats okay? Oh, and don't you need it sized?" she asked, looking at my credit card with a perplexed expression.

"They are all sixes, right? That is standard?" God, I hated the fact that I knew this. This was to be my first marriage. Amelia didn't count anymore.

"Yes, that's right," she answered.

"Well, it turns out my girl's left ring finger is a size six, so wrap it up," I said.

Ten minutes later, I had the ring. I got a chill as I walked out of the jewelry store. I felt like someone was watching me. It was an odd feeling and as I made my way to the market, I couldn't help feeling like I was being followed.

After a beautiful dinner that I prepared, Julia handed over the ten dollar bill and gave me a smacking kiss.

"That was awesome spaghetti." She rubbed her belly and burped.

"Nice," I beamed as I took a sip of my wine. She got up to get the wine bottle, noticing that my glass was empty. I strategically placed her ring in its box in front of her cleared plate and waited.

When she sat back down, she poured our wine and sat back. Only seconds passed before she saw it and gasped.

"Holy hell, that is a big piece of ice, Brennan," she squealed. She tore it out of the box and I got down on one knee.

"Julia, I love you. You know that too much has kept us apart for too long. I want you to be my wife, take my name, and have a family with me. I will follow you to the ends of the earth for just one kiss. But right now, I just want one word. Please marry me, my love?"

She wasn't even looking at me when she said yes. She was inspecting the fucking ring. I barely saw the damn thing when buying it and now she looked at it like it was her favorite toy. I inched it away from her.

"Tell me yes, lady. Say it to my face! Tell me!" I shouted with animation.

"Yes, Brennan Curtis. I want to be your wife. Right now. Can we be husband and wife right now? Let's go to Vegas!" She screamed right back at me. We were yelling and excited and so fucking in love.

Despite my absolute joy, I shook my head and tsk'ed her as I leisurely put the ring on her left ring finger. She and I kissed peacefully deep. I noticed a flash of light come from outside. We both looked up.

"Heat lightning?" Julia asked, as she appreciated the ring again with the biggest smile I had ever seen on her face. God, she was so fucking beautiful. And she was mine. I never thought it would happen. I never thought I would be this happy again. I can be with Julia every day of our lives.

I shrugged at her question and went back to kissing her. As I picked her up and took her to our bedroom, I noticed another huge flash of light come from outside the window, and I tried to look out to see the sky.

"It must be," I said through my kisses. It didn't occur to me until we were about to fall asleep in each other's arms that it was a clear sky that night. That flash was from someone watching us.

I put the camera system in the following day and watched every magazine for months. Someone had stolen our moment and I would seriously hurt whoever it was.

EPILOGUE

FALL 2014

VANCOUVER

<u>JULES</u>

I watched my two nieces' faces as they watched me shimmy into my A-lined wedding gown made especially by some Italian designer my mother said I needed to call. It was gorgeous. It fit all of my curves perfectly and the low dip in the front would give Brennan a little eye candy for later.

I decided to marry him in Vancouver because Kent's land was beautiful and we wanted to get off the island in the fall. It would draw to much attention to the island and we loved everyone there, even Stephanie, the jeweler that clearly had a thing for my fiancé.

Brennan had picked the Justice of the Peace. I asked Kent to give me away. Joanie and Kelly were there with bells on. *Literally*. I made them wear light plum dresses and they were sporting bells on their heels. It was fitting for the lesbians that they were. They were both my maids of honor and when I asked them, they shut down the business for a much needed vacation to the Pacific Coast. They were going to head out to Astoria, Oregon after our party. They were so excited that I think they would have worn a garbage bag if I had asked.

Brennan and I chose Hawaii for our honeymoon since we were on this side of the States. We looked forward to a full month of sunning, sexing, and eating.

My mother and Kent walked into his bedroom.

"It looks like everyone is ready for us," Kent said handsomely in his tuxedo. "Brennan can't wipe the shit eating grin off his face."

I swear there was something up with him since we got here yesterday. He was acting overly jubilant. It was nice and I was happy too but he was a little over the top and when I mentally questioned him, he would just kiss my ring finger.

Joanie handed me my bouquet of red roses and I took my brother's arm. We walked out to a beautiful lawn made into a white and red glorious wedding scene. There were maybe twenty people there. His parents were there but not together. I had met them and their respective spouses during the summer when Brennan invited them out.

Both were a little wary at first but after I cooked and tried like hell to appear halfway normal, they grew to like me. His mom had told me last night that she was happy to gain a new daughter. I beamed at Brennan as he looked shocked. I think his parents were unhappy when he had gotten divorced.

Everyone saw the love we had for each other, especially as I walked down the aisle to him. He was crying when I got to him. With a quivering lip, he thanked Kent and took my hand. He leaned in and whispered, "You look like a gorgeous angel."

So then I started to cry. That is when I saw our heavily tattooed justice of the peace. Yes, he was in a suit but it probably was the only one he owned. The guy was clearly a tattoo artist. How Brennan decided on him was beyond me. Luckily it was a short and sweet ceremony. When it came to exchange the rings, Brennan started laughing.

"Who wants to go first?" the tattooed guy asked.

"Um. I don't have your ring, Brennan. Shit. Did we even buy rings?"

Everyone was a little confused then and they probably couldn't hear our muffled conversation. I felt like such an asshole in that moment. How did we overlook that very important detail?

"Then you should go first," Brennan said as tattoo guy took the backdrop sheet down to show a tattoo space set up. *What. The. Fuck.*

"What is going on?" I asked with clear alarm in my voice.

"You are going to accept my ring. My inked one," he said. All humor had left his face. He knew I didn't do tattoos. I heard people start talking as they started to understand what was happening. Brennan's expression pleaded with me to make this the one and only time to get ink.

I exhaled loudly and went to sit. Within fifteen minutes, I had an Irish Celtic Knot tattooed around my left ring finger. It hurt like a mother fucker but Brennan kept me busy by kissing my other hand and feeling up my thigh. Brennan's tattoo was done a little faster and he didn't even blink as the needle scraped through his skin.

We both held up our antibacterial ointment covered fingers to the crowd as the tattooed guy announced us Mr. and Mrs. Brennan Curtis. Our kiss was beautiful. The applause was startling. I still wasn't used to hearing that sound again. Flashes went off over and over. He and I made our way to the other part of the lawn to take our first dance.

We had decided on *I've Been Loving You* by Otis Redding. It was so fitting. We sang it to each other and when it was over, we made sure to top it off with yet another panty dropping kiss. I couldn't wait to get him alone. Everyone else fell away and that day, as I became Mrs. Brennan Curtis, I had hope for a beautiful life ahead.

I felt the aching from my finger but it was a small pain to notice after a day like today. Everything was perfect. That night as we lay in bed after mind numbing sex, I gave him my wedding present.

He jumped up like a little kid to get his. I frowned at him.

"Mine isn't wrapped," I said.

"Baby, you know that is okay, just give it to me," he said with a soft tone on my bare neck.

"Well, there you have it. You gave it to me and yes, it is a baby," I said just as soft back to him.

He stilled and then his curious eyes lifted to find my smile.

"A baby? We are having a baby?" he asked in surprise. His head dipped to look at my stomach which hadn't grown yet. I was only six weeks along but I was pregnant. I felt it. Hunger cravings and a bit bitchy. Brennan just thought I was stressed about the wedding. No one even noticed when I didn't take a real sip from the champagne today.

I nodded and claimed, "Get ready, Daddy. Loves is going to be jealous when he realizes he will have to share your time with your child."

Brennan crawled on top of me and then jumped off, worried that he was going to hurt me. I laughed and tugged him back on top of me.

"Totally isolated, honey. You can't hurt the baby." I smiled. He was *already* such a great dad. He would be the father I always wanted for myself. It was going to be amazing to be a witness to Brennan and his child.

He was also so protective of me. When he told me about the possible camera flashes and his unease about someone following us, we had a state of the art camera and security system installed. Since then there hadn't been any more instances of Pierre–like activity and I didn't mind signing a statement to the police that Johnny Lennox was stalking me. I imagined he received the notice to stop or he would get a restraining order from me. There had been radio silence from the lawyers and from the police. We lived out the rest of the summer in engagement harmony.

"Well, this isn't as exhilarating but I hope you like it," he said as he grasped the wrapped box and handed it to me.

I shredded open the paper to find a book. I rotated it over and over until it hit me what it was.

"Losing Grace" By Julia Curtis donned the cover.

"This is my... Brennan what is this?" I probed. I was astounded as I considered at the cover of my book. *My* book. Holy shit. It was unbelievable.

"I stole your manuscript in August when you said you were done. I had it edited and then I published it. I did the cover graphics myself after I read it. It is a beautiful story, Julia."

It was a pretty solid story. After talking to my brother about visiting Grace's father in prison, I also requested to see him. Brennan went with me because I was more than mortified to actually sit across from a murderer. He was a rapist. He is the rapist of a little girl. It was horrific to go but I knew it was only for research and maybe some closure to that time period in my life.

I was able to watch his body movements, his eccentricities, and anything that said that he was clearly someone to distrust. Besides his sudden urge for turrets when speaking about Grace, he appeared to be a normal person if he got a haircut and got rid of the orange prison jumpsuit.

I also got in touch with Emily and Angela's parents to get current information on my old childhood friends.

When I spoke with Angie's dad, he had said that she had moved to a small town in the mountains of Colorado and she didn't have a phone. He also commented that she was not connected to the internet. I got the impression that she was isolated. When I spoke with Emily's parents, they were just as enthusiastic about Emily as they ever were. She was living right outside of Boston with her new husband. They gladly gave me her phone number.

"Hi Emily? This is Jules Delaney. I don't know if you remember me... " I started before Emily cut me off.

"Oh, wow! Jules Delaney from the Love Sick Ponies. My husband, Michael would call me crazy. He is a big time lawyer, and oh my gosh, he loves your music. I can't wait to tell him you called," she boasted. I didn't correct her that I was no longer with the band.

My conversation with Emily was ninety five percent about her new husband and the other five percent was about how she hardly remembered the whole situation with Grace.

Both were dead ends but I was pleased with myself that I had tried. Brennan and I researched for two full weeks and were able to come up with enough information to call it a fictional novel based on true events. He was a huge help with his knowledge of information research. I was extremely surprised that he never was able to find me with everything he knew. I sat in my office for ten days straight and wrote. Brennan was respectful of my space at first but after three days, he came in to rock my world on my desk and then we went back to our day. *Horn dog.*

I looked at the dedication page and all it said was, "For my sexy ass husband, Brennan" and I laughed out loud. He grabbed a pen from the bed side table.

"Sign it for me?" he asked. I was still laughing and slapped *my* book on his shoulder. "Sign it, sweetheart. As Julia Curtis. First one is for me." The pride I saw in his face was amazing. I loved him so much.

Tears were falling from my eyes as Brennan gave me room to open the front cover and sign my new name on the title page. I flipped through the pages and after all that had happened today, I started to bawl.

"What is it? What's wrong? Did I fuck up?" Brennan asked sincerely concerned.

I shook my head.

"You and I are going to be so unbelievable as parents, lovers, and partners in life. I am so damn proud to call you my husband. Thank you for loving me through all of this. We went through so much and I guess I am just so thankful that we are finally here."

Brennan rubbed the back of his hand on my cheek, wiping away some tears. He slowly bent down and kissed my belly and then kissed the book.

"I am so proud of you, Julia. You are the woman that all women strive to be. Don't ever change, my love. I love all of you." He smirked with a knowing look. Yes, I still had my moments.

I knew he did. I believed him because I loved myself. I liked the woman I had become and I was proud of the work I had done to get what I deserved in life. No one could ever take that away from me.

Ever since I was twelve, and probably even before that, I always lived my life for the attention of others. I lost friends, I disgraced my body, and I hurt so many people including myself. Being the typical rock star was right in line with my persona. Tear the place and people up and move on to the next party. Every rock star knows that you get your one two hour set. The other twenty two hours? Yeah, people don't often get that part.

Since I met Brennan, the ultimate love of my life, all of those memories and disgraces caught up with me and slowly I became a person with depth. A human being that cares, that thinks of others, and who would rather feel the pain than numb it out with pills or sex. Today I realized that I was not only surrounded by family and friends that I loved but people who have never tried or succeeded in purposely hurting me or my reputation. Brennan showed me that I needed to change parts of me that would eventually kill me. He did it in a really fucked up way but we did eventually turn a shit ass situation totally around to make it into something pure and untouchable from others. No one could get between Bren and me anymore. We were solid as a rock. There was *nothing* plastic about us.

Slowly, my confidence molded into pure gold and in so many ways, I am appreciative of my path. It was what I went through that got me to the place I am now. Sure, I wish there were a few situations I could change. I would have called Emmy and Angie after that fateful day when we were twelve. I would have tried to remain friends. I wouldn't have said yes to Johnny when he proposed, knowing that deep down I really didn't feel the burning feelings I had felt for Brennan. Last, but not certainly not least, I would have called Brennan the moment I realized that I wanted, not needed, him in my life again. I wouldn't have left it to fate to bring us back together. I would have taken the high road and spoken up for what and who I believed in.

I am in passionate love and I believe in me. There is nothing plastic about that. *Rock on.*

MUSICAL PLAYLIST FOR
PLASTIC CONFIDENCE

Metallica–Fade to Black

The Cult–Sweet Soul Sister

Guns N' Roses–November Rain

Dinosaur Jr.–Out There

Smashing Pumpkins–Cherub Rock

Coldplay–Speed of Sound

The Shins–New Slang

Radical Face–Welcome Home

Van Morrison–Into the Mystic

Otis Redding–I've Been Loving You Too Long

Plastic Confidence is the first book in the Goodbye Series. If you liked this book please read Alisa's other books and follow Alisa Mullen at the following links.

#1–Plastic Confidence
https://www.goodreads.com/book/show/220076 95-plastic-confidence

FB Fan Page–http://tinyurl.com/l5jgo2b

Goodreads Page–http://tinyurl.com/m69qsof

Amazon BIO Page–http://tinyurl.com/l9plrxr

Twitter–@alimullenbooks

Google Plus–
https://plus.google.com/+AliMullenbooks/about

Website:
http://alimullenbooks.wix.com/alisamullenbook s

Blog: http://alimullenbooks.wordpress.com/

Books By Alisa Mullen

The Chosen Series

Unsettled

Unchosen

Unrequited

Unmarked–Due out Fall 2014

Novellas and Short stories

One Missing Link–Novella

Act As If–Sinners Saints Anthology

Please enjoy the first chapter of Book Two, Artificial Love, due to release in the fall of 2014.

ARTIFICIAL LOVE

Book Two of *The Good Bye Trilogy*

By Alisa Mullen

ONE

<u>Johnny Lennox</u>

I heard a whimper from the other side of my bed. Female. I turned my throbbing head slightly to the left to see a head of long dark brown hair. Jules. I placed my hand on it and started to pet it like she was a fucking kitten. I knew it wasn't Jules, but in my drunken splendor every night, I made sure I brought home the one that most closely resembled her.

Female turned over and I flinched. Bad idea. She had piercings in every part of her face. Four in the eyebrows, one septum, and three–I kid you not–in the cheek, and one in the lip. I scrubbed my hands over my eyes and told myself once again that I had to stop fucking

Jules by proxy. It wasn't working. I stretched and looked at the clock.

Damn, I had an appointment with Dr. Snooze in less than twenty minutes. I grabbed a smoke, a new habit I had picked up since Jules left me over two years ago, and threw on whatever to head out.

"Where are you going?" Female looked sad that we weren't going at it again, I was sure.

"I have an appointment with my shrink," I answered as I looked at the wall of Jules. I had printed over seven hundred photos at the local Walgreens and plastered them to my wall. Some were from when we were just getting to know one another. Some were of her on stage. Some were of us as we played guitar together on the tour bus and then a lot of them were of the photos Mark, my private investigator, had taken on Martha's Vineyard where she has been living all this time.

As part of my therapy, I took one photo down. It was a duplicate anyway. There were four more exactly like it still taped to the wall but Dr. Butt-munch didn't need to know that.

"Why are there so many pictures of Jules Delaney on your wall?" Female asked as she started to pull up her halter dress. Ugh, piercings everywhere. *Everywhere*. I mean, Jules' piercing were tasteful and stunning. I loved them. She was so beautiful.

"Research," I answered flatly.

"Wow, she is so beautiful. I didn't get a chance to her in concert before she left the band. But Ethan is definitely a good fit for Love Sick Ponies now," she went on.

I was going to lose it on her. Ethan was a terrible replacement for Jules. He couldn't sing the songs like her. He certainly didn't wear the low cut, plaid schoolgirl skirt I grew to love. I.Grew.To.Love.

"Yeah, he is alright. Listen, I got to go. It was nice to um... get to know you?" I asked. Normally, they were gone by morning but I must have been too fucked up to tell her to get out when I realized she wasn't Jules.

"Sure." She looked pissed as she flew by me and opened the door. "My name is Christine by the way. You might want to learn a girl's name instead of screaming out Jules when you come."

Hell, I knew I did that. She wasn't the first to get pissed and she certainly wouldn't be the last. I called out Jules. That was my form of dealing. Dr. Scratch-a-Dick said we would get to *that* after we tackled the photo wall.

Luckily, I had remembered to charge my phone the night before. I plugged the ear buds in and started my Jules playlist. She sang to me everywhere I walked in downtown Manhattan. It didn't matter if it was snowing or raining. Her voice got me through each walk. It was a necessity that I had not told Dr. Pickle Cock about yet and I still wasn't sure if I was going to.

I made my way down Madison Avenue and noticed that a few people pulled out their phones to take pictures of me. I pulled my Red

Sox hat down lower and steeled my expression for the public. No, I was not depressed, like the magazines kept writing. No, I was not still in love with Jules Delaney. Lie. No, I was a happy bassist for the popular band, Love Sick Ponies. Yes, I was happy. I made attempts at a grin while I listened to Jules belt out *One Leg Up* and I tried not to show the normal tear that fell down my face when I heard her last beautiful illustrious note. She was an angel. An angel that I had turned into a saint the very night that she left my apartment forever.

Lionel Ritchie played about the sun and the rain as I stepped into the low lit office. I took a seat and grabbed the first magazine I saw. I was five minutes late but sometimes the good doctor had real whack jobs that required a few extra minutes. I could tell the level of crazy when they came out of his office either looking like they had just been probed by aliens or their cat had just died. I never walked out looking like either.

I only had a few months left with this state mandated therapy crack nut until I was done.

My mother, the loving therapeutic figure that she is, said that Dr. Goldman was one of the best. Golden she had described him. Then she laughed and I didn't. He hadn't done much for golden material since Jules had not come back to me and Jules had not realized that she still belonged to Love Sick Ponies. So, when I ran my car into a ditch after seeing her with Brennan kissing in their elaborate estate in Vineyard Haven, the cops said that my alcohol level was too high to give me just a warning pass. Instead they fucked me. I was tested for drugs weekly. I was not allowed to drive a car for like forever and I had to see Dr. Fucktard every week for almost a year.

I flipped through Fan Date magazine and my heart stopped when I saw her beautiful smile. She was so happy and looking down at her white wedding gown while holding a bunch of wild flowers. I tore the page out but not before I saw her grinning down to her tattooed finger. She never wanted a tattoo. Obviously, Brennan made her get it. *Asshole*. The guy totally manipulated his way into her life. He didn't deserve her at all. He was a total douche that hurt her way more than I did. Well, at least as much. Okay, maybe cheating on her twice did trump a lot of bad relationship etiquette but fuck it. She was mine.

My heart warmth dropped at least twenty degrees as I read "Mrs. Jules Curtis" as the headline. Was that supposed to be funny? That was nowhere near a fucking joke. She wasn't a Curtis. She was a Lennox. My Lennox. *My name.* My leg started the nerve shake when Doc came out to see me with ripped up pieces of the magazine and a scowl on my face.

"Good Morning, Johnny," he said as he took in my disheveled look.

"Morning, Doc," I answered numbly as I pulled myself up from the chair and threw the magazine down on the table. I put the ripped photo of Jules in her wedding dress in my pocket and breezed past him to go find the chaise lounge that I had fallen asleep on countless times. Today, I was too fucking pissed to even imagine sleeping. I probably wouldn't sleep for days after knowing that my girl was officially married. *Happily married.* I was so fucked.

15596447R00240

Made in the USA
San Bernardino, CA
01 October 2014